A TWISTED MIND

By Eva Carmichael

A TWISTED MIND

Published in paperback, 2021 in association with:
JV Publishing
Tel: 07860213358
jvpublishing@yahoo.com

ACKNOWLEDGEMENTS

Grateful thanks to John & Vicky (JV Publishing) for enabling me to get this book to market. Your continued encouragement and patience are beyond thanks.

Again, I have to thank my beta readers, Mary, Maureen, Lindsey and Bill. Your contributions were invaluable.

A big thank you to Billy and Judith, who have gone out of their way to help me promote my books this year on Redcar Market.

Thank you also to my husband, Derek, who's still providing the tea, coffee and occasionally wine, and my family for their continued encouragement.

Last but by no means least, I would like to thank the people of Redcar and the surrounding area who have bought my books over the last eighteen months. The wonderful comments of support I have received make all the hard work worthwhile. Thank you.

PROLOGUE

The child crept slowly towards the marmalade cat sprawled on top of the garden wall. "Here, kitty, kitty," the child coaxed. The cat ignored the child, choosing instead to meticulously groom its front paw. Satisfied, it stretched and meowed contentedly.

The child moved closer. "Come here, kitty, that's a good cat." Inches away now, heart racing, eyes glistening with excitement, the child raised the knife above its head. This was going to be fun, much more fun than killing birds and frogs.

Suddenly, the silence of the afternoon was broken.

"Darling, tea's ready," the woman in the doorway of the house said. "Hurry up. You don't want it to get cold."

Startled, the child turned to face Mother, silently cursing at the interruption. The distraction had only been for a fleeting second, but it was long enough for the cat to leap down from the wall and make its escape into the lane. The child glared at Mother. It was her fault the cat got away. Someday she'd be made to pay dearly for that.

The child sulkily replaced the knife in the hiding place beneath one of the trees. Killing the cat was a pleasure that would have to wait for another day.

"Coming, Mother," the child said, running towards the house. "What's for tea?"

A TWISTED MIND

1

Saturday, 10ᵗʰ August 2002 – Rosie made her way along Redcar's crowded beach, dragging the twins' pushchair behind her. Bobby, her ten-year-old son, was in front, carrying a blue and white deckchair. As they got closer to the sea, Rosie stopped. "This looks perfect," she said. "Let's sit here."

Bobby quickly assembled the deckchair for his mother. "Can I go and play now?" he said, waving at several boys playing in the sea. "My mates are over there."

"All right," Rosie said, smiling. "But don't go too far. I don't want you getting lost." She watched as he raced down the beach to the water's edge before readjusting the sunshade over the pushchair. Both girls slept as she sank into the deckchair and removed a magazine from her bag.

Ten minutes later, she heard a faint murmuring as they began to wake up. Rosie gently lifted Daisy out of the pushchair and sat her on the blanket before placing Poppy next to her. The girls giggled as Rosie handed each of them a small bucket and spade. She watched contentedly as they began to dig in the soft sand.

"Rosie? I thought it was you."

Startled, Rosie turned to face the newcomer. "Cheryl?" she said. "What a lovely surprise. But what are you doing here? I thought you hated the sand."

Cheryl bent and kissed Rosie on the cheek. "I do," she said. "My company is holding a teambuilding exercise in Redcar. We're all staying at the Royal."

"How long are you here?"

She shrugged. "Not long. We should be done by Tuesday."

Rosie squinted against the bright sunshine and put her hand over her eyes for protection. "Teambuilding, you say. That's all very modern, isn't it?"

Cheryl screwed up her face. "It's the new CEO's idea. He used to work in America where it's all the rage." She knelt on the sand next to the twins and gently ran her fingers through

Daisy's soft, blonde curls. "The girls are looking gorgeous," she said. "They've grown since I last saw them." She filled one of the buckets with sand and quickly turned it over, making a perfect castle. Daisy promptly hit it with her spade, causing it to collapse, much to the delight of Poppy.

"The girls love playing in the sand," Rosie said. "I bring them down here almost every day in the summer."

"I love their dresses," Cheryl said. "Cornflower blue is a perfect match for their eyes."

Rosie blushed. "I made them myself. I make most of their clothes."

"You always were good with a needle. You should think about taking up dressmaking seriously."

She laughed and raised her arms. "Where would I find the time? I'm far too busy with the children to think about a career."

Cheryl tilted her head and smiled. "It must be hard with three kids," she said. "When's your next baby due?"

Rosie automatically put her hand protectively on her stomach and gasped. "Is it obvious? I didn't realise I was showing yet."

"How far are you? Three months?"

"Four," she corrected. "After this one, Eddie says he's having the snip."

"Is he still working on the markets?"

"He's over at Stockton today, but he's thinking about packing in and getting a shop in Redcar. That way, he won't be away from home so much."

"It would make life a lot easier for you if he did," Cheryl said. "By the way, where's Bobby today? Isn't he with you?"

Rosie pointed in the direction of the shoreline. "He's over there with his friends. That boy loves the water. I can't keep him away."

Cheryl waved, but Bobby was too preoccupied to notice. "How is he these days? Have the tantrums stopped?"

Rosie frowned. "He seems a lot better," she said. "He's

been awarded a scholarship in London. He'll be starting in September."

"I heard something about that," Cheryl said. "Let's hope it straightens him out." She stood up and brushed the sand from her skirt. "Well, it's been lovely seeing you again, but I have to go."

"Why don't you come to the house and have dinner later?" Rosie said. "Eddie would love to see you."

Cheryl sighed and shook her head. "Sorry, I can't. I'm meeting some of my company's senior executives this evening."

"You're turning into quite a career girl, aren't you? Who would have thought our lives would work out like this when we were at school? Me, a full-time mum and you…"

"Me, a buyer for one of the biggest clothing retailers in Europe. Crazy, isn't it?"

Cheryl reached into her bag, took out a business card and handed it to Rosie. "We really must make an effort to keep in touch. Ring me whenever you feel like a chat, okay?"

Rosie nodded, reached out for the card, and placed it in her bag. "I will, I promise."

She watched as Cheryl walked up the beach until she was swallowed into the crowd. Then, a few minutes later, Bobby came running towards her. "Mum," he called, "Mum, can I have an ice cream, please? My friends have one."

The twins giggled. The word ice cream was one they recognised. Rosie looked around for the vendor and saw the van parked on the promenade. "Can you manage to carry three cones by yourself, Bobby?" she asked.

He frowned and shook his head.

"In that case, you stay here and watch the girls while I get the ice creams."

"But, Mum, I—"

Rosie wagged her finger. "You're not having one without the girls having one too. That wouldn't be fair. Now, stay here with the girls and don't let them wander off. I won't be long."

"But, Mum."

Daisy gave out a shrill cry. "There, darling," Rosie said. She picked the sobbing child up in her arms and gently wiped the sand from her eyes with a tissue. "It's all gone. That's my brave girl." She turned to Bobby. "I'll take Daisy with me. You stay here and watch Poppy."

Rosie carried her daughter up the beach and joined the queue for ice cream. It was a long queue, and it was almost ten minutes before she got served. She strolled back along the beach carrying the three cones with Daisy toddling happily beside her. In the distance, she spotted the pushchair next to the striped deckchair and the discarded buckets and spades on the sand, but there was no sign of Bobby or Poppy.

Frowning, she placed Daisy in the pushchair and gave her an ice-cream cornet. She looked around frantically for her missing children as Bobby came running towards her. "Oh, I wanted a flake in mine," he whined. "My mates have all got a flake."

She inhaled and grabbed Bobby by the shoulders. "Where's Poppy?" she said hysterically. "Where is she?"

Bobby pulled away and shrugged. "I don't know. She was on the blanket playing with her spade, so I went to see my friend. He'd caught a jellyfish and—"

"I don't care about his bloody jellyfish," Rosie yelled. "Where's Poppy?" She ran towards the sea, calling her daughter's name.

A woman approached. "Whatever is the matter?" she asked.

"My little girl has disappeared. I can't find her. She must be here somewhere. Her name is Poppy."

The woman reached out and touched Rosie's arm. "Don't worry," she said. "She can't have gone far. We'll find her."

Within minutes, large groups of people began scouring the beach for the little girl. Two lifeguards joined in the search along with the lifeboat, which searched the coastline. Still, despite everyone's efforts, there was no sign of little Poppy Lee.

2

Rosie sat in the back of the police car, tightly clutching Daisy on her knee. Bobby was in the front seat, busily pressing buttons and pretending to steer. The young female officer, sat beside Rosie, handed her a tissue as tears streamed down Rosie's face.

"Where is she?" Rosie said. "Where's my baby?"

"Calm down, Mrs Lee," the police officer said. "We'll find her. Kids are always wandering off by themselves."

Rosie sobbed. "But it's been over an hour," she said, slowly rocking backwards and forwards. "Why haven't they found her?" Daisy attempted to wriggle free, but Rosie tightened her grip on the infant. "I only went to get ice cream. Poppy was playing with Bobby on the sand."

The vehicle's rear door opened, and a man indicated for the officer to get out of the car. He took her place beside Rosie.

"Mrs Lee, I'm Detective Inspector Andrew Bainbridge," he said. "PC Cooper will drive you and the children home. There's nothing you can do here."

"No," Rosie said. "I can't leave. I have to find Poppy."

"We'll find her," Bainbridge said. "It's best you wait at home with your other children. Your husband has been told what's happened. He should be at the house shortly."

She lifted her tear-stained face towards him. "You will find her, won't you? You will find Poppy?"

Bainbridge opened the door. "We'll do everything possible, Mrs Lee. PC Cooper will stay with you, and I'll be along later."

Rosie nodded and blew her nose loudly.

"Come on, young man," Bainbridge said, addressing Bobby. "Climb into the back seat with your mum. That's a good boy."

Bobby grabbed the steering wheel firmly. "No," he said. "I want to drive."

Rosie leant forward and grabbed her son by the arm. "Do as you're told. Sit back here with your sister and me."

The boy glared at Bainbridge and reluctantly climbed into the back of the car.

"Bobby, did you see what happened to Poppy when your mum left to get the ice cream?" Bainbridge asked.

He shrugged and stared through the window. "She was playing on the sand. I told her not to move."

"You left her on her own?"

"I wanted to see the jellyfish," he said. "Poppy should have done what she was told and stayed on the blanket."

"Did you see anyone near her after your mum had gone?"

He shook his head. "No. I was in the sea with my mates. We caught three jellyfish and—"

Rosie roughly grabbed hold of her son by the shoulders. "Will you shut up about those bloody jellyfish? I told you to watch your sister. This is your fault she's missing, you stupid boy."

He wriggled free and turned angrily to face his mother. "No, it isn't. It's your fault. You should have taken Poppy with you."

Ten minutes later, the police vehicle pulled up outside Hudson Gardens, a tree-lined cul-de-sac in one of the town's smart new developments. Number 14 was a mirror image of the other houses in the street. Rosie, still carrying Daisy, took the key from her bag and opened the door.

Cooper glanced at the neighbours standing at their front gates.

One of the neighbours, a middle-aged woman with brown hair tied in a neat bun, came over to her. "How's Rosie?" she said, straining to see beyond the police officer and into the house. "Is there any news? Have you found the poor little mite?"

"Enquiries are continuing," Cooper said as she half-closed the front door.

"If there's anything I can do," the woman said. "My name's Mary. I live across at number 11 and—"

"Thank you, Mary, but there's nothing you can do for the moment," she said and closed the door behind her.

"You have a lovely home, Mrs Lee," Cooper said as she entered the lounge. "You'd never think you had three children living here."

"Eddie likes everything tidy," she said. "He hates mess." She walked back into the hall carrying her daughter. "Daisy is exhausted. I'll take her upstairs and put her in her cot." She turned to her son. "Bobby, come and play quietly in your room. That's a good boy." Rosie slowly ascended the stairs with Daisy in her arms, Bobby following closely behind. Five minutes later, she returned to the lounge.

"Sit down and rest," Cooper said. "I've made you a cup of tea." She handed Rosie a mug.

Rosie shook her head and sniffed. "No thanks. I don't drink tea. Funny isn't it, me not liking tea with a name like Rosie Lee? Everyone finds it hilarious."

"I know what you mean. My name's Jilly."

Rosie arched an eyebrow. "Jilly? What's funny about that?"

"My surname is Cooper. So you can imagine the comments I get."

Rosie smiled weakly but said nothing.

"By the way, your neighbour from across the street offered her help. She said her name was Mary."

"Mary? Oh, that'll be Mary Biggins."

"Is she a friend of yours?"

Rosie shook her head. "Not really. The only time she comes to my door is to complain about Bobby playing with a football in the street."

"Well, at times like these, you'll find people can be really kind. Everyone will want to help."

The sound of a key in the front door caused both women to turn. Eddie Lee bounded into the room, a thunderous look on his chiselled face. "What the hell's happened?" he said. Where's Poppy? Why weren't you watching her?"

"Eddie, please, I—"

Cooper put her hand on Eddie's arm and steered him away from Rosie. "Mr Lee, this really isn't helpful. Everything possible is being done to find your daughter."

He turned sharply to face Cooper, pointing his finger. "Why aren't you out there looking for her? My kid's missing, and you're sat here drinking bloody tea."

Cooper stood her ground. "Every available officer is searching for your daughter. If she's on the beach, we'll find her."

"And what if she isn't? What if she's been swept out to sea or taken by some pervert?" He turned and glared at his wife. "Well? How did you manage to lose our daughter?"

Rosie sat huddled on the couch. "I... I left her with Bobby for a few minutes while I went to fetch ice cream," she whispered. "I wasn't gone long, but when I got back, Poppy was missing."

"Don't you dare blame Bobby for this," he said. "He's only a child. This is your fault, not his."

There was a sharp rap on the door. "That'll be DI Bainbridge," Cooper said. "He's the policeman you met earlier, Rosie."

Cooper went into the hall and opened the front door.

"Well?" Eddie demanded as the DI entered the lounge. "Have you found her? Have you found my daughter?"

"Sit down, Mr Lee," Bainbridge said. Eddie slumped onto the couch next to his wife, his arms folded tightly across his chest.

Bainbridge perched on the arm of a chair opposite. "Every available officer is out there searching for your daughter. If she's on the beach, we'll find her." He turned to face Rosie. "Mrs Lee, do you recognise this?" He removed an evidence bag from his pocket containing a child's pink sandal.

Rosie shrieked and put her hands to her face. "That's

Poppy's. I bought those sandals last week."

"Are you absolutely sure?"

"Of course, I'm sure. Daisy has an identical pair."

Eddie leapt forward. "Are you saying my kid is in the water? You think she's been swept out to sea?"

"It's early days," Bainbridge said, placing the evidence bag back into his pocket. "But I'm afraid it is a possibility."

Rosie put her head in her hands and howled. "No. Please, god, don't let this be true."

Cooper put her arm comfortingly around Rosie's shoulders.

"I will need statements later," Bainbridge said. "In the meantime, PC Cooper will act as temporary FLO. I will arrange for a permanent FLO later today."

Eddie scowled. "What the hell's an FLO?"

"A Family Liaison Officer," Bainbridge said. "She'll stay with you and keep you informed of progress. Please feel free to ask her any questions which you might have."

Eddie hunched his shoulders and stretched out his arms, palms up. "Is that it?" he said. "My baby is missing, and all you're doing is sending some FLO?"

"I assure you, everything possible is being done to find your daughter," Bainbridge said. "I'll call back later this evening. Hopefully, I'll have more news by then."

Eddie banged his fist hard on the table. "Fuck this. I'm going to the beach to find her myself. You lot are bloody useless."

Bainbridge stood and stepped forward, blocking Eddie's path. "I would advise you not to do that, Mr Lee. You should stay with your wife and family. We'll keep you informed of progress."

Rosie fell onto her knees, cradling her head. "You will find her, won't you?" she said, sobbing. "You will find my little girl?"

"We'll do our best," Bainbridge said. He opened the front door, walked along the drive, and glanced back towards the house. Eddie Lee stood glaring at him through the window.

3

It was eight o'clock that evening when DI Bainbridge returned to Hudson Gardens. He was in the company of PC Helen Taylor, an experienced FLO.

Eddie Lee met them at the door. "Well?" he demanded. "Have you found her?"

"Let's go inside," Bainbridge said, making his way into the house.

Rosie was asleep on the couch with Cooper seated in an armchair opposite. At the sound of the newcomers entering the room, she opened her eyes and attempted to sit up.

"How are you feeling, Mrs Lee?" Bainbridge asked.

Rosie smiled weakly. "Have you found my baby yet?"

Bainbridge sat next to her on the couch. "Not yet, but everyone is out there looking for her." He turned to PC Taylor. "This is Helen. She is going to stay with you for the next few days. If you have any questions, just ask her."

Rosie nodded an acknowledgement at the police officer.

"The doctor called earlier," Cooper said. "He's given Rosie a sedative to calm her down. She was in a terrible state."

"She'll be in a worse state if anything bad has happened to my daughter," Eddie said through clenched teeth.

Bainbridge stood up and walked towards the window. "The search for your daughter is intensifying," he said, "but so far, no-one has come forward claiming to have seen her by the shoreline."

Eddie moved towards Bainbridge. "But you found her sandal in the sea. She must have been swept away."

Bainbridge sighed and hunched his shoulders. "That seems the most likely explanation, but we have to look at alternatives."

Eddie's eyes narrowed. "What are you saying? That my daughter was abducted?"

"I'm saying that it's an avenue we have to explore."

"Oh god, no, not my baby," Rosie said. "Please, not my

little girl."

Bainbridge returned to the couch and sat next to Rosie. "Mrs Lee," he said. "Are you sure you didn't see anyone acting suspiciously around you and the children?"

"What do you mean, suspiciously?"

"Did you notice anyone watching you or a stranger trying to get into conversation, for instance?"

"No, there was just me, Bobby and the two girls."

"You're sure about that?" Bainbridge said.

"Yes, I… Oh, I forgot. I did speak briefly with Cheryl Lewis. She's an old school friend. We hadn't seen each other in ages."

"Does Cheryl live in Redcar?"

Rosie frowned and shook her head. "No. I think she's still in Newcastle, but this has nothing to do with her. She'd been gone ages before… before Poppy disappeared."

"I'm sure you're right, but we'll need to speak with her. Maybe she saw something." Bainbridge took out his notebook. "What was Cheryl doing in Redcar?"

"She's taking part in some teambuilding exercise with her company," Rosie said. "They're all based at the Royal." Rosie delved into her bag and retrieved Cheryl's card. "She gave me this so we can keep in touch."

Eddie scowled. "Cheryl Lewis? What the hell did she want? I never did like that woman."

"That's not fair," Rosie said, the colour rising in her cheeks. "Cheryl was my best friend at school."

Eddie grunted. "I don't like her, and I don't want you mixing with her either. Do you hear me?"

"May I see the card?" Bainbridge asked and took it from Rosie. He wrote the details in his notebook before handing the card back. "I'll send a car around tomorrow morning to take you both to the station to make a statement."

Eddie huffed as he lit a cigarette. "What the hell for? Rosie's told you everything that happened. Why aren't you out there looking for our daughter?"

"I assure you, Mr Lee, everything possible is being done to find her," Bainbridge said, walking towards the door. "Helen will take care of the children tomorrow when you're at the station."

Cooper smiled. "Try and get some sleep, Rosie," she said softly as she followed Bainbridge into the hall. "I'll see you tomorrow."

Bainbridge drove the vehicle to the police station. "What do you make of them?" he asked after a few minutes. "Do you think they're involved?"

Cooper shook her head. "No. Rosie is genuinely devastated by what's happened."

"What about the husband?"

"Eddie's angry with his wife," she said, "but that's understandable, I suppose."

Bainbridge wrinkled his nose. "Mm, I suppose so, but there's something about that bloke I don't like. By the way, the wife's staying at her sister's tonight. Can I come round to yours later?"

Cooper smiled as she gently squeezed his knee. "DI Bainbridge," she said, "I thought you'd never ask."

"I'm going out for some air," Eddie said as he pulled on his jacket. "I won't be long." He stomped through the front door and down the street towards the park. Sitting on a bench, he took out his mobile phone and rang a number.

"It's me," he said. "What the fuck were you doing in Redcar today talking to Rosie? Are you trying to stir things up? … We agreed it was over, and you'd stay away… One of the girls has disappeared, and the police are speaking to everyone who was on the beach. They'll be coming to see you, so make sure you keep your mouth shut about us, okay?"

4

"Any news, Duffy?" Bainbridge asked as he walked into the incident room half an hour after leaving the Lee's house. "How did you get on rounding up the local pervs?"

"In hand, sir," Sergeant Steven Duffy said, hurriedly putting out his cigarette. "We've interviewed half a dozen already, and there are three more waiting."

"Any joy?"

Duffy shook his head. "Not yet. Those we've spoken to all have alibis for this afternoon."

"Keep at it. Somebody must have seen something."

"You don't think…"

"Think what?"

"Well, sir, you don't think that the girl was washed out to sea? The currents are pretty strong in Redcar."

Bainbridge frowned. "It's probably what did happen. But I have to be sure. If somebody's holding that kid, we have to find her."

"If she's out there, we will," Duffy said. "I hear half of Redcar has joined in the search."

"Have the press been in touch?"

"Just the local rag, so far."

"Well, let's hope it stays that way. I don't want this girl's disappearance turning into a media circus."

"No, sir," Duffy said. "Oh, by the way, I hear congratulations are in order."

"Eh?"

"Your promotion to Detective Chief Inspector."

Bainbridge scowled. "How did you hear about that? It hasn't been made official yet."

"Oh, you know how it is," Duffy said, lightly tapping the side of his nose with his finger. "Somebody knows somebody who's heard a rumour."

"Well, make sure you keep schtum until it is made official, okay?"

"Yes, sir," Duffy said. "Does this mean you'll be moving away from Redcar once you're promoted?"

Bainbridge shrugged. "I'm not sure. I've heard DCI Shaw is taking early retirement, so there could be a vacancy here, but you haven't heard that from me."

Duffy gave a sly wink. "Of course, sir," he said. "My lips are sealed."

Bainbridge picked up the daily incident book and quickly scanned through it. "Nothing else much happening in town today." He replaced the logbook on the table.

"No, sir, it's been very quiet." Duffy walked over to the water dispenser and filled a plastic cup. "Will you be sitting in on the remaining interviews?"

Bainbridge shook his head. "No. I'm whacked. I think I'll have an early night. It's going to be another long day tomorrow." He walked towards the door and then turned sharply to face the sergeant. "Before I forget," he said, "I want you to do a thorough background check on Eddie Lee."

"The kid's dad?"

Bainbridge nodded. "Yes. There's something about that man I don't like."

"I'll get on it straight away, sir."

"Thanks, Duffy. See you tomorrow."

When Bainbridge left the room, Duffy rushed over to the CCTV screen in the office and flicked onto the car park camera. He watched as Bainbridge opened the front door of his own car and Jilly Cooper climbed in. Stroking his chin, he began to chuckle. "Lucky buggar."

5

Rosie and Eddie Lee arrived at Redcar Police Station at nine-thirty on Sunday morning. Rosie was taken to interview room one and Eddie to a room across the corridor.

"Would you like tea, or a coffee, Mrs Lee?" the young police officer standing by the door asked.

She shook her head and wilted into one of the wooden chairs. "No, thank you. I'm fine."

The door opened, and Bainbridge strode into the room. "Good morning, Mrs Lee," he said, taking his seat at the bolted-down metal table. "Thank you for coming in this morning."

"Please, call me Rosie," she said.

Bainbridge smiled and nodded. "How are you feeling? Did you manage to get any sleep?"

"A little," she said as she nervously twisted her hair between her fingers. "Is there any news about Poppy yet?"

"No, not yet, but everyone is out there looking."

Rosie sighed. "There were three reporters at the door this morning."

"I hope you didn't speak with them?"

She shook her head. "No. Eddie told them to piss off, but they were taking photographs of us getting into the police car."

Bainbridge leant forward. "Rosie, I'm sorry, but I have to ask you more questions about yesterday."

She raised her head, her eyes meeting those of the policeman. "I don't know what else I can tell you. I left Bobby looking after Poppy while I went to get ice cream. I took Daisy with me. I was only gone a couple of minutes. When I came back, Poppy... Poppy was gone."

"You say you left your daughter with Bobby. Where was he when you got back?"

Rosie furrowed her brow. "He was mucking about in the sea with some lads he'd met. He was excited because one of them had caught a jellyfish."

"Bobby's your stepson, isn't he?"

"Yes, that's right. He's Eddie's son."

"Where's Eddie's first wife, Bobby's mother?"

"Oh, they weren't married," she said. "They met when Eddie was working in London. Claudia was a model back then." Rosie clenched her hands tightly into fists. "She walked out, leaving Eddie to take care of Bobby by himself. The lad was only seven at the time. What sort of mother does something like that?"

Bainbridge stroked his chin. "How long after Claudia left did you and Eddie get married? It can't have been long."

Rosie shrugged. "A few months, that's all," she said quietly. "Eddie needed someone to help take care of Bobby."

"How did Bobby feel about having a new mum so soon?"

Rosie's eyes narrowed, and she threw back her head. "I don't know what you mean. Bobby is a good boy."

"Was he resentful at having to share his dad with you and the two girls?"

"What are you implying? Bobby loves his baby sisters."

"Not enough to keep Poppy safe."

"That's unfair," she said, tears running down her cheeks. "It's my fault she's missing, not his. I should never have left Poppy in Bobby's care. He's only a child himself."

Bainbridge handed her a tissue, then, leaning back in his chair, waited until she had regained her composure. "Tell me about your friend, Cheryl Lewis. You say you met by chance on the beach?"

She sniffed loudly and, taking out a tissue from her bag, blew her nose. "Yes, that's right. I hadn't seen her in ages."

"You were at school together, weren't you?"

"Yes, but I left school when I was sixteen. Cheryl went on to college. She's doing really well for herself."

"Her card said she was a fashion buyer."

Rosie nodded. "Her company is *Chic Fashions*. They're a French clothing company. Perhaps you've heard of them?"

Bainbridge shook his head.

"Their clothes are fantastic, but they are expensive."

"Your husband doesn't seem to like Cheryl."

Rosie sighed. "I don't understand why." She smiled. "He hardly knows her really."

"You say she lives in Newcastle?"

"As far as I know, but like I said, I haven't seen much of her since I had the twins."

Rosie glanced at her watch and looked towards the floor. "Is there anything else you want to know, inspector? I really have to get home to the children."

"I think that's about all for now," he said. He indicated the young female officer standing by the door. "PC Jarvis will take your statement, and then you're free to leave. I'm going to speak with Eddie now."

Rosie frowned. "Why? Eddie wasn't even in Redcar when Poppy disappeared. He was at Stockton Market. He's told you that."

"So he did, Rosie," Bainbridge said. "But in a case like this, I have to check every detail." He stood up and walked towards the door. "Can I get one of my officers to get you a cup of tea?"

Rosie shook her head. "I don't drink tea. I wouldn't mind a glass of water, though, if it's not too much trouble."

PC Jarvis left the room and returned a couple of minutes later with a plastic cup containing water from the dispenser.

"Here you are, Rosie," she said, handing her the drink. "Let's get your statement down, then you can leave."

6

Eddie Lee paced anxiously around the small, windowless interview room. Finally, Inspector Bainbridge entered and took a seat. Duffy stood by the doorway.

"Sit down, Mr Lee," Bainbridge said. "This shouldn't take long."

Eddie plonked himself down on the chair at the metal table. "What the hell am I doing here in the first place? I wasn't even in Redcar when Poppy disappeared. It's Rosie you should be talking to."

"I've spoken with your wife," Bainbridge said. "But there are one or two matters I need to clear up with you."

Eddie tilted his head and frowned. "What sort of matters?"

"I need to know your whereabouts yesterday."

"I've told you where I was. I was at my stall on Stockton Market, just like I am every Saturday."

"Were you at your stall the whole day?"

"Yes, of course I was. I didn't leave until that copper came and told me that Poppy had gone missing."

"What time did you set up your stall that morning?"

"Eight o'clock. You're not allowed on until eight."

"Was anyone with you?"

Eddie frowned again. "Only young Franky. He helps me out at most of the markets."

"That's Franky Symonds, I take it?"

Eddie nodded. "Yeah, that's right. Franky's a bit slow upstairs, if you know what I mean. I let him help as a favour to his mum."

"Very noble of you, I'm sure," Bainbridge said with a hint of sarcasm. "Tell me, would you say Franky is an honest sort of lad?"

Eddie flung back his head and began to laugh. "Honest as the day is long. I don't think it would ever occur to him to lie. I don't think he'd know how."

"So, if Franky told one of my officers that you left the stall at twelve o'clock and did not return until quarter past two, you would agree he was telling the truth?"

Eddie's posture stiffened. "He said that?" He banged his fist on the desk. "After all I've done for the ungrateful little twat."

"Where were you, Mr Lee?" Bainbridge asked. "Where did you go for over two hours yesterday at the time your daughter disappeared?"

Eddie's eyes narrowed into slits as he leant back into his chair. "Piss off. I don't have to tell you anything."

"If you refuse to answer my questions, you will be arrested on suspicion. You do understand that?"

Eddie glowered at him but remained silent.

Bainbridge leant forward. "Oh, by the way, Franky also said that your absence from the stall on Saturday afternoon was a regular occurrence."

Eddie took a deep breath and lowered his head into his hands. "I went to meet someone," he said quietly.

"Who did you meet?"

"A friend."

"What's your friend's name?"

"She's nothing to do with it. I just call round and see her every Saturday when I'm in Stockton."

"How long have you been visiting this woman?"

"About six months, maybe seven."

"I take it she's married?"

Eddie nodded. "Her husband's a mechanic. He works at a garage in Middlesbrough."

"So, you go round to keep this woman company every Saturday lunchtime?"

"No, mate, I go round to shag her, not that it's any of your business."

"I'll need her name and address."

"Piss off."

"Mr Lee, speak to me like that again, and I'll arrest you for obstruction. Do you understand? Now, stop messing about and give me this woman's details."

Eddie lowered his head and ran his fingers through his hair. "Her name's Sharon. She lives in the flat above the hairdressers on Concorde Road."

"Does Sharon have a phone number?"

He nodded.

Bainbridge produced a sheet of paper and pushed it over the desk towards Eddie. "Write it down. I'll need to speak to her."

He scribbled down Sharon's number. "You will be… discreet?" he said. "Her husband mustn't find out she's been playing away, or he'll kill her. Sharon's a nice kid. I don't want her getting dragged into this shit."

Bainbridge took the paper from Eddie. "Tell me about your relationship with Rosie."

"What do you mean relationship? Rosie's my wife."

"Would you say you are happily married?"

"Of course, I am. I love Rosie to bits."

"Your wife is a beautiful young woman. I find it difficult to understand why you would want to cheat on her if you are happily married like you claim."

"That's none of your bloody business," Eddie said, screwing his hands tightly into fists.

"Under the circumstances, I'm making it my business," Bainbridge said. "Now, answer my question."

He glared at Bainbridge, then, sighing, leant back in his chair, clasping his hands behind his head. "Rosie is… Rosie is obsessed with the kids," he said. "Every waking hour she's fussing over them. She never has time for me. Sometimes I feel… I feel invisible."

Bainbridge raised an eyebrow but remained silent.

"I know it sounds pathetic, being jealous of her taking care of my kids, but it's almost as if I don't exist."

"Tell me about Bobby's mother."

"Claudia? What do you want to know about that bitch for? She fucked off years ago."

"What made her leave?"

Eddie shrugged. "Who knows? I came home from work one night, and she was gone. She'd left Bobby with a neighbour and just disappeared."

"Do you know where she went?"

Eddie shook his head. "I have no idea. She probably went back to London where I met her. Claudia always did like the city life, the clubs and the bright lights. I don't think Middlesbrough was ever her cup of tea at all."

"So, you have no idea where she went or where she is now?"

"No, and I don't want to know. That woman's dead to me."

"What sort of person was she?"

Eddie shrugged. "Claudia suffered from her nerves. She was always edgy. She hardly ate, and she drank too much."

"And it was shortly after Claudia left that you met Rosie?"

"Yeah, that's right. Rosie was the answer to my prayers. We married and moved over to Redcar to live by the sea after she got pregnant with the girls. Kids like the seaside."

"How did Bobby react to having a new mum? It must have been hard for him."

"Bobby? What's he got to do with Poppy going missing?"

"Mr Lee, right now I'm trying to piece together what sort of family you are. I need to know your background, to help me understand."

Eddie leant forward. "Understand what? Look, mate, all you have to do is find my little girl."

"That's what I'm trying to do," Bainbridge said. "Now, tell me about Bobby."

"He's a bright lad. In fact, he's a bloody genius." Eddie's face softened. "He's just been awarded a scholarship to a private school near London, did you know that? He's got brains coming out of his ears, that lad."

"You must be proud of him?"

Eddie grinned. "Of course, I am. What father wouldn't

be?"

"Mr Lee, can you think of anyone who might hold a grudge?"

"A grudge? Poppy's two years old, for God's sake."

"I meant a grudge against you or Rosie?"

He shook his head. "That's crazy. We're just two people trying to do the best we can for our kids. We don't have enemies." He ran his hands through his hair again. "What are you going to do about Sharon?" he said. "You will be careful? Not a word to her husband or to Rosie?"

"Mr Lee, your private life is none of my business as long as it doesn't appertain to our enquiries," Bainbridge said as he got up and walked towards the door. "Sergeant Duffy will take your statement, and then you are free to leave."

Twenty minutes later, Eddie walked down the corridor into reception, where his wife was waiting. "Come on, Rosie," he said, taking her by the arm. "Let's get out of here. The kids will need feeding."

7

It was eleven o'clock when Bainbridge and Cooper arrived at The Royal Hotel. As they walked towards reception, a slim, dark-haired woman wearing a light-grey trouser suit approached them. "Are you the police?" she asked.

Bainbridge nodded and introduced himself and Cooper.

"I'm Cheryl Lewis. I've been expecting you." She indicated for them to follow as she made her way to a designated smoker's area facing the sea. "I heard what happened," she said quietly as the three of them sat down. "I was only talking to Rosie yesterday on the beach, but of course, you know that, don't you?"

"What did you do after you had spoken to Rosie?" Bainbridge asked.

"I left the beach and walked along the promenade. I called into the Beacon Lounge and had a glass of wine, then went back to the hotel."

Bainbridge narrowed his eyes. "Did you leave the hotel at all that evening?"

Cheryl shook her head. "No. I got showered and dressed, then went into a working dinner at about seven-thirty. It would be after eleven before I went to bed."

"Tell me about Rosie. How long have you known her?" he said.

Cheryl smiled. "Since we were twelve. We were in the same class at school." She took out a packet of cigarettes from her bag and offered one to the officers. They both declined. She lit her cigarette and drew heavily before continuing. "Rosie's dad had just died, and I suppose I felt sorry for her. We've sort of kept in touch on and off ever since."

Bainbridge leant forward. "What can you tell me about Rosie? What sort of a person is she?"

It was several seconds before she spoke. "Rosie was… is… very attractive. Men notice her."

"Did she have many boyfriends before she met Eddie?"

Cheryl shook her head slowly. "None that I know of. Her mother was strict. She didn't like Rosie mixing with boys. That's why I wasn't surprised when Rosie got married soon after the old bat died. She hadn't known Eddie more than a couple of months."

Cooper jotted something on her notepad. "How well did you know Eddie?"

Cheryl took another long draw on her cigarette before answering. "I met Eddie through Rosie just before they got married. But, if I'm honest, I'm afraid I didn't like him much."

Bainbridge arched an eyebrow. "Oh? Why was that?"

"I suppose I found him a bit controlling. He seemed to make all the decisions, and Rosie just went along with everything he said."

"Is there anything else you can tell me about them as a couple?" he said.

Cheryl inhaled deeply. "Rosie is a lovely person, but… well, she isn't too bright. I'm sure you've noticed that. At school, they used to call her dozy Rosie."

Bainbridge frowned. "Kids can be cruel."

Cheryl brushed cigarette ash from her lapel. "I suppose so, but you don't have to know Rosie that well to realise she is a bit dim."

"That's not the impression I got," he said. "What makes you say that?"

"Well, for a start, just look at the girls' names, Daisy and Poppy. Who calls their kids after flowers these days? Her mother was called Lily, would you believe?"

Cooper continued taking notes. "I think the names are sweet," she said.

Cheryl huffed but said nothing.

"Did you keep in touch with Rosie over the years?" Bainbridge asked.

"No, not really. I bumped into her in Newcastle when she was pregnant with the girls, and we met up a couple of times after that, but too much water had gone under the bridge to form a real friendship."

Bainbridge slowly stroked his chin. "How did Rosie seem when you saw her on the beach?"

Cheryl smiled. "She seemed content to be surrounded by kids, but that's Rosie all over. She's a natural carer, a real Mother Earth. Did you know she's expecting again?"

Bainbridge widened his eyes. "No, I didn't know that."

Cheryl stubbed out her cigarette and took another from her bag. "Rosie was sixteen when she left school to take care of her mother. The old bat had had a heart attack or a stroke or something." She lit the cigarette and drew heavily. "I warned her she was ruining her future, giving up on her education. I told her the authorities would take care of her mother. That's what we pay our taxes for, right?"

"I take it you didn't like Rosie's mother?"

"No, I did not. She was a nasty, selfish woman. The poor kid was little more than a domestic servant to her."

Bainbridge frowned. "Going back to yesterday. Is there anything you can remember that could help our enquiries? Anything at all?"

Cheryl sighed heavily before shaking her head. "No, I'm sorry," she said. "When I left Rosie, the girls were playing on the sand, and Bobby was with some lads splashing around in the sea."

"Okay, we'll leave it there, but if you think of anything else."

Cheryl stubbed out her half-smoked cigarette in the ashtray. "Have you heard what people are saying?" she said, lowering her voice. "They're blaming Rosie for poor little Poppy drowning. They're saying she was negligent."

"Do you think that's true?" Cooper said.

Cheryl shrugged. "How would I know? I wasn't there. But what is it they say, no smoke without fire?"

Bainbridge rose from his chair. "Well, I think that's all for now, Miss Lewis. I will need you to make an official statement. Perhaps you could call into the station tomorrow?"

She walked with the officers back into the hotel foyer. "Yes, of course. The lectures finish for the day at four o'clock. Perhaps I could call about five if that's okay?"

Bainbridge nodded. "I'll see you then."

Bainbridge turned to Cooper as they got into the car. "Well, what's your opinion of Cheryl Lewis?" he asked.

She scowled. "I'm afraid I don't like Cheryl Lewis very much. She came across as being vindictive, not a nice person at all."

Bainbridge turned on the engine. "I had Duffy check her out. She arrived at the hotel alone, like she said and was in the hotel all night. She certainly didn't have Poppy with her."

Cooper shrugged. "I'm not saying she's involved in the abduction, but I think Rosie could do with choosing a new friend."

8

"It's one o'clock," Bainbridge said as he steered the car into the pub car park. "Let's have a quick lunch at the Crown. I don't think I can stomach the works canteen two days in a row."

"I'll get my coat," Cooper said as she removed her jacket from the car's boot.

The pub was busy, but they managed to secure a small table at the back of the room.

"What do you fancy?" Bainbridge asked after scrutinising the menu. "I think I'll have the Ploughman's."

"Sounds good," Cooper said. "I'll have the same."

Bainbridge went to the bar and placed their order, returning with two glasses of coke. He flopped down heavily into the chair and sighed.

"What is it, Andy? Is something the matter?"

He lowered his head. "Jilly," he said quietly, "I'm sorry, but this… we… have to stop."

"Stop? What do you mean? Is it something I've done?"

"No, of course not. It's just—"

"I thought we had something special?" She reached out and touched his arm.

"We do… we did, but… well, I suppose I can tell you now. It's going to be all over the nick tomorrow. I'm being made up to DCI."

"That's great news. You deserve it, but why…?"

"Do you have any idea how it would affect my career if it came out about you and me? It wouldn't do your career any good either."

"I don't understand. We've always been discreet. Nobody suspects."

Bainbridge ran his hand through his hair and sighed. "Steve Duffy does."

"What's he said?"

"It's not so much what he said as the way he looks at me

sometimes."

"Don't you think you're a little paranoid?"

"I'm sorry, but I've made up my mind. We have to stop seeing each other."

"But, Andy, we work together. You can't just ignore me as if I don't exist."

"I'm hoping to stay on in Redcar when my promotion comes through. I think it's best if you apply for a transfer."

Cooper's posture stiffened. "I don't want a bloody transfer. I like it here."

"Please, Jilly, don't make this more difficult than it already is. These last few months have been fun, but it can't go on. I'm married. I have responsibilities."

"You had responsibilities when you were climbing into my bed, but it didn't seem to bother you then."

"Things are different now. Surely you can see that?"

Cooper clenched her fists, her eyes brimming with tears. "What I see is a selfish, lying bastard."

"When have I ever lied? You knew our relationship didn't have a future."

"I knew nothing of the kind. I thought you loved me."

Bainbridge shook his head. "No, Jilly. I love my wife."

Cooper took out a tissue and dabbed her eyes. "What if I refuse to transfer? You can't make me."

Bainbridge reached over the table and grabbed her wrists, pulling her towards him. "You will transfer," he said. "You'll put your request in today. Understand?"

She winced in pain, and Bainbridge released his grip. "Sorry," he said softly. "I didn't mean to hurt you, I just—"

"Forget it," Cooper said, rubbing her wrists. "I'll put in for a transfer if that's what you want, but I'll never forgive you, Andy." She got up from the table and hurried towards the toilets.

When she returned five minutes later, the waitress had placed their lunch on the table.

"It's the right thing to do," Bainbridge said. "You'll come

to realise that in time." Cooper remained silent as she slowly sipped her coke and prodded at her food.

Once they were back in the car, he turned to her. "I'm sorry," he said, "but it's for the best, for both our sakes, yours as well as mine." He turned on the engine. "We'd better get back to the station, or tongues will be wagging."

9

"Any news?" Bainbridge asked Sergeant Duffy as he arrived back at the office.

"There are a couple of statements on your desk from this morning, sir, and a report from one of the officers involved in the search," Duffy replied. "It doesn't look good for Rosie, I'm afraid."

Bainbridge walked into his office, giving a cursory glance at Rosie and Eddie's statement before picking up the report. His body tensed as he began to read. "Bloody hell," he said. "I don't believe this." He rushed into the incident room. "Where's Cooper? I need her to come with me to the Lee's house right away."

"She's signed out, sir," Duffy said. "She's on half-day. Her shift finished at two."

Cursing, Bainbridge left the building and headed towards Hudson Gardens.

PC Taylor lounged in an armchair, reading the newspaper when he arrived. Rosie sat on the couch, cuddling Daisy on her knee while gently brushing her soft curls. She looked up expectantly when she saw Bainbridge. "Have you found her?" she said. "Have you found my baby?"

"No, I'm sorry, Rosie," Bainbridge said. "Not yet."

Eddie slouched on the couch beside his wife and took a drink from a can of lager. He put it down on the table with a loud bang. "You're wasting your time," he slurred. "She's gone. The sea got her, my poor baby." He began to sob loudly, his large shoulders heaving.

"Don't cry, love," Rosie cooed as she reached out to comfort him. "They'll find her."

Eddie pulled away. "Don't fucking touch me," he said, snarling. "You killed my Poppy. She's gone because of you."

"I'm sorry," she said. "I'm so, so sorry."

"Come on, Eddie," Bainbridge said firmly. "This isn't

helping, is it?"

Eddie wiped his eyes on the back of his sleeve. "Leave me alone," he said through gritted teeth. "Keep away from me, all of you." He got up from the couch and staggered towards the hall. "I'm going for a lie-down," he said, dragging himself up the stairs.

Bainbridge glanced at the small and fragile figure of Rosie brushing her daughter's hair.

"Rosie, I have more questions, I'm afraid," he said, perching on the couch next to her.

"I'm sorry, but there's nothing more I can tell you," she whispered, not bothering to take her eyes off her child. "I told you everything that happened in my statement yesterday."

"Yes, I know, but I need to talk to you about what happened last Wednesday."

She stopped brushing Daisy's hair and looked directly at him. "Last Wednesday? I don't know what you mean."

"You were on Redcar beach with the children, weren't you?"

"Yes, I take them to the beach most days when the weather is warm."

"An eye witness has told us the girls were seen floating out to sea in an inflatable. A young man brought the craft back to the beach."

She frowned. "It was a pink unicorn. I'd bought the girls a pink inflatable unicorn to play with on the beach."

"But they weren't on the beach, Rosie. They were inside the unicorn floating in the sea. How did that happen?"

She shook her head slowly. "I... I don't know," she said. "One minute the girls were playing on the sand, jumping in and out of the inflatable. And the next... a man brought the girls over to me and told me what had happened."

"He said you were asleep."

Her frown deepened. "Yes, but only for a minute. I was so tired. The girls were struggling with their back teeth and cried most of the night, the poor little mites. I hadn't had much sleep, and I was exhausted."

"So, you left them to their own devices?"

She lowered her head. "They were playing with Bobby. He must have wandered off and left them for a few minutes. I... I feel really bad about what happened, but the girls weren't hurt."

"I understand you're expecting again. Congratulations."

Rosie raised her head and smiled weakly. "Thank you."

"How does Eddie feel about another child?"

"What do you mean?"

"Three children must put a strain on your marriage. A fourth child is..."

"That's none of your bloody business," she said. "Why are you wasting time asking questions like this when you should be out there looking for Poppy?"

"In an investigation of this type, we have to examine every piece of your life," Bainbridge said. "We have to determine what is significant and what isn't."

"It seems like prying to me," she said.

"Believe me, it's necessary. That's why I need you to tell me about your consultation at the Marie Stopes Clinic."

Rosie gasped. "How did you know about that? I only enquired, I didn't—"

"You didn't go ahead with an abortion? I know that, Rosie, but you were considering it, weren't you?"

"This has come from Mary Biggins's daughter, hasn't it? She's a nurse at the clinic. It was supposed to be confidential. She had no right to..."

Bainbridge studied her as the colour drained from her face. "Tell me what happened."

She pulled Daisy closer to her. "There's nothing to tell. When we found I was pregnant again, Eddie hit the roof. He said he didn't want any more kids." Rosie gasped and put her hands to her face. "Oh, god. You're not thinking Eddie's done something to Poppy? That's crazy. Eddie's a good dad. He was just worried because money's a bit tight at the moment, that's all."

"So, what happened?"

"He made an appointment for me to go to the clinic a couple of months ago. We talked about my options and… and I just couldn't go through with it."

"How did Eddie react when you refused the abortion?"

She shrugged. "He was angry at first, but he's fine about it now. In fact, he's quite looking forward to having another son."

"It's a boy?"

She smiled and put her hands protectively on her stomach. "Yes. It's a boy."

"Rosie, there's something else." Bainbridge cleared his throat. "I've seen the girls' hospital files. They seem to have had a few accidents recently. Daisy had a cut lip, and—"

"She fell off her trike," Rosie said. "It tipped over on the drive."

"Then Poppy had a bruised back and cuts to her legs."

"The front bar came loose on the swing, and she fell out. It was a second-hand swing Eddie had picked up on the market. We threw it away after the accident."

"Didn't Daisy get splashed with boiling water?"

Rosie sighed. "I was boiling some potatoes, and the pan fell off the stove. I couldn't have put it on properly," she said. "It didn't do any real damage. The water just sprayed her hand."

"She still had to have treatment," Bainbridge said, arching an eyebrow. "The girls seem to have a lot of accidents, don't they?"

"No more than any other kids their age," Rosie said. "It's not easy keeping your eye on two of them. They get into everything."

Bainbridge looked down at his phone as it vibrated. "Excuse me. I have to take this… Yes, what is it?" he said and walked into the hallway.

"Sir, there's been another one," Duffy said.

"What?"

"A five-year-old girl, this time, snatched from the back alley in Queen Street."

"I'll be right there," Bainbridge said, hurrying out of the house towards his car.

10

Bainbridge arrived at the police station within ten minutes. When he arrived, Sergeant Duffy and two other officers were wrestling with a man at the front desk.

The man was in his forties, tall and thin with a sandy coloured goatee beard and long hair tied in a ponytail. He was dressed casually in jeans and a green t-shirt.

"Take him to the cells," Bainbridge ordered. The two constables escorted the man away. Bainbridge turned to Duffy. "Where's the girl?"

"She's in the interview room with her mum," Duffy said. "Her name's Jodie Brammer. She seems to be all right, sir. The ME was already in attendance at the station on another matter. He says the kid's not been interfered with."

Bainbridge rushed to the interview room. A young woman with short black hair hugged a small girl, sobbing hysterically.

"Is Jodie all right?" Bainbridge asked. "I understand the doctor said there was no assault on your daughter."

The woman shrugged. "Maybe not, but I bet he was going to, the filthy pervert."

"Can I get you anything? A cup of tea?"

The woman shook her head. "No thanks. I just want to take Jodie home. She's been scared to death."

Bainbridge nodded. "Of course. We'll arrange that shortly. I just need a clear picture of exactly what happened."

"That bastard grabbed her off the street and drove off with her in his car. That's what happened. If my neighbour hadn't seen it and got the car's number, God knows what would have happened."

"Well, Mrs Brammer—"

"Miss," she corrected. "I'm not married. Call me Julie."

"Julie, when Jodie's up to it, I will need to speak to her about what happened."

She shook her head. "I don't know what Jodie's dad's gonna say when he finds out some kiddy fiddler tried to take her. He'll kill him."

"Where is her father? Would you like me to explain things to him?"

She shuffled in her chair.

"Julie, where is her dad?"

"If you must know, he's inside," she said. "He got six months for housebreaking last week."

"Oh, I see," he turned his attention to the child. "Hello, Jodie." He smiled. "My name's Andy, and I'm a policeman." The girl had stopped crying and was clinging tightly to her mother's neck. "Can you tell me what happened?"

The girl sniffed loudly and buried her head in her mother's chest.

Julie scowled. "Can't this wait? You can see she's upset. I want to take her home."

"All right," Bainbridge said. "I'll get a police car to drive you home. Would you like a ride in a police car, Jodie?" he said.

Julie shook her head. "No, she bloody wouldn't," she said. "I don't want a cop car outside my house."

"In that case, I'll get one of the officers to drive you home in an unmarked car. I'll speak to Jodie tomorrow."

Julie picked her daughter up and headed towards the door. "All right, if you must," she said. "Can we go now? I have stuff to do."

After arranging for their transport, Bainbridge walked through to the main office, where Sergeant Duffy and several officers were gathered. "Well?" he said. "What do we know about the bloke in custody?"

"His name's Raymond Miller," Duffy said, handing Bainbridge a sheet of paper. "He's a known paedophile. According to our records, Miller lives in South Bank, or he did before he got sent down. He got eighteen months for indecent assault. He was released last week."

"Who made the arrest?"

"I did, sir," said a young officer.

"And you are?"

"Police constable 1439 Beaumont, sir."

"Well, PC Beaumont, tell me about the arrest."

"Well, sir, in company with PC Brooke, I was proceeding along—"

Bainbridge frowned. "For goodness sake, man, you're not in court now. What happened?"

Beaumont's cheeks flushed. "A call came over the radio that a young girl was seen being dragged into a blue Mondeo in Queen Street," Beaumont said. "We were given the registration number of the car and told it was last seen heading towards Warrenby."

"And you immediately gave pursuit?"

"Yes, sir. We picked up the car just as it was entering the caravan site."

"Where was the child?"

"She was in the front passenger seat in a distressed state, sir. Her hands had been bound with tape, as had her mouth."

"Did Miller make any comment?"

"He told us to fuck off," Brooke said.

"Do you know which caravan he was heading for on the site?"

"No, sir. We brought Miller straight back here."

"Well done, both of you," Bainbridge said. "Did Miller have any keys on him when you nicked him?"

"Yes, sir," Beaumont said. "Sergeant Duffy has them."

Sergeant Duffy handed a keyring containing three keys to Bainbridge. "He had these, a mobile phone and a wallet containing twenty-three quid on him," he said. "I was just about to log them in."

Bainbridge took the keys and handed them to Beaumont. "Take these, and find me his caravan," he said. "He could have young Poppy Lee in there. Take a team with you and inform CSI."

"Yes, sir," Beaumont said. "If she's there, we'll find her."

Bainbridge turned to the sergeant. "Duffy, I want you to accompany me when I interview this scumbag," he said.

He smiled. "It'll be a pleasure, sir."

11

Raymond Miller was placed in interview room one. He was drumming his fingers nervously on the table and staring at somewhere on the far wall when Bainbridge and Duffy entered the room. Bainbridge turned on the tape and introduced himself, and Duffy did likewise.

"For the benefit of the tape, can you give your name, please?" Bainbridge asked.

"Fuck off," Miller replied.

"Are you Raymond Miller?" Bainbridge continued.

"Fuck off," Miller repeated. "I want a solicitor."

"Did you abduct Jodie Brammer from Queen Street earlier today?"

Miller scowled. "What do you mean, abduct? I was just taking her for a ride, that's all."

Bainbridge sneered. "A five-year-old girl?"

"Yeah, why not? It was all perfectly innocent. The kid looked bored. I thought she might like a ride in my car."

"Why did you tape her hands and mouth?"

"Because she kept messing with the gear stick and the buttons on the dashboard, that's why. I told her to stop, but she wouldn't."

"Why tape her mouth?"

"I got fed up with telling her to stop, so I slapped her. After that, she started screaming and crying, so I taped her mouth to keep her quiet."

Bainbridge leant forward, steepling his fingers. "Where were you planning on taking the girl?"

"To my caravan."

"Which is your caravan? There are over thirty on the Warrenby site."

"Mind your own fucking business. I didn't take the girl to the van, so you stay away."

"What were you going to do with her, Raymond?" Bainbridge asked. "What were you going to do with a five-year-old girl in your caravan?"

Miller hunched his shoulders. "I had some pop and biscuits. I was going to give her some and then take her back where I found her."

Bainbridge frowned. "I think you had other plans for that little girl. I think you were going to sexually assault her."

Miller threw back his head. "Bullshit. You can't prove that because nothing happened. Ask her. She was still wearing her knickers when you found her, wasn't she?"

"Tell me about the other girl," Bainbridge said.

Miller shrugged. "What other girl?"

"The girl you took from the beach on Saturday."

"The kid that went missing? That was nothing to do with me. I'd nothing to do with that."

"Where were you on Saturday?"

"What time?"

"Midday onwards."

Miller grinned. "Oh, that's easy," he said. "I went to watch a pre-season friendly. Newcastle was playing Middlesbrough at the Riverside."

"Can anyone confirm that?"

"Yeah, as a matter of fact, they can." He leant back in his chair. "I got nicked for fighting in a pub. Two wankers from Newcastle tried it on, and I gave them a pasting. Then the cops came and arrested me. The bastards didn't release me until after the match was finished."

Duffy got up from the table and went towards the door. "I'll check," he said.

"You do that," Miller goaded. "I'm saying nothing else until I have a solicitor. By the way, is there any chance of a cup of tea? I'm parched."

Duffy put down the phone and sighed. "Well, his alibi holds out. He was definitely locked in a cell in Middlesbrough at the time Poppy disappeared."

"Have we found his caravan yet?"

"Yes, sir, Beaumont has just radioed in. CSI officers are over there now. There's no sign of Poppy, though."

Bainbridge sighed. "I think we can rule Miller out," he said. "I don't think he had anything to do with Poppy Lee's disappearance."

"No, sir. It's looking more like the poor kid drowned after all."

12

Bainbridge arrived at the caravan site in Warrenby just after six. He made his way to the small caravan in the middle of the site. "Is this it?" he said, addressing Leo Cutts, the newly appointed forensics officer.

Cutts was carrying two sealed evidence bags. "Yes, sir. Not exactly home and gardens, is it?"

"What's in the bags?"

"Mostly porn," Cutts replied. "Under the counter stuff."

"Anything else?"

"We found two small dolls inside, cheap versions of the Barbie doll."

Bainbridge raised an eyebrow. "Now, what could a grown man possibly want with those?" he said. "I don't suppose there's any sign of Poppy Lee?"

Cutts shook his head. "No, sir, not yet, but we're running tests. I thought that kid drowned. Everyone at the stations thinks so."

"I'm not ruling anything out yet," Bainbridge said as he walked over to the door of the shabby, two-berth caravan. "Is it all right to go inside now?"

"Yes, sir, we've taken fingerprints and tested for DNA."

"Good. Let me have the results as soon as you can."

Bainbridge climbed the two metal steps into the caravan and pushed open the cream painted door. He was immediately struck by the acrid smell inside, a mixture of urine, body odour, and stale food. He gave a cursory glance around the kitchen area and at the small sink and drainer full of dirty crockery. The stove was covered in thick grease with a fat-filled frying pan and a dirty saucepan on top. Above, a small wall cupboard contained tins of beans and spaghetti hoops, along with four cans of lager.

Bainbridge walked further into the van, where a couch had been pulled out to form a bed. There was no sheet, just a dirty duvet with no cover and a couple of pillows piled in one corner. Various items of men's clothing were scattered across the floor, along with a pair of trainers.

He huffed. "I see Miller was living the dream," he said as he was joined by PC Beaumont.

"Yes, sir," Beaumont replied.

"Well, if that bastard has had kids in here, they're not here now. We'd better get back to the station."

Bainbridge arrived back at the police station twenty minutes later.

"No sign of young Poppy?" Sergeant Duffy asked when Bainbridge walked into the Incident Room.

Bainbridge shook his head. "I don't think Miller's involved with Poppy's disappearance," he said. "We'll charge him with the abduction of Jodie and see what else CSI find in his flea-ridden caravan."

Duffy shrugged. "I was just about to put the kettle on. Do you fancy a cuppa?"

Bainbridge shook his head. "No thanks. I'm done for today. I'll leave our friend Raymond Miller in your capable hands, sergeant."

"Okay, sir. See you tomorrow."

"Goodnight."

13

Four weeks later, newly promoted Detective Chief Inspector Bainbridge was in his office going through the monthly crime figures when Duffy tapped on his door and entered the office.

"We're going down to the Crown tonight, sir, if you fancy joining us," Duffy said.

Bainbridge looked up. "What's the occasion? We had my piss up last week."

"It's Jilly Cooper, sir. She's transferring to Durham next week."

"So soon? I knew she'd applied for a transfer, but…"

"Confirmation only came through this morning. She's a bright girl is Jilly. She takes her sergeant's exam next month."

"Well, let's hope she does well. What time are you meeting at the Crown?"

"About seven."

"All right, I'll be there. By the way, Duffy, have we any more witness statements to come in regarding Poppy Lee's disappearance?"

"No, sir, everything we have has been passed on."

"There doesn't seem to be a statement from Cheryl Lewis, Rosie's friend. Did she come into the station?"

Duffy shrugged. "Do you want me to chase it up?"

"No, leave it with me. I'll give her a call."

Duffy leant on the door jamb. "The lads think it's a foregone conclusion that the coroner will pronounce a verdict of death by misadventure. It's been almost a month since the kid disappeared."

Bainbridge shrugged. "You're probably right," he said, "but if there's the slightest chance she didn't drown."

"Sir, we've interviewed every ponce within a ten-mile radius of Redcar. If that kid had been snatched, we'd have heard about it by now."

Bainbridge leant forward. "I hear the family are having a rough time of it."

"Yes, they've been getting quite a bit of hate mail, and someone put their window through the other night."

"Arrange for a marked car to patrol their street every night for the next couple of weeks. Hopefully, things will start to calm down by then."

"Yes, sir," Duffy said as he made to leave the office. "You heard that Mrs Lee had a miscarriage?"

Bainbridge nodded. "Yes, the poor woman. I feel sorry for Rosie. She's not a bad person. She's just—"

"Dim?"

"I was going to say mentally exhausted."

"Young Bobby Lee was in the paper this week. He's got a scholarship to some private school just outside London. According to MENSA, his IQ is through the roof."

Bainbridge ran his hand through his hair and sighed. "Personally, I thought he was an arrogant little sod. We never contacted his mother, did we? Claudia, I think her name is."

Duffy shrugged. "There didn't seem much point, sir. Eddie said she got married soon after they split up, and she moved somewhere on the south coast. He's had no contact with her since."

Just after seven o'clock, Bainbridge put on his jacket and prepared to join his colleagues in The Crown. He was passing through the incident room when PC Beaumont came dashing out of interview room one.

"Sir," he said breathlessly, "I think you should hear this."

Bainbridge frowned. "What is it?" he said. "I was just about to leave."

"It's Simon Wray, sir. He's been arrested for possession of a Class A drug."

"Surely you can deal with that? It's straightforward enough."

"Yes, sir, but Wray wants to make a deal."

"What sort of a deal?"

"He says he knows something about Poppy Lee's

disappearance, sir."

Bainbridge rushed past the young officer and entered the interview room. "I hear you have some information about a missing child?"

Simon Wray sat at the table drumming his fingers, a look of arrogance on his pale, gaunt face. "That depends," he said.

"What do you mean by that?"

"It depends on whether we can do a deal."

Bainbridge's eyes narrowed. "I think you watch too much telly, Mr Wray. This isn't America. We don't do deals."

Wray smirked. "You will when you know what hand I'm holding."

Bainbridge leant over the table and grabbed Wray's arm. "If you know anything, anything at all, about the disappearance of that little girl, you must tell me."

"I don't have to do anything," he said. "You get me off this trumped-up drug charge, and maybe we'll do business."

Bainbridge turned to Beaumont. "Well, constable," he said, "tell me what happened."

"I was proceeding... I saw the defendant's van being driven at speed along the Coast Road, sir. I gave chase, and along with PC Brooke, we managed to bring the vehicle to a halt." Beaumont gave a nervous cough and cleared his throat. "PC Brooke and I were of the opinion that the driver, Mr Simon Wray, had been drinking alcohol, and we proceeded with a breathalyser test. This proved positive."

Wray flung back his head. "I'd had a couple of lagers, that's all. I wasn't drunk."

"Continue," Bainbridge said.

"On searching the vehicle, I found a plastic bag containing a substance which I believed to be heroin. Mr Wray was subsequently arrested and brought to the police station."

"Has the substance been identified?"

"Yes, sir. It is heroin."

"What do you say to that, Mr Wray?"

Wray shrugged. "I was just holding on to it for a mate,

that's all. It isn't mine."

"Don't kid a kidder, Wray."

"But I know stuff… about the kid who went missing. You let me go, and I'll—"

"You'll what? If you know anything about the disappearance of Poppy Lee, you tell me now, or I swear to God, I'll make sure you never see daylight again."

"If I tell you what I know, will you speak up for me in court? This is the first time I've been nicked."

"It might be the first time you've been caught, but I bet it's not the first time you've been dealing."

Wray huffed. "You can't prove that."

"I can try. Now, tell me everything, and we'll see what can be done. That's the best I can do."

There was an uneasy silence. It was several seconds before Wray spoke. "All right, you win, but you promise to put a word in to the court?"

Bainbridge nodded. "Well?"

Wray cleared his throat. "The day the kid went missing, I was in my van in Majuba car park."

"What were you doing there? Dealing drugs?"

Wray shook his head vigorously. "No, nothing like that. I'm a carpet fitter by trade. I'd just finished a job in one of those swanky new houses in Beach View Road at Marske. I came over to Redcar for a couple of pints. The pubs in Marske are a bit pricey."

"Were you alone in your van?"

Wray smirked. "If you must know, I was with a woman."

"What's her name?"

"How the fuck do I know? I'd met her in a pub on the seafront."

"So, you met a woman in a pub. Then what happened?"

"She got in the van, and I drove up to the car park at Majuba. We climbed into the back of the van and… and did the business. Afterwards, I got into the front seat to get a can of lager. That's when I saw the kid."

"Are you sure it was Poppy?"

"Oh yeah, it was Poppy, all right. She had an ice-cream cornet in her hand."

"Who was she with?"

"I couldn't see properly. They were standing at the other side of the vehicle leaning in. My van's windows were a bit steamy, and... anyway, whoever it was fastened the kid into one of the baby seats."

"One of the seats?" Bainbridge said. "You mean there was more than one?"

"Yeah, I could see two, but to be honest, it was the vehicle that caught my eye, not the kid. I remember thinking what a stupid thing to do, letting a kid have ice cream in the car. It was bound to make a mess."

"What about the vehicle? What sort was it?"

"It was a dark-blue Range Rover. One of the new models. I was thinking of getting one myself, but they cost a bomb."

Bainbridge stared at Wray. "I don't suppose you got the number?"

"No, why would I? Anyway, I didn't get the chance. My... my lady friend had got her second wind by this time, if you know what I mean." He laughed coarsely. "All I can tell you is it was a dark-blue Range Rover."

"Why didn't you come forward with this information earlier?"

Wray shrugged. "I wasn't supposed to be in Redcar that day. If my missus finds out what I was up to..."

"I'll need you to make a statement to PC Beaumont," Bainbridge said.

"What about our deal?"

"What deal?"

Wray banged his fist on the table. "You bastard. You promised."

"Like I told you before, Mr Wray, this isn't America. We don't do deals."

"Not even if I tell you what the person who took the kid

dropped before they drove off?"

"What?"

"About that deal… Are you going to speak to the court and tell them I co-operated?"

"I'll see what I can do," Bainbridge said. "Now tell me what was dropped."

"Money," Wray said. "They dropped money."

Bainbridge frowned. "Money? How is that going to help find Poppy?"

"Whoever took the kid must have just come back from their holidays. The money they dropped was euros. Six fifty-euro notes."

"Are you sure it was dropped by the Range Rover's occupant? It couldn't have been from someone else?"

"No. I saw the money shortly after the vehicle drove off. It was near the driver's door."

"Do you still have the notes?"

Wray scowled and shook his head. "Of course I don't. I took them to the bank and exchanged them for real money."

"Can you remember what country they were issued in?"

"Oh yes. The euros were definitely French. Now, do we have a deal?"

Bainbridge nodded. "I'll see what I can do," he said.

On leaving the interview room, Bainbridge walked into Superintendent Kevin Naylor's office and relayed his conversation with Simon Wray.

"We'll get all the CCTV in that we can," Naylor said, "but I'm not hopeful after four weeks."

"I'll get the team out asking after the Range Rover," Bainbridge said. "Somebody must have seen it. It's not your average run-of-the-mill, is it?"

Naylor rubbed his chin. "If that stupid bastard had told us this on the day. Of course, Wray could be mistaken. If he saw a child at all, it might not even be Poppy."

Bainbridge frowned. "It's a possibility. But if he's right,

this is the first sighting we have had of her."

"Unofficial sighting," Naylor corrected. "Let's not get carried away."

"No, sir," Bainbridge said as he left the superintendent's office then made his way to the Communications Room.

14

Bainbridge returned to his office and opened up Poppy Lee's file. He retrieved the details from the business card Cheryl Lewis had given to Rosie and rang the number. It wasn't until the fifth ring that the phone was answered.

"Hello?" said a well-spoken female voice.

"Cheryl Lewis? This is Detective Chief Inspector Bainbridge from Redcar and Cleveland Constabulary."

"Good evening," she said.

"Ms Lewis, I see that you did not come into the station to make a statement like you were asked."

"No, I'm sorry about that. I was called back to the office on an emergency the day after we spoke, and I'm afraid I forgot all about it."

"I will need your statement, Ms Lewis," Bainbridge said.

She exhaled. "That's going to be difficult at the moment, I'm afraid. I'm flying to France tomorrow for a meeting, and then my itinerary is just crazy. I have to go to Italy the following day, then Germany and—"

"I'm still going to need your statement," Bainbridge insisted. "I think help finding that little girl is more important than buying and selling a few frocks, don't you?"

"But why do you need me to make a statement? I've told you already, I only spoke with Rosie on the beach for a couple of minutes. I was at the hotel when the child went missing."

"Do you go to France regularly?"

"Once, sometimes twice a month. Chic Fashions is a French company, after all. Why do you want to know that?"

"What make of car do you drive?"

"A Renault Megan. It's a company car."

"Do you own, or have you ever driven a Range Rover?"

"Why on earth would I want a Chelsea tractor? I live in the city."

"I take it that's a no."

"Yes, detective chief inspector. It's a no."

"I must insist that you call at the station after your tour of Europe."

"All right." Cheryl sighed heavily. "I'll come to the station as soon as my itinerary permits if that's okay, but I doubt I'll be able to tell you anything that will help your enquiries."

"Perhaps not, but all the same, I do need a statement from you. Oh, one more thing—"

But Cheryl Lewis had already hung up.

15

There was a knock on the door, and Rosie hurried into the hall. She didn't get many visitors these days. "Cheryl," she shrieked in delight, throwing her arms around her friend and kissing her on the cheek. "What are you doing in Redcar?"

Cheryl hugged her. "You poor darling. I can't believe what's happened. You must be out of your mind with worry." She followed Rosie into the lounge. "Has there been any news about Poppy?"

Rosie shook her head. "The police think she was washed out to sea."

"You poor thing," Cheryl said. "I hear you miscarried too. I'm so sorry."

"The doctors said it was caused by all the stress."

Cheryl removed her coat and flopped onto the couch. "Well, if there's anything I can do, please let me know."

Rosie sighed as she sat next to Cheryl. "That's kind, but there's nothing anyone can do. Would you like something to drink? A tea or coffee?"

Cheryl grinned and reached into her large bag. "Actually, I've brought some wine. I thought you could probably do with a proper drink."

"I... I don't know," Rosie said. "I have Daisy upstairs."

"Don't be such a prude and get a couple of glasses. One drink won't hurt you. In fact, it will do you good."

"All right, I suppose you're right," Rosie said and went into the kitchen, returning with two wine glasses. She handed them to Cheryl. "Just a small one."

Cheryl half-filled the glasses and handed one to Rosie. "Here, drink this," she said. "You'll feel better."

Sinking back into the couch, Rosie began to sip the wine. "What brings you back to Redcar? I didn't think you were a fan of the seaside."

"I'm not," she said, "but that damned policeman insisted I come to the station to make a statement."

"Why? You weren't even there when Poppy went missing."

Cheryl smiled. "That's what I told them. It was a waste of my time really, but at least I get to see my friend again."

"It's a pity it couldn't have been under happier circumstances," Rosie said. "Life's pretty awful at the moment." She reached for a tissue and blew her nose.

Cheryl took a cigarette from her bag. "Do you mind?" She lit it before Rosie could respond. "Where's Eddie?"

"He's working on Redcar Market today. He should be home soon."

"How's he dealing with things? Is he okay?"

Rosie shrugged. "Eddie's upset, but I think he's starting to come to terms with what's happened. I don't think I ever will."

Cheryl leant forward and gently squeezed Rosie's arm. "Don't give up hope. They haven't found her body, so until they do, Poppy may be still alive somewhere."

Rosie smiled weakly but said nothing.

"By the way, you'll never guess who I bumped into in Newcastle a couple of weeks ago."

"Who?"

Cheryl exhaled. "Martin Lowry."

"Martin Lowry from school?"

She nodded. "Guess what he's doing now?"

"I've no idea. I haven't seen him in years."

"He's a paramedic."

"Good for him. Martin always was good at first aid, wasn't he?"

Cheryl drew heavily on her cigarette. "Yes. If it hadn't been for his quick thinking in the school lab that day, things could have been much worse."

Rosie put her hands to her face and grimaced. "Oh, Cheryl, please don't remind me. It was terrifying. I still don't know how the accident happened. One minute I was holding the bottle firmly, and the next…"

Cheryl winced. "And the next, I was being splashed with sulphuric acid. If Martin hadn't had the presence of mind to douse me with water as quickly as he did…"

Rosie lowered her head. "I still have nightmares about that day. I really am sorry. I know it was my fault, but I honestly don't understand how it happened."

Cheryl leant forward and took Rosie's hand. "Don't worry about it," she said softly. "Accidents will happen. I had a couple of skin grafts, and I'm as good as new." She sipped her wine. "Anyway, Martin sends his regards. He says he hopes your daughter is found safe and well."

"That's kind of him."

Cheryl drank the remnants from her glass and winked. "Should we have another?"

Rosie glanced at the mantle clock. It was three-thirty. "All right. Just a small one, then I really must make a start on dinner. Eddie will be home at five."

Cheryl poured the wine and handed a glass to Rosie. "How's Bobby getting on at his new school?"

At the mention of Bobby, Rosie's face lit up. "He loves it," she said. "He telephones almost every night. He's really settled in well."

"So, he's not homesick then?"

"He doesn't seem to be."

"Does the scholarship extend until he's eighteen?"

"Yes, thank goodness. Eddie and I could never have afforded the school fees otherwise."

"Well, let's hope he does well."

Rosie got up from the couch and walked towards the kitchen. "I'd better start dinner. Would you like to stay for something to eat?"

Cheryl shook her head. "No thanks, I have to get back to Newcastle. I have an early flight tomorrow."

"Where are you going this time?"

"France."

Rosie clasped her hands. "Oh, you're so lucky. Sometimes,

I wish I'd travelled more before settling down."

Cheryl drained her glass. "It's not half as glamorous as you might think, believe me. What you have here with your family is real, Rosie. Never forget that." She got up from the couch and reached for her coat. "Now, I really must be making tracks. Oh, is that Daisy I can hear crying?"

Rosie rushed into the hall. "Yes, she's had her nap. She's missing her sister, poor little thing."

"Well, you go and see to your daughter." Cheryl walked towards the front door. "I'll see myself out."

Rosie walked over to her friend and hugged her. "We must make an effort to keep in touch. I really do miss our friendship."

Cheryl smiled. "Me too. I'll call you in a day or two."

Rosie watched as her friend climbed into her Renault Megan and drove out of the cul-de-sac.

16

It had been two months since Poppy Lee had disappeared. Sergeant Duffy walked into the briefing room to hand out the shift's assignments to his officers. He raised an eyebrow at the sight of Bainbridge standing at the front of the room.

"Before Sergeant Duffy takes the roll call, I have some information," Bainbridge said. "It has been decided to officially wind down the search for Poppy Lee." There was a faint murmuring amongst the officers present. Bainbridge raised his hand. "It's unfortunate, I know, but we have to accept that the little girl was swept out to sea off Redcar beach."

PC Beaumont stepped forward. "But, sir. What about the sighting of the girl in the Majuba car park?"

Bainbridge shook his head. "That can't be verified. Simon Wray was an unreliable witness. He's off his head most of the time on drugs."

"But what about the Range Rover, sir?" Beaumont continued. "Surely CCTV will have picked it up?"

Bainbridge sighed. "All the tapes have been wiped. Nobody in the vicinity recalls seeing a vehicle of that description."

"But sir—"

"Enough, PC Beaumont," Bainbridge said. "If I thought there was the slightest chance of finding that little girl alive, I would—"

"What about the money, sir? Three hundred euros is a lot of cash."

"There's no proof where that money came from. It's probably somebody's left-over holiday money."

"Then why not take it to a bank and exchange it for sterling? Simon Wray did. Don't you think it's possible that the person kept the money in euros because they would be revisiting France in the near future?"

"I take it you're referring to Cheryl Lewis, Rosie's friend?"

Beaumont nodded. "Yes, sir. She was on the beach around the time Poppy was taken, and she visits France regularly."

Bainbridge exhaled. "Cheryl Lewis did not abduct Poppy Lee," he said. "Her alibi has been thoroughly checked. She was at The Royal Hotel that day with several of her colleagues, and she most definitely did not have a child with her." He began to walk towards the door and then turned. "Neither, I might add, does she drive a Range Rover."

Beaumont shrugged. "She could have had an accomplice?"

Bainbridge reached the door. "That's all from me this morning. Sergeant Duffy will give you your assignments."

The sergeant duly took up his position at the front of the room and began to read out the day's rota.

It was late morning when Duffy entered the DCI's office. "I thought you might like a cuppa," he said, handing him a mug of tea.

"Thanks," Bainbridge said, putting down the bundle of papers he had been scrutinising on his desk. "Tell me, sergeant, what do you think about the Lee case?"

"Well, sir, I think that little girl wandered into the sea and was drowned. It only takes one wave to knock a two-year-old off her feet, and once she was down…"

"It just worries me that nobody saw anything. You'd think somebody would notice a small child alone by the shoreline."

Duffy shrugged. "I think people were just too busy enjoying the sunshine. It's not every day the temperature gets that high. And the kid was wearing blue, don't forget. You can't see blue clearly in the water."

The DCI sipped his tea and sighed. "Yes, I suppose you're right."

"Let's just hope that when Daisy grows up, she does her parents proud."

"Yes, let's hope so," the DCI said, returning to the papers he had been working on. "Let's hope so."

17

Sixteen years later – Jilly Cooper gave a contented sigh as she gazed around her sea-view apartment in Redcar. It had been sixteen years since she had last worked here as a police constable. Now she was returning. Not as a constable this time, but as a newly promoted detective inspector.

She flitted through her wardrobe before finally settling on a black skirt and pale blue jacket. Glancing at her watch, she noticed it was eight-thirty. She inhaled deeply and curled her hands into fists. In just over an hour, she was due to report for duty at Redcar Police Station, where Detective Chief Superintendent Andrew Bainbridge was in charge.

"Welcome back," Bainbridge said as she entered his office. "I'm so glad to see you again." He leant over the desk and shook her hand. "Congratulations on your well-deserved promotion."

"Thank you, sir," she smiled weakly. "It's good to be back."

"Please, take a seat," he said, indicating the chair across from his desk. "I'm sorry I wasn't here to meet you first thing. I had a meeting in Middlesbrough this morning, and you know how these things go on."

Cooper smiled as she smoothed down her skirt and placed her hands on her lap. "The sergeant has filled me in on everything that's been happening. I see there have been several mysterious disappearances of young women over the last eighteen months."

"That's right. The third young woman disappeared only last month."

"Were these women in the vulnerable category?"

"You mean were they sex workers?" Bainbridge shook his head. "No, they were not. They were young but appear to have led perfectly normal lives."

"But it's not being treated as a possible murder

investigation?"

Bainbridge frowned. "Not at the moment. It's been decided to continue treating each case as a missing person for the time being."

"I see, sir, but—"

Bainbridge raised his right hand. "Jilly, why don't we dispense with this sir business when we're alone? I think we've gone way over the line to be so formal, don't you?"

"I… Andy, what happened between us before is history. We're different people now. I'm a detective inspector and you… you are a detective chief superintendent."

"Who's about to retire in six months. You do know that?"

Cooper gave a faint nod. "Yes, I heard. I was surprised you were retiring so early though. I thought you might have stayed on for another five years."

He shrugged. "I thought about it, but—"

There was a sharp rap on the door and Sally, the newly appointed typist, came into the room.

"These are the files you asked for, sir," she said.

Bainbridge indicated a small table against the wall. "Put them over there," he said.

"Yes, sir," Sally said, putting down the files. "Is there anything else before I go to lunch?"

He shook his head. "No, that's all, thanks."

Sally hurried across to the door, giving a courteous nod to Cooper before closing it quietly behind her.

"The poor kid looks terrified," Cooper said.

"Oh, Sally's all right. It's just first-week nerves."

Cooper shrugged. "I know how she feels."

"I've got a special task I'd like you to carry out," he said. "We'll discuss it in detail after lunch. It's turned twelve. I don't know about you, but I'm starving."

Cooper smiled. "I'll get my coat."

18

It was a fifteen-minute drive to The Coppers Inn, an eighteenth-century, stone-fronted building set back from the main road. Bainbridge parked the car alongside a silver Audi.

Cooper climbed out of the car and stared at the building. "Didn't this used to be called The Crown?" she asked.

Bainbridge grinned. "That's right. Steve Duffy owns it now. You do remember Sergeant Duffy, don't you?"

"Yes, of course. I'd heard he'd retired, but I didn't know he'd bought a pub."

As soon as they entered the building, Duffy came hurrying towards them, a broad smile on his chubby face. "Well, if it isn't Jilly Cooper," he said. "You haven't changed one bit." He put his arms around her and hugged her tightly. "Andy told me you were coming back to Redcar. Welcome back."

She grinned and leant forward, kissing Duffy on the cheek. "It's lovely to see you again. How do you enjoy being a landlord?"

Duffy shrugged his hefty shoulders and winked. "It beats working. Now, what can I get you to drink?"

After enjoying the cod and prawn pie, Bainbridge ordered two coffees. "Let's go into the lounge bar," he said. "It's quieter there." They walked through the double doors, choosing a table close to the window. A few minutes later, a young waitress brought them their coffee.

Cooper sighed. "It doesn't seem sixteen years since we were here last. Where does the time go?"

Bainbridge sipped his coffee and leant towards her. "I think it's time I explained what happened that day," he said quietly. "Why I did what I did."

Cooper sat bolt upright and inhaled deeply. Her lips tightened, and she clasped her hands together on the table. "If you don't mind, Andy, I'd rather not discuss it. Like I said before, it's in the past."

He shook his head slowly and, reaching out, took hold of Cooper's hands. "You don't understand," he said softly. "I had to end our relationship. I had no choice."

Cooper quickly withdrew her hands onto her lap. "I understand your career meant more to you than I did. I thought we had something special. It just shows what a crap detective I was back then."

Bainbridge fixed his eyes on her. When he spoke, there was a faint tremor in his voice. "She knew about us," he said.

"Who knew?"

"My wife. She had known for a few weeks. She had pictures of us together."

"No, how could she?" she whispered.

"My wife was a resourceful and vindictive woman. She'd hired a private detective to have me followed. She threatened to wreck both our careers if—"

"If what?"

"If I didn't end our relationship and get you transferred. I couldn't let her do that to you, Jilly. That's why I said those things."

"Does your wife know I'm back in Redcar?"

"She's dead," he said quietly. "She suffered a massive stroke last year."

There was an uneasy silence. "Thank you for telling me," Cooper said softly, "but that doesn't change anything. What happened between us is history." She sipped the last of her coffee. "Perhaps we should be getting back to the station?"

Five minutes later, they were back in the car, heading in the direction of the police station.

"Duffy's looking well," Cooper said in an attempt to lighten the mood. "How long has he had the pub?"

"He retired five years ago and bought it soon after that."

"Good for him," she said. "Is there a Mrs Duffy?"

"There was," he said, "but they split up soon after Duffy retired. I heard she moved to Australia. Duffy never got involved with anyone after that, as far as I know." Bainbridge turned into the police car park. "By the way, did you notice the waitress?"

"The young blonde girl? What about her?"

"That was Daisy Lee," he said. "It was her twin, Poppy, that went missing sixteen years ago."

"Of course, the little girl that drowned."

"The family are still living in Redcar. Her mother is convinced Poppy is still alive."

Cooper exhaled. "Poor woman," she said. "Losing a child like that must be impossible to come to terms with."

Daisy Lee had watched through the window as the two police officers got into their vehicle and drove out of the car park. Duffy stood by her side. "So, that's the policeman who tried to find Poppy?" she said.

He nodded. "Yes, that's Andy Bainbridge. He's a good man, Daisy. If Poppy had been taken, Andy would have found her. You can be sure of that."

Daisy gave a deep sigh. "My mother thinks Poppy is still alive somewhere."

He put his arm affectionately around the girl's shoulders. "It's a terrible tragedy what happened," he said softly, "but your sister was swept out to sea. That's a fact." He turned and walked towards the bar. "Hurry up and clear the tables, then you might as well get off home. It looks like it's going to be a quiet day."

Daisy collected the coffee cups and took them to the kitchen, then returned to the main bar.

"It's your night off tonight, isn't it?" Duffy said as the girl began clearing more tables. "Are you doing anything special?"

She shook her head. "Not really. Bobby's up from London for a few days, so Mother wants us all together."

"How is Bobby? I haven't seen him in years. I heard he was doing well for himself."

She shrugged and reached for her coat. "We don't see

much of him either. We used to be close, but he always seems too busy these days."

19

Cooper was at her desk later that afternoon when Bainbridge entered her office. He was carrying three buff-coloured files.

"I want to discuss these with you," he said, placing the files on her desk. "They are the witness statements regarding the missing women."

She pushed her papers to one side as Bainbridge took a chair across from her and opened the first file. "Deborah Jenkins was the first," he said. "She was last seen leaving the Boardwalk Nightclub in Redcar on Christmas Eve, eighteen months ago." He slid Deborah's photograph towards Cooper.

"She's a pretty girl. Did she have a job?"

"She was between jobs," he said. "She worked in retail."

"Any convictions?"

"Two. Both for possession of marijuana."

"So, Deborah liked to take drugs?"

Bainbridge shrugged. "We couldn't get much out of her friend, Maria McGuire, other than Deborah had been drinking heavily all evening. I suspect drugs were involved."

"Do we know of any reason why she would walk away from her life?"

Bainbridge shrugged. "All we know is that she had been sofa-surfing for a couple of months before she disappeared and had been staying at Maria McGuire's flat over the Christmas period."

"It's possible she decided to move on, I suppose," she said. "After all, there doesn't seem to be much to hold her here."

"Maybe, but I'd like you to interview her friend again. See if she remembers anything else." He opened the second file. "Suzie Graham disappeared about a year ago," he said, handing her photograph to Cooper. "She was walking her boyfriend's dog one night and never returned."

"Are you sure the boyfriend wasn't involved in her disappearance?"

Bainbridge shook his head. "No. We soon wrote him off

as a suspect. Sam Carter seemed genuinely upset about Suzie's disappearance."

Cooper scanned the file. "I see Sam is ten years older than Suzie."

"Yes, that's right," he said. "I'll put money on her being shacked up with some younger bloke."

Cooper closed the file. "Who is the third girl?"

"Her name is Janette Walsh." He handed the file to her. "Janette went missing about four weeks ago."

Cooper scanned the summary report. "I see she is just eighteen. An art student at the local college."

"That's right. She lived at home with her parents. She went missing after going to meet friends in Locke Park."

"She certainly likes her tattoos and piercings," Cooper said, noting the diamond studs through Janette's nose and bottom lip.

"I think that's supposed to be arty. Why a young woman wants to disfigure herself like that is beyond me."

"Tattoos are the in-thing now, Andy. I was thinking of getting one myself."

Andy arched an eyebrow but said nothing.

She smiled. "Just kidding. I think I'm too old for that sort of thing now. They are best on young people."

Bainbridge frowned. "Yes, but young people turn into old people. That's when they look even more stupid." He stood up and walked towards the door. "I'll leave you to it. Let me know when you've re-interviewed the witnesses. I'd like your opinion."

"I take it you don't think there's anything sinister about these disappearances?"

"No, I don't. I think the most reasonable explanation is that they chose to leave, but the chief constable wants to make sure we don't have some maniac running around Redcar abducting young women."

Bainbridge made his way back to his office, leaving Cooper to study the files in more detail.

Ten minutes later, there was a tap on her door, and Sally entered, carrying a mug of tea. "I've brought you a drink, ma'am," she said and placed the mug down on the desk. "Detective Chief Superintendent Bainbridge said you didn't take sugar."

Cooper smiled. "Thank you. How are you enjoying working here, Sally?" she asked. "It's your first job since leaving school, isn't it?"

Sally blushed. "Yes, ma'am. I love it." She turned to leave and then spun back around. "Ma'am …" She faltered, moving closer to Cooper's desk. "May I ask you something?"

"Of course. What is it?"

"It's about my friend who's missing. I just wondered if you'd heard anything?"

"What's your friend's name?"

"Janette Walsh," she said. "I'm so worried. Nobody's seen her in almost a month."

"How well did you know Janette?"

"We were best friends at school. She went to Art College, so I haven't seen as much of her as I used to."

The telephone gave out a shrill ring. "Oh, I have to take this," Cooper said. "I'll speak with you later." Sally nodded and hurriedly left the room.

"Detective Inspector Cooper… Yes, sir, right away."

20

Rosie and Eddie Lee were finishing their supper in the dining room of 14 Hudson Gardens, along with their children, Daisy and Bobby.

"That was delicious, Mum," Bobby said as he laid his knife and fork across his empty plate. "I wish my wife could cook like you."

Rosie tutted. "You'd better not let Karen hear you say that," she said.

"But it's true. She set fire to boiled rice once. It ruined the pan." There was a faint ripple of laughter.

"Where is Karen?" Eddie asked. "We haven't seen her in months. I thought she would be coming up here with you."

Bobby hunched his shoulders and frowned. "She's really busy. She got a promotion at the bank, and her workload has doubled. She doesn't have time to visit anyone at the moment."

Rosie tutted once more. "That girl works too hard. She should make time to relax. You too, Bobby. There's more to life than work."

Bobby dabbed his mouth with the napkin and pushed back his chair. "Work is important, Mother. You only get out of life what you put into it."

Daisy threw out her hands and glared at Bobby. "Oh, here we go again. Another lecture on how to succeed in life. You forget, Bobby, we didn't all have the benefit of the education you had."

Bobby scowled as he got up from the table. "If pulling pints in a pub is your life's ambition, Daisy, that's fine. But you could do so much better. Achieve so much more."

She stuck out her chin defiantly. "I like working at the pub. I meet all sorts of interesting people."

He scoffed. "Interesting drunks more like."

Daisy flung her napkin on the table. "Actually, I met someone interesting today."

"Oh, who was that?" Bobby said.

Daisy turned to face her mother. "Mum, you remember that policeman who dealt with Poppy's accident? He had lunch at the pub today. Duffy pointed him out to me."

Rosie gasped. "Detective Inspector Bainbridge?" she said, her hands curling tightly into fists.

Eddie reached over and patted Rosie's hands. "Don't get upset, love. That's all over now. New beginnings, remember?"

"He's a Detective Chief Superintendent now," Daisy said. "I don't think he knew who I was, though."

"Actually, there's something I need to discuss with you all," she said. "It's about Poppy."

Eddie scowled and banged his fist on the table. "What have I told you?" he said. "Poppy is dead. There's nothing to discuss. Is that clear?"

Rosie got up from the table and walked over to the dresser. Opening a drawer, she removed a large buff-coloured envelope and returned to take her place. "I got this letter yesterday," she said, removing the envelope's contents. "It's from the television people."

"What television people?" Eddie said, snatching the document from Rosie's hands.

"The producers of *Where Can They Be?* have invited us onto the show to make an appeal. If Poppy is out there somewhere, she might see it and realise who she is. Somebody else might see it and recognise her or—"

"So that's why you asked me to come up for a few days?" Bobby said. "To take part in this bloody appeal?"

Eddie's nostrils flared, and his mouth tightened as he read the letter. "It says they received information from a witness that Poppy was seen being put into a vehicle the day she disappeared," he said. "That's bloody rubbish. Why didn't this person tell the police?"

"He did," Rosie said. "He made a statement, but they didn't believe him."

"Where's this witness now? Why has he waited until now

to tell us this?"

"The man from the television programme said he has been in jail for the last ten years. It was when he was dying that he made the statement and sent it to them. He wanted money for his family."

"I don't believe it." Eddie screwed up the letter and threw it on the floor. "The man's a bloody liar."

Bobby picked up the crumpled letter. "If we agree to do this appeal, it could open up all the animosity again towards the family. You do know that, Mum?"

Rosie nodded and tilted her head defiantly. "I don't care," she said softly. "If my baby's out there, I need to know."

Daisy got up from the table. "I'm going for a walk. I need some air."

"I'll come with you," Bobby said. "We have to think this through."

Daisy and Bobby walked along Redcar's seafront, arm-in-arm.

"It's good to see the funfair's still here," Bobby said. He smiled. "This place is like stepping back in time."

Daisy frowned. "What do you mean? The council have spent millions on modernising Redcar."

"Oh, I can see that. I meant the funfair has hardly changed." He inhaled deeply. "The smell of hot dogs and candyfloss are exactly the same as I remember when we were kids." Bobby squeezed Daisy's arm. "Do you fancy a go on the rollercoaster?" he said, a broad grin on his face. "It's been years since we rode the big dipper."

Daisy shook her head and grimaced. "No thanks. I hate the big rides. I have done ever since I fell off the galloping horses when I was seven and broke my arm."

Bobby frowned. "I told you to hold on tight, but you got too excited and let go."

They hurried by the amusements and headed towards the town centre. "Let's go to the pub," she said. "We need to talk about this bloody appeal."

"Okay, but I've given up booze."

"You have? Whatever for?"

"Because I prefer a clear head," Bobby said. "Should we go to The Coppers Rest? Maybe you could introduce me to some of the interesting people you were talking about?"

"The Coppers Inn," Daisy corrected. "No, I don't want to go there tonight. I'm there enough with work. Let's go to the Beacon."

Bobby screwed up his face. "I thought they were going to pull it down years ago."

"Rubbish. It's part of the landscape," Daisy said, laughing. "In fact, people have become remarkably fond of it over the years."

He shrugged. "If you say so," he said as he followed his sister through the glass doors into the pub.

They found a booth close to the door, and Bobby went to the bar, returning a few minutes later with a coke for himself and a large white wine for Daisy. "So," he said, a broad grin on his handsome face. "What do you think about going on the telly? Personally, I think Mum is bonkers. Everyone knows Poppy drowned."

"But what if she didn't? What if she was taken by someone like that bloke said?"

"Why would anyone take a two-year-old girl?"

Daisy shrugged and fidgeted with the beermat. "Maybe someone who couldn't have a baby of their own and…"

Bobby put his hands over Daisy's. "Poppy drowned," he said. "She was washed out to sea. They found her shoe at the water's edge, don't forget."

"Someone could have put it there to make it look like she had drowned."

Bobby pulled his hand away and scowled. "You're being ridiculous," he said. "If Poppy had been taken, it would have been by a paedophile. Do you really think our parents want to know that? Imagining what the weirdo would do to our baby sister?"

Daisy gave an involuntary shudder. "Stop it, Bobby. For God's sake, stop it."

"I think we should dissuade Mum from making the appeal. It will save heartache in the end. Don't you agree?"

She took a tissue from her bag and dabbed her eyes. "I don't know," she whispered. "If there's a chance, even a tiny chance that Poppy is still alive."

"There isn't. I was there that day, don't forget. I saw what happened."

"What exactly did you see? Please, tell me. Mum won't talk about that day."

Bobby ran his fingers around the rim of his glass for a few seconds, a faraway look in his eyes. "There's not much to tell. You and Poppy were playing on the sand. Mum went to fetch us all an ice cream." He picked up his glass and sipped his drink. "For some reason she took you with her and left Poppy on the beach."

"What happened after Mum left?"

"Some lads I'd been playing with had caught a jellyfish, so I went to have a look." He lowered his head into his hands. "Mum came back with the ice cream, and… and Poppy was gone."

"Didn't you notice anyone hanging about? Didn't you hear Poppy cry out? You must have seen or heard something."

"Well, I didn't," he said and took another sip from his glass. "I know I should have, but I didn't."

Daisy reached over and patted his arm. "You're not to blame for what happened," she said.

"Aren't I? I was supposed to be a super-intelligent ten-year-old. I should have seen something. If I hadn't been so obsessed with those bloody jellyfish."

"You were a child. Nobody blames you for what happened."

"I think Mum does. I see her looking at me sometimes, and I wonder."

"You're imagining things. She couldn't be prouder of you."

Bobby shrugged but said nothing.

Daisy sipped the last of her wine. "So, big brother, what does it feel like to be working in London?"

Bobby smiled. "It feels good. It's hard work, of course, but rewarding."

"It's a pity you live so far away. We'd all like to see you more often."

"London's not a million miles away. I get up to Redcar as often as I can. I was here only last month."

"I know, but it's not the same. I get lonely sometimes, and it would be good to have you to talk to."

"I'm a phone call away. You know that." He drained his glass. "Another drink?"

"Sure, why not?" she said. "There's nothing else to do."

It was almost ten o'clock when Bobby and Daisy returned to Hudson Gardens. Their mother sat on the couch, gently rocking backwards and forwards, gazing into the distance. Snooker played silently on the television.

"I didn't know you were a snooker fan," Daisy said, taking off her jacket.

Rosie started. "Snooker? Oh, I hadn't noticed. The television was just on."

"Where's Dad?"

"He's gone to the police station. He wants to find out exactly what the witness said about seeing Poppy."

Bobby flopped down in an armchair. "You're not seriously going ahead with this bloody appeal, are you? I've told you, Mum, it will cause more harm than good."

Rosie got up from the couch and walked into the kitchen. "Would anybody like a drink?" Both Daisy and Bobby declined. A few minutes later, Rosie emerged from the kitchen, a mug of steaming hot chocolate in her hand. "It helps me sleep," she said.

Bobby went to the window and lifted the blinds. "How long has Dad been gone?"

Rosie shrugged. "About an hour, I think. He left soon after you two went out."

"Mum, that was three hours ago. I'm going to the station to find him."

"I'll come with you," Daisy said.

"No, you stay here with Mum. I won't be long." Bobby walked into the hall and went through the door into the night.

Daisy sat on the couch next to her mother and put her arm around her shoulders. "It'll be all right, Mum," she whispered. "Everything will be all right."

21

Bainbridge sat at home watching snooker on the television and enjoying a fish supper when the telephone rang. He glanced at the clock. It was nine o'clock. "Damn!" he muttered and picked up the receiver. "Bainbridge," he said.

"Sir, it's Sergeant Brown. I'm sorry to disturb you at this hour, but I think you should come back to the station right away."

"Why? What's up?"

"It's Mr Lee, sir. He insists on speaking with you. He says it's urgent."

Bainbridge rubbed his chin and sighed. "All right, sergeant. Tell him I'll be there in fifteen minutes." He put down the receiver and turned off the television.

Eddie Lee paced the waiting room as Bainbridge arrived at the station. "Good evening, Mr Lee," he said. "I understand you wished to see me urgently?"

Eddie nodded but remained silent.

"We'll go to my office," Bainbridge said. "We won't be disturbed there." Eddie followed him along the corridor until they reached the door marked *Detective Chief Superintendent Bainbridge*. He turned to Eddie. "Can I get you anything? Tea or coffee, perhaps?"

"No thanks," he said. "I'm fine."

Bainbridge indicated for him to sit in one of the armchairs to the side of his desk. He sat in the other. "Well, what can I do for you?"

Eddie took out the crumpled letter received from the television programme and thrust it towards Bainbridge. "It's about this. Is it true? Did someone see my little girl being taken?" He leant forward, his breathing rapid, as beads of sweat formed on his brow. "It claims there was a witness who saw Poppy being taken, and the police did nothing about it."

Bainbridge took a deep breath and leant back into his chair

as he read the letter. He sighed. "It is true that a man claimed to have seen a little girl matching Poppy's description being put into a vehicle. But I can assure you this claim was thoroughly investigated at the time, and there was no evidence to substantiate what the man said."

Eddie threw up his hands. "You can't be sure he was lying, though, can you? Suppose this bloke was telling the truth? Suppose he did see someone taking my daughter?"

"Mr Lee... Eddie, believe me, lengthy enquiries were made at the time. But unfortunately, the witness was unreliable. A convicted drug addict. You can see from the letter that he died in prison."

"Just because he was a wrong 'un doesn't mean he was lying."

"The man only offered the information about Poppy in an attempt to make a deal for himself. He'd been arrested on serious drug offences."

"So, you're saying he was lying to save his own skin?"

"That's exactly what I'm saying, Eddie. All the evidence says that your daughter was swept out to sea." Bainbridge walked over to the wall cabinet, took out a whisky bottle, and poured two glasses. He handed one to Eddie.

"Thanks," Eddie said as he took the glass and slowly sipped the contents. He lifted his head and looked directly at Bainbridge. "Tell me the truth. If you were me, would you do this appeal?"

He shook his head slowly and sighed. "That's something only you and Rosie can decide. But you must realise you'll be putting yourself and your family through a terrible ordeal if you do. Remember what happened last time?"

"People blamed Rosie," Eddie said. "It nearly destroyed her."

Bainbridge drained the contents of the glass. "Come on, Eddie. Go home to Rosie. She needs you."

Eddie lowered his head into his hands. "I don't know what to do. I just have this feeling that maybe..."

"Think carefully before you decide," Bainbridge said. "Do you really want to dredge this all up again? People can be cruel."

"Yes, they can, can't they?" Eddie said as he walked towards the door and silently left the room.

After Eddie left, Bainbridge poured himself another drink. "Damn you, Simon Wray," he cursed. "Damn you."

22

Cooper arrived at the station at eight-thirty. Bainbridge was already working in his office, so she knocked lightly on his door before entering.

"Good morning." She smiled. "It looks like it's going to be a lovely day."

Bainbridge did not look up from his desk. "Close the door, Jilly, and take a seat."

She sat across from him and frowned deeply. "Is everything all right, Andy? You look… you look harassed."

He put down his pen and looked up. "I had a visit from Eddie Lee last night. He's talking about making a public appeal on the television about his missing daughter."

"Why would he do that? I thought that case was settled."

"It was until Simon Wray wrote to the producer of *What Became Of?* claiming to have seen the child being abducted."

Cooper shook her head. "But Simon Wray's allegation was investigated. There was no evidence to support his story."

"I know that, but what if Wray was telling the truth and Poppy was abducted?"

"Andy, Poppy Lee was swept out to sea. She's dead. She's been dead for sixteen years."

Bainbridge sighed. "Perhaps, but what if we got it wrong and Poppy is out there somewhere."

"That's nonsense. You know it is."

"Well, the Chief Constable doesn't think it's nonsense. He's agreed for me to appear on the programme on Friday."

"What?"

Bainbridge leant back in his chair and waved a dismissive hand. "Anyway, enough talk about Poppy Lee. Have you had a chance to go through those statements I gave you?"

"Yes," she said. "I'm going to re-interview the witnesses again. There's just a chance they might remember something."

"All right, but don't spend too much time on it. Like I said, the most likely explanation is that they've moved on."

Sally was working on her computer when Cooper stopped next to her. "Sally," she said, "can you come through to my office, please?"

Sally stopped typing immediately and followed her.

Cooper indicated a chair in front of her desk. "Sit down," she said. "I want to talk to you about your friend who disappeared."

"Janette? I don't know what happened to her."

Cooper sat poised her pen over her notebook. "You said you were at school together?"

"Yes, ma'am, that's right. We sort of lost touch when she went on to Art College."

"When was the last time you saw her?"

Sally pondered. "It must have been about two weeks before she disappeared. I bumped into her in the high street in Middlesbrough."

"What was she doing?"

"Shopping, ma'am, same as me. We went into the burger bar for a snack and a catch-up."

"What did you talk about? Can you remember?"

Sally frowned. "Yes, ma'am. Janette had bought some black patent stilettoes."

"Stilettoes?"

Sally's frown deepened. "I thought it was a bit odd, but Janette said she had a weekend job, and she wanted to look smart."

"Did she say what the job was?"

Sally lowered her head. "No, not exactly. Just that it paid good money. Some of our friends joined us in the burger bar, so I didn't get a chance to ask her anymore."

"Is there anything else you can tell me about Janette? Anything at all that you think might help me find her?"

She shook her head. "No, I'm sorry, ma'am. Like I said, I came to work here, and Janette went to Art College." She smiled. "She's a very talented artist."

Cooper sighed as she placed her pen and notebook back

into her bag. "Thank you. You've been extremely helpful."
    Sally hurried out of the office and back to her computer.

23

Maria McGuire lived in a newly renovated ground-floor flat on the outskirts of Marske. Cooper knocked on the door, and it was opened immediately.

"Miss McGuire? Miss Maria McGuire?"

"Who are you?"

Cooper produced her warrant card. "I would like to speak with you about Deborah Jenkins."

Maria put her hands to her face. "Oh my God, have you found her? Have you found Debbie?"

"Let's go inside," Cooper said as she gently guided Maria through to the lounge.

"Have you found Debbie?" Maria repeated.

Cooper shook her head. "No, I'm sorry we haven't," she said. "I need to ask you more questions about the night she disappeared."

Maria huffed as she flung herself onto the couch. "More questions? I've told the police all I can remember."

Cooper stood by the window. "I understand Deborah was staying here with you in the flat?"

Maria nodded. "She didn't have anywhere else to go, so I let her stay here for a couple of weeks until she got herself sorted."

"Is there anything here that belonged to Deborah? A phone or laptop, perhaps?"

Maria shook her head. "No. The police took her phone. Debbie didn't have a laptop. And by the way, her name is Debbie. She hates to be called Deborah."

Cooper gave a slight nod. "What about Debbie's clothes? Do you still have them?"

"No, I'm afraid not. There wasn't much. She travelled light. I gave all the casualwear to the charity shop."

"You gave all Debbie's clothes away?"

Maria looked down at the floor and shrugged. "Not all," she said, colour beginning to rise in her cheeks. "I kept a couple of sweaters for myself. After all, she owed me a ton of rent."

"Was there anything else?"

"There was an expensive red-sequined dress and matching shoes. I sold those on eBay."

"Why wasn't she wearing the dress on Christmas Eve?"

Maria shrugged. "She said it was for work only."

"What sort of work?"

Maria stood up and walked over to the fireplace. "She had a job working weekends somewhere. Dressed up to the nines she was when she went out."

"Do you know what this job was?"

"I've no idea. I do know it was cash-in-hand though, and quite a bit of cash at that."

Cooper frowned. "There's nothing about this in the statement you made. Why didn't you mention this to the police when she disappeared?"

Maria folded her arms. "I wasn't going to drop her in it with the taxman, was I? I didn't know she was going to go missing for eighteen months."

"Tell me again what happened that night," Cooper said. "Tell me everything you can remember."

Maria sighed heavily. "Like I told you lot before, I was at the Boardwalk nightclub on Christmas Eve with Debbie and a group of friends. I'd got a few bottles of cider in my flat, so about one o'clock I suggested we all come back here to continue the party."

"Are you sure Debbie was amongst the group when you left the club?"

"I don't remember seeing her," she said, "but she must have been. We were all a bit drunk, to be honest."

"Do you know if she had been taking drugs that night?"

Maria tensed. "I... I don't think so."

"Maria, it's important you tell me the truth."

"She took a couple of pills in the club," she said, "but she was okay. She always pops a couple of pills when she's on a night out. Debbie certainly knew… knows how to party."

"When you walked home, did you go along the beach or along the road?"

"I was on the beach with a couple of friends, but the rest of the group were walking along the roadside. Debbie must have been amongst them."

"Did she have a boyfriend?"

Maria shook her head and smiled. "No. She liked to play the field."

"So, there was no one special that you know of?"

"She'd been out a couple of times with Peter Crosby, he's a footballer at Middlesbrough, but it was nothing serious. Like I said, she liked to play around."

"Do you know if Debbie was worried about anything?" Cooper eyed Maria as she looked away from the officer's gaze. "What is it, Maria?" she asked. "It's important that you tell me everything."

Maria sniffed and returned to the couch. "She was upset about losing her job at the jewellers just before Christmas. I think she was worried about getting another job without a reference."

"Why wasn't she given a reference?"

Maria frowned and began to fidget with one of the cushions on the couch.

"Why didn't she have a reference?" Cooper repeated.

Maria gave a deep sigh. "Well, if you must know, she'd been sacked. She was found stealing a bracelet from the stockroom and was dismissed."

Cooper scowled. "The police weren't informed of this."

"That's because Manuel's Jewellers didn't want the bad publicity. They'd got their stuff back, and that was that."

Cooper looked up from her notes. "Had Debbie stolen before?"

"I… I don't think so. She—"

"Maria, I have to know everything about Debbie. You're not being disloyal. You're helping me find out what happened to her. Now please, answer my question. Was Debbie a dishonest person?"

Maria turned her attention back to the cushion. "She did go shoplifting sometimes," she said quietly, "but she'd never been caught."

Cooper closed her notebook. "Is there anything else you can tell me? Anything at all?"

Maria shook her head. "No, nothing," she said. "You think Debbie's dead, don't you?"

"We haven't found a body, so—"

"I think she's dead," Maria said. "She's been missing eighteen months. She must be dead."

"It's possible that she wanted to get away from everything. Make a fresh start."

Maria shook her head. "No, Debbie's dead. I can feel it."

Cooper parked outside the basement flat on Redcar seafront that had been the home of Suzie Graham. The front door's green paint was peeling. A striped cotton sheet was fastened on the inside of the rain-streaked window. Inside the flat, she could hear a dog barking in response to her knock. After the third knock, the door was finally opened by a tall, thin man, dressed in jogging bottoms and a white vest.

"Sam Carter?" Cooper asked.

"Yeah, that's me," he said, rubbing his eyes with his knuckles. "Who are you?"

Cooper took out her warrant card and introduced herself.

"Oh, come in," he said, yawning. "Sorry, I'm still half asleep. I've been working all night."

She followed him into the untidy flat. Sam hurriedly picked up an empty pizza box and a couple of lager cans off the table and put them in a waste bin before removing a pile of discarded clothes off the armchair and putting them on top of the dresser. "Sorry about the mess," he said, indicating for the officer to sit in the chair. "The place is a bit of a pigsty, I'm afraid."

Cooper sat down and opened her notebook. "I have a couple more questions about Suzie Graham's disappearance."

He yawned once more and leant forward to stroke the black Labrador at his feet. "I've told the police everything. I don't know what else I can tell you."

"Suzie took the dog out that evening, didn't she?"

"Yeah. It was me that usually took Bruno for his evening walk, but I had the flu, so Suzie took him. I wish to God she hadn't. If I could turn the clock back…"

"How long had it been from Suzie leaving to the dog returning to the flat?"

He screwed up his face in concentration. "About an hour. I was beginning to feel uneasy because it usually only took half an hour."

"Tell me about Suzie. Where did you meet?"

"I was working in Scotland, a little village outside Edinburgh," he said. "I went for a drink one night with some of the lads and… and there she was. The prettiest girl I'd ever seen."

"There's a big difference in your ages, I see. Didn't that cause problems?"

"You'd think so, wouldn't you? But we got on like a house on fire from day one."

Cooper glanced at her notes. "I understand Suzie worked in a nursing home. Did she enjoy working with older people?"

"No, not really. It was the only job she could get at the time."

Cooper leant forward. "Sam, is there something you're not telling me? Something you didn't mention to the police earlier?"

He lowered his head as he ran his hand through his hair.

"Well, Sam?" the officer prompted.

"All right, we had a row the night before, if you must know," he said.

"What was the row about?"

"I'd been working over in Manchester," he said.

"Go on," Cooper encouraged.

"I was ill. I had the flu. I couldn't stop shivering, so I decided to come home a couple of days early. My phone was bust, so I couldn't let Suzie know." He sniffed loudly and reached for a tissue in his pocket. "It was one o'clock in the morning when I got to the flat. Suzie wasn't here." He reached out and picked up an open can of lager from the floor. "Suzie walked in about four that morning. She'd been drinking, and she was dressed in some glitzy silver frock that was halfway up her arse." He stood up and began to pace the room. "I accused her of being with some bloke. We argued, and... and I hit her." He clenched his hands into fists. "I've never hit a bird before," he said. "I was so angry."

"So, what happened?"

"Suzie said she'd been hosting at a party and that it was all innocent. I was really ill the next day, so I stayed on the couch. That's why she took the dog out that night instead of me."

"Did Suzie tell you where the party was?"

"All she would say was she had been earning money as a hostess. She had over three hundred quid." The dog began to whine and scratch at the door. "Oh, I better let Bruno out into the yard. I haven't walked him yet." He got up and opened the door leading into the small backyard. The dog yapped appreciatively as it bounded through the open door. "Suzie wanted somewhere bigger to live," he said, returning to the couch, "somewhere with a decent garden. I was on a zero-hours contract, so money was tight. It still is."

"Do you think Suzie decided to go back to Scotland?"

He shrugged. "I don't know. The atmosphere between us was pretty tense, but I know she didn't like living in Scotland."

"Do you still have her things?"

"Yes, they're in the bedroom," he said. "There's not much, I'm afraid. Three pair of jeans, half a dozen t-shirts, a couple of hoodies and a drawer full of knickers."

"What happened to the silver dress?"

"I ripped it up that first night," he said. "I didn't like to see her dressed like a tart. I put the stilettos in the bin too."

"Does Suzie have a laptop or mobile phone?"

"She doesn't have a laptop, but she had her phone with her that night. It's ringing unobtainable now."

He lifted his head. "Something's happened to Suzie," he said. "I know it has. Something bad."

24

Cooper pulled into the car park of The Coppers Inn. She had just enough time for a sandwich before her appointment with Janette's parents.

She found a table at the back of the pub and picked up the menu. Duffy hurried forward, smiling. "Jilly," he said, holding out his hand. "It's lovely to see you again. No Andy today?"

She shook her head and smiled. "No, he's getting ready for his appearance on the telly."

"Daisy's been telling me about the appeal. It's a waste of time if you ask me, building Rosie's hopes up like that."

"I think so too, if I'm honest."

Without waiting to be asked, Duffy pulled up a chair and sat across the table from her. "You don't really think it's possible the kid got taken, do you? I was involved in that case. We both were. There's no way we could have missed anything, I'm sure there isn't."

She gave a deep sigh. "You're probably right, but at least it will put the family's mind at rest, once and for all."

"It will open up old wounds," he said. He frowned. "There are some people who still haven't forgiven Rosie for leaving Poppy alone on the beach."

Cooper shot Duffy a quick glance. "She wasn't alone. Her brother was with her."

Duffy scraped back the chair and stood up, signalling for the waitress to come over. "Bobby was just a kid. He could barely look after himself, let alone a two-year-old girl."

Before Cooper could respond, Daisy Lee came over to her table. "Yes?" she said, "what can I get you?"

"A coke, please," Cooper said, "and a ham sandwich on brown bread."

"Do you want ice in your coke?"

"No, thank you."

Daisy scribbled furiously on her notepad. Finally, she turned as if to leave and then spun around to face Cooper.

"You're that policewoman who worked on the case when our Poppy disappeared, aren't you?"

"Yes," Cooper said. "I was involved in the search."

"You know Mum's going on television with an appeal on Friday?"

"So I understand."

"Will you be going on the telly as well?"

She shook her head. "No, but DCS Bainbridge will. He led the enquiry."

Daisy turned and went through the door leading to the kitchen while Duffy busied himself, clearing abandoned tables.

When Cooper finished her food, she made her way towards the car park. Duffy was in the doorway smoking a cigarette. "Bloody stupid law, stopping folks smoking in pubs," he said.

She shrugged. "It doesn't bother me. I gave up years ago."

"I wish I could, but I've been smoking since I was fourteen. It's too late now."

"It's never too late."

He huffed as he threw down the half-smoked cigarette and stubbed it out with the toe of his shoe. "Too late for me, my love. My bad habits are here to stay, I'm afraid."

She smiled and then walked towards her car. Duffy followed. "So, what are you up to without Andy?" he asked.

She opened the car door and climbed into the vehicle. "I'm taking a second look at the three women from Redcar who've gone missing."

"I heard they'd just buggered off. You don't think they've been murdered, do you?"

She turned on the car's ignition. "We haven't found any bodies."

Duffy huffed again. "Young girls nowadays go wandering the streets at all hours by themselves, dressed in next to nothing. You could say they deserve all they get."

She turned to him and scowled. "That's a terrible thing to say. Anybody should be able to walk the streets in safety. How they choose to dress is their business."

He turned and walked back towards the pub. "We'll have to differ on that, I'm afraid," he said over his shoulder. "Give Andy my best."

Elizabeth and Robert Walsh were at home in their smart mid-terraced house when Cooper arrived. Elizabeth came to the door.

"Oh, come in, dear," she said after Cooper introduced herself. "We've been expecting you."

Cooper walked into the neat sitting room, one wall of which was covered in framed paintings.

"Janette painted those," Mrs Walsh said, noting Cooper's admiring glance. "She's got a real talent, our girl."

"They're lovely," Cooper said, sitting on the couch and taking out her notebook. "Mrs Walsh, I—"

"Oh, call me Elizabeth, dear," she said. "Would you like some tea?"

"No, thank you. I'd like to ask you some further questions about Janette. I know you've spoken to the police already about your daughter, but I'm here to see if there's anything else you can add."

Mrs Walsh shook her head. "I've told the police everything. Janette was a good girl. She was high-spirited, but artistic, and artistic people are always headstrong, aren't they? It's part of their temperament."

Robert Walsh sat in an armchair by the television, the local newspaper on his lap. He stood and threw down his paper. "For goodness sake, stop blabbering and tell the truth. Janette was unruly. She was out of our control. She had been for years."

Cooper frowned. "Unruly? What do you mean by that, Mr Walsh?"

"You just have to look at the way she dressed and those

ridiculous tattoos and piercings. Janette did exactly what she wanted to do, despite what we said." He stomped towards the front door and, opening it, went out into the street, slamming the door loudly behind him.

"You'll have to excuse Robert," Mrs Walsh said. "He's taken Janette's disappearance a lot harder than he's letting on."

"Was there conflict between them?"

"I suppose so," she said. "Father and daughter stuff. Robert's a good man, but he hasn't got an artistic bone in his body, I'm afraid. He couldn't understand some of Janette's choices. I kept telling him it was a phase she was going through, that she'd grow out of it, but... well, you can see how he is."

"You told the police that Janette was meeting friends at Locke Park the day she disappeared."

"Yes, some students from college. She was always out and about with friends. Me and her dad couldn't keep track."

"Extensive enquiries have been made at the college, and I'm afraid we can't find anyone who had arranged to meet Janette in the park."

She frowned and shook her head. "No, that can't be right. My daughter doesn't tell lies."

"Had Janette ever mentioned leaving home?"

"Well... a couple of weeks before she disappeared, she had a terrible row with her dad, and she did threaten to leave, but she didn't mean it. The trouble is they both have fiery tempers."

"What was the row about?"

"Janette had stayed out all night. She said she had been at a friend's, but her dad thought she had been out drinking. It wasn't the first time she'd done that."

"Did she say which friend she had stayed with?"

"Sally Lomax, probably. They used to be close at one time before Janette went to college."

"Does Janette have a boyfriend?"

Mrs Webster inhaled deeply and shook her head. "No, she would have told me. We have no secrets. I don't know where my girl is, but wherever she is, she didn't go there willingly."

"May I see her room, please?" Cooper asked, putting her notebook into her bag.

"It's the room at the end," she said. "I'll show you." She walked into the hall with Cooper.

"Can I ask you to wait downstairs, Mrs Walsh? I won't be long."

"My daughter and I have no secrets," she said, pursing her lips. "Our relationship was more like sisters than mother and daughter."

"Nevertheless, I would appreciate it if you waited downstairs." Mrs Webster huffed but turned and went back into the lounge.

Cooper surveyed the tidy room. She smiled, remembering the rows she had had with her own mother when she was a teenager about the state of her bedroom. She opened the wardrobe door and looked at Janette's clothes hung in colour-coordinated sections. Light colours to the left and dark ones to the right. A second smaller wardrobe had shelving housing her footwear. Trainers, sandals, boots and a pair of brown flat-heeled shoes stood in neat rows. She sighed loudly and then began her search.

Cooper returned to the lounge ten minutes later.

"Well?" Mrs Webster said, "did you find anything helpful?"

"No, not really." She returned to the couch and perched on the edge. "Elizabeth, when Janette left to go to Locke Park, did she have a bag with her?"

"She probably had her black shoulder bag. I'm afraid I can't remember."

"Does Janette have a computer? I didn't see one in her room."

"She has a tablet and a mobile phone, but they're always with her."

Cooper took out her notebook. "When I was looking around your daughter's room, I couldn't find her patent stilettos. Do you know where they are?"

"My daughter doesn't own a pair of stilettos. She wears trainers mostly, like most of the other girls her age. Why…?"

"Are you sure? I was told—"

"Of course, I'm sure. I clean Janette's bedroom thoroughly every week. I know everything she owns. She most definitely does not own a pair of patent stiletto shoes. What is so important about these shoes?"

"It's just part of the enquiry," Cooper said. 'Forget about it."

Mrs Webster leant forward about to speak.

Cooper held up her hand. "Does Janette have a part-time job?"

Mrs Webster shook her head. "She did mention getting a job once, but her dad soon put a stop to that. He said she had to concentrate on her studies and forget about money. He'd make sure she had everything she needed."

"How did she react to that?"

"She sulked at first, but she soon got over it, and she never mentioned it again."

Cooper closed her notebook and put it into her bag. "Well, I think that's all for now. If you think of anything else."

"I've told you everything I know. Just find my daughter. Please bring her home."

25

Cooper was busy typing up her report when Bainbridge tapped on her door and entered. "It's six o'clock," he said. "Isn't it time to stop work?"

She looked up from her computer and frowned. "Andy, I need to talk to you about these disappearances. There's something not quite right."

Bainbridge stood at the threshold. "What do you mean?"

"It doesn't mention it in the report, but all three of these young women had one thing in common. They all had a job that nobody knew about."

"And?"

"Debbie had been found stealing from her employer. She had been sacked and not given a reference, but she told her friend that she had something lucrative lined up."

"I don't see how—"

She tapped her pen on the desk. "But what sort of job? Maria said every couple of weeks she went off somewhere and came back with a lot of cash. She even wore an expensive dress to go to work in."

"You're not suggesting she is a sex worker."

She shook her head. "I don't think so, at least not on the streets."

"What about the others?"

"Suzie worked in a care home, but her boyfriend, Sam, said the night before she disappeared, she had been working as a hostess until the early hours."

"What sort of hostess?"

"The sort that made a lot of cash. According to Sam, she had over three hundred pounds."

"Jilly, I made enquiries with the Scottish Police about Suzie Graham. Like I said before, she has a history of running away."

"Oh?"

"She absconded twice from the children's home where she

had been placed after her mother died. When she was fourteen, she ran away from her foster parents. She was missing for almost a week."

"This isn't the same thing, though," she said. "Suzie had no reason to leave. She was happy living with Sam."

"According to Sam, but we only have his word for that." Bainbridge leant back against the door frame. "What about the third girl, Janette Walsh?"

"I spoke with her parents this afternoon. Her mother knew nothing about Janette looking for work."

"Well then, that kicks your theory into the long grass, doesn't it?"

"I spoke to Sally, our typist, earlier. She and Janette are friends. Sally said Janette had bought a pair of stiletto shoes just before she disappeared."

"What's that got to do with anything?"

"Janette told Sally they were to make her look smart for a weekend job."

"The job that no one knows about?"

"Possibly. But when I searched her room earlier today, there was no sign of the shoes. Her mother said she didn't own such a pair."

"Where are you going with this, Jilly?"

"Janette lied to her mother about meeting friends at Locke Park. None of her fellow students knew anything about a meeting."

"Maybe she was going to meet a boyfriend and didn't want her parents to know?"

She shook her head. "I don't think so. I think she had a secret that she didn't want anyone to know about. Perhaps all of the missing girls did. The more I dig into their lives, the more convinced I am that something bad has happened to them."

He leant forward. "Jilly, we have one girl who appears to be drug-dependent, another who has a history of taking off on a whim, and a third who has a bohemian lifestyle by anyone's standard."

She shrugged. "All I know is we should be treating their disappearance as suspicious."

He leant back again and rubbed his chin. "I'm not convinced, and we don't have the resources for a full-scale enquiry based on a theory."

"I was thinking of putting up posters around the town. That wouldn't impact too much on the budget," she said.

"No, but it would cause panic, linking the three disappearances."

She remained silent.

He threw open his arms. "Come on, Jilly, you've got to admit it's pretty flimsy grounds for a full investigation."

"I'm sorry, but I disagree. I have found no reason for any of the women to walk away from their lives. I want to continue with my enquiries."

He stood upright and, thrusting his hands into his trouser pockets, turned towards the door. "All right, keep digging, but don't waste too much time. Real crimes are being committed in this town which need dealing with."

She stared at the door as it slammed shut.

26

Bainbridge arrived at the television studio in Newcastle at six-thirty the following evening. Rosie and Eddie Lee, together with Bobby and Daisy, arrived at the studio ten minutes later.

"Good evening," greeted a young woman dressed casually in jeans and a t-shirt carrying a clipboard. "If you all follow me, I'll take you to the green room." The party followed the young woman into a small room off the corridor. "Please help yourself to tea or coffee," she said, indicating the paraphernalia on top of the unit on the far wall. "Mr Roberts will be with you shortly."

Five minutes later, Jacob Roberts, a local presenter and regular host of *Where Can They Be?* came into the room and introduced himself. Jacob Roberts was tall and slender with collar-length sandy hair and a neat beard. "So glad you've all agreed to appear on the show," he said, a broad smile on his heavily fake-tanned face. "Let's see if we can find Poppy, shall we?"

Bobby, stood by the window, with his hands thrust deep into his trouser pockets, groaned. "It's a bloody waste of everybody's time. Poppy's gone. She drowned."

Rosie looked up. "Don't you dare say that. Poppy was taken. I know she was."

Daisy put her arm around her mother's shoulders. "Don't get upset, Mum," she said. "If Poppy is out there, we'll find her, won't we, Mr Roberts?"

"Of course we will," Roberts said. "We've got everything ready. The photographs you sent of the girls, as babies, are a great help, Mrs Lee. The reconstruction on the beach yesterday might help jog someone's memory."

Bobby snorted. "After sixteen years? I don't think so."

Roberts turned sharply to face Bobby. "You'd be surprised what people remember, even after sixteen years. Now, let's go through to the studio and get the show on the road."

The group took their allotted seats as Roberts made the

opening introductions. "Two-year-old Poppy was last seen on Redcar Beach about lunchtime on Saturday, 2 August 2002," he began. A photograph of Poppy appeared on the screen behind him. Roberts looked into the camera. "Do you remember seeing this little girl?" he said.

Roberts turned to Rosie. "Poppy and Daisy are identical twins, aren't they?" he said. "I understand people found it difficult to tell them apart."

Rosie smiled and nodded. "I had trouble myself sometimes. Especially when I dressed them in matching outfits."

"But there was a slight difference between the girls. Isn't that right, Rosie?"

"Oh, you mean the birthmarks?" she said. "Yes, both girls have a small birthmark in the shape of a question mark."

"Where exactly were these birthmarks?"

"They're behind their ears. Daisy's mark was behind her left ear, and Poppy's behind her right. They were... are quite distinctive." She turned to her daughter. "Show them, Daisy. Show them your birthmark."

Scowling slightly, Daisy pushed back her hair, revealing an inch-long birthmark in the shape of a question mark behind her left ear.

"So, if Poppy Lee is out there somewhere, she will have the same mark but behind her right ear?" Roberts said.

The camera then panned in on Daisy's face.

"Poppy can't look much different to her sister," he said. "Do you know a young lady who looks similar to Daisy Lee? A young lady with a birthmark in the shape of a question mark behind her right ear?"

Roberts turned to Bainbridge. "DCS Bainbridge," he said, "shortly after Poppy Lee vanished, I understand a man claimed to have seen the little girl being placed into a motor vehicle. Would you care to comment on this?"

Bainbridge cleared his throat and took a deep breath before replying. "Someone did indeed come forward claiming to have seen a child being put into a Range Rover," he said. "An investigation was made at the time but came to nothing."

"The Range Rover was never traced?"

Bainbridge shook his head. "No, despite vigorous enquiries, no one reported seeing such a vehicle."

"But surely, if the police had widened their investigation, checked on all vehicles matching the description given by…" He glanced down at his clipboard. "Mr Simon Wray."

Bainbridge leant forward, staring straight into the camera. "Extensive enquiries were made but without success. Mr Wray did not make his statement until several weeks after Poppy had disappeared." He clenched his fists. "There were no other sightings reported, no CCTV, just Mr Wray's version of events."

"You didn't believe Mr Wray's statement, did you?"

Bainbridge shook his head. "No, I did not. Simon Wray only mentioned seeing the girl being put into a car after being arrested on drug-related charges. In my opinion, his story was merely a way of getting the charges against him reduced."

"And were they?"

"No, they were not. Like I told Mr Wray at the time, this isn't America. The police don't do deals."

Roberts walked towards camera one and smiled. "Well, that's it for another week. If you have any information that can help find Poppy Lee, please notify your nearest police station. You have been watching *Where Can They Be?* The programme that prides itself on finding missing loved ones. Please tune in next week for another unsolved missing person's case."

He turned to the second camera. "Goodnight, and thank you all for watching."

"How do you think it went?" Eddie said to Bainbridge ten minutes later when they were outside the studio. "Do you think it will get results?"

Bainbridge shrugged. "It's just a waiting game now. If

Poppy is out there, somebody may recognise her."

Rosie gave a slight shudder. "It was eerie watching that video on the beach. It was almost like I was back there."

Eddie took Rosie's hand. "Come on, love," he said. "Let's go home. There's nothing more we can do here." He turned to Daisy. "Are you coming home with me and your mother, or driving back with Bobby?"

"I'll drive her," Bobby said. "We can call for a drink on the way, can't we?"

Daisy smiled and nodded.

Bainbridge unlocked his car door. "Well, goodnight, everyone," he said. "Let's hope the programme has jogged someone's memory."

Bobby climbed into his car and turned on the engine. "I still think it's a waste of time. Poppy drowned. I know she was. I was there."

27

"I thought you did great," Bobby said to Daisy as he pulled the car up outside The Coppers Inn. "Now, let's go and enjoy a drink and forget about that bloody programme." He managed to secure a small table just as the occupants got up to leave. "White wine?" he asked as Daisy sat down. She nodded. Soon Bobby was back with the wine and a coke for himself. "That bloke behind the bar was asking how we got on," he said. "Is he your boss?"

She smiled and gave a slight wave. "Yes, that's Duffy. He used to be a police officer." She took a sip of her wine. "Oh, he's coming over."

Duffy bounded over to their table and plonked down on the wooden chair. "This must be Bobby," he said, a broad grin on his chubby face. Bobby raised an inquisitive eyebrow. "You won't remember me," Duffy continued. "You'd have been about ten the last time I saw you."

Bobby smiled weakly but remained silent.

"So, Daisy, how did you enjoy being on the telly? Did you meet any celebrities backstage?"

She frowned. "I wasn't there to meet celebrities. I was trying to get information about my missing sister."

"Our missing dead sister," Bobby corrected as he sipped his coke. "Poppy drowned that day. Everybody knows that, and it's about time Mother accepted it."

Daisy sighed and took a sip of her wine. "You know she walks the beach almost every day? I think she's still searching for her."

Duffy tutted and shook his head. "It's a sad business, but it's over and done with now. Maybe your mother will finally get some peace when she realises Poppy isn't coming back."

Daisy turned to Bobby. "I'll get us another drink. I don't want to go home yet."

"I'll get these," Duffy offered, hurrying towards the bar. He returned a few minutes later with the drinks. "Give your parents my regards," he said and picked up the empty glasses from the table. "Why don't you take a few days off, Daisy? Spend some time with your brother. I can manage."

She shook her head. "Thanks, but Bobby's going back to London tomorrow and, to be honest, I prefer to be working rather than just sitting around the house."

"Suit yourself," he said. "The offer's there if you change your mind."

When Duffy had gone, Bobby turned to his sister. "I'd invite you to come down to London to stay with Karen and me, but... well, we're both out of the house working so much and..."

Daisy reached over and patted Bobby's arm. "Later, maybe. Mum won't admit it, but she needs me. God knows how she'll react to people's responses to the appeal. Bainbridge has warned us to be prepared for the nutters."

Bobby smiled and squeezed his sister's hand. "Try not to worry. There's nothing we can do about it." He put his glass to his lips and drank the remnants. "Now hurry and drink up. It's getting late. I've got an early start tomorrow."

28

Cooper knocked and entered Bainbridge's office. "It looks like the appeal was a waste of time," she said, sitting on the chair across from his desk. "We've been inundated with calls. Some of sympathy for the family and some condemnation of Rosie; but there's been no real information."

"It's only been four days," Bainbridge said as he gathered papers off his desk and placed them carefully into his briefcase. "The show went out on *catch-up* last night, so let's wait and see."

Cooper huffed. "Andy, that kid is dead. I know that, and so do you."

He picked up his briefcase. "I'm going to visit the Lee family. Do you want to join me?"

"Of course, I'll come," she said. "Give me five minutes to finish up in my office, and I'll be right there."

"Good, I can do with all the moral support I can get."

Twenty-five minutes later, Bainbridge and Cooper pulled up in front of 14 Hudson Gardens.

"Leave the talking to me," Bainbridge said as they approached the house.

The door opened, and Eddie Lee rushed towards them. "Don't say anything, mate," he said. "We knew it was a longshot, somebody remembering something from that day. You're not to blame."

Rosie joined Eddie on the doorstep. "Come in," she said. "We want to thank you for all the help you have given."

Both officers walked through into the immaculate lounge.

"Please, sit down," Eddie said. "Can I get you a drink? What about you, DI Cooper?"

Bainbridge frowned as he sat on the couch, Cooper beside him. "Mr Lee," he began.

"Eddie, please. Surely we've known each other long enough to dispense with the formalities?"

"I'm Andy," he said, "and this, as you already know, is Jilly."

Eddie nodded and walked towards the refrigerator. "Beer okay?" he said, taking out a couple of bottles.

"Beer's great," Bainbridge said. "It's been a long day."

Eddie turned to Cooper. "Would you like a beer, Jilly? Or maybe some wine? We have some white wine that's been chilled."

"Thanks, I'd love a glass."

Rosie poured two glasses of wine and handed one to Cooper. "I know it sounds strange," Rosie said, leaning back into the couch, "but doing that appeal the other day, it's like a weight has been lifted off my shoulders. I somehow feel more... more relaxed."

"Good," Cooper said. "You can get on with your life now, Rosie." She looked around the room. "Where's Daisy?"

Rosie smiled. "She's at work. She loves working at the pub."

"I had hoped she'd do something more with her life than work behind a bar," Eddie said. "She's a bright girl. She could do so much better."

His wife tutted and placed her hand on his arm. "Daisy's doing all right. She won't be a barmaid forever." She turned to face Cooper. "Her boss thinks she has potential. So, he's going to train her up for management."

Eddie's frowned. "I still think—"

He stopped as the shrill ringing of a mobile filled the room.

"Excuse me," Bainbridge said. "I have to take this." He walked through into the hallway. When he returned to the lounge, his face was ashen.

Cooper got to her feet and walked towards him. "Is everything all right? You look like you've seen a ghost."

"Something urgent has come up. I have to get back to the station."

Eddie put down his beer and moved towards him. "Is it about the appeal? Has someone got information?"

"I'll ring you," Bainbridge said and walked out of the house, closely followed by Cooper. He climbed into his car before Eddie could reach him.

Cooper got into the car beside him. "What is it, Andy? What's happened?"

His hands trembled as he turned on the ignition. "A young woman has just walked into Redcar Police Station. She's claiming to be Poppy Lee."

29

Daisy was busy collecting glasses in The Coppers Inn when her mobile rang. She frowned, not recognising the number. "Hello?" she said.

"Daisy? Daisy, it's me, Karen."

Daisy put the glasses on a table. "Oh, how lovely to hear from you. It's been ages. How are you?"

"I'm fine," Karen said. "Has there been any news about Poppy? I saw the appeal on television."

Daisy sighed. "No, not really, but none of us were expecting any, except Mother, that is."

"I do feel sorry for Rosie. She's never got over losing Poppy, has she?"

"She still feels guilty about what happened."

"Please give her my love and tell her I'm thinking of her."

"I will," Daisy said. "We were disappointed you didn't come up to Redcar with Bobby the other day. It's been ages since you were last here."

The line went silent, and Daisy glanced at the screen before putting the phone back to her ear. "Hello? Are you there, Karen?"

"Yes, I'm here. I... I was just surprised at what you said, that's all."

"What do you mean surprised? I don't understand."

"Bobby and I have separated. I thought he would have told you that."

Daisy plonked down heavily on one of the chairs. "Bobby hasn't said a word to any of us."

"We're getting divorced," Karen said. "I assumed Bobby would have said."

"But you can't get divorced. You and Bobby are made for each other."

"No, we're not, Daisy. Not anymore."

"I can't believe this. What... what went wrong?"

Karen inhaled deeply. "Where do you want me to start?

Has Bobby told you he walked out on his job two weeks ago? He said he'd had enough."

"But we thought he was doing so well. What happened?"

"He just quit," Karen said. "I blame it on the booze."

"What do you mean, booze? Bobby doesn't drink alcohol. He only had coke when he was here."

"Bobby is on the way to becoming an alcoholic. And he gambles. We lost almost everything because of that."

Daisy gasped. "I can't believe what you're saying. Bobby wouldn't do that."

"You don't know what your brother is capable of, Daisy. Believe me."

"If Bobby isn't living with you, where is he living?"

"I have no idea. The last I heard, he was lodging somewhere in Greenwich with a friend from his university days."

"Why don't you come up to Redcar and let's try and sort this out? I know Mum and Dad would love to see you."

"I'm sorry, Daisy. I know Bobby's your brother, but... I have to go. I just wanted to wish the family well with the appeal. Let me know if there are any developments, won't you? And Daisy..."

"Yes?"

"Maybe it's best not to mention our conversation to your mother. She's got enough to worry about right now."

30

Bainbridge, accompanied by Cooper, arrived at the police station at exactly nine-thirty. Sergeant Duncan Brown was behind the main desk of the Incident Room, a look of excitement on his usually bland face. "She's in interview room one, sir," he said.

Bainbridge glanced at the handful of constables hovering around the incident room. He scowled. "Don't you lot have work to do?"

"Yes, sir," chorused the three officers as they hurried away.

Bainbridge took a deep breath as he gripped the door handle and walked into the interview room with Cooper close behind.

A well-dressed young woman stood by the window, looking out into the street below. The silk lilac dress and co-ordinating bolero jacket had certainly not been purchased in any high street shop. Her golden-blond hair had been coiled along the top of her head, held in place by a sparkling diamante slide. The unmistakable fragrance of Chanel perfume wafted around the small room.

"Good evening," Bainbridge said. "I'm Detective Chief Superintendent Bainbridge, and this is my colleague, Detective Inspector Cooper." The woman did not turn around but continued to gaze out of the window into the street.

"Please, take a seat, Miss...?"

"Davereaux. Catherine Davereaux," she said with a faint French accent. The young woman turned and walked gracefully over to the table, sitting directly across from him. Bainbridge studied the woman's features. Her flawless skin with expertly applied make-up and her eyes the colour of cornflowers. There was no mistaking the similarity. They were precisely the same colour as those of Daisy Lee.

"I'm here at the insistence of friends," the woman said. "They watched that television programme the other night and are convinced that I am the missing child from the beach. It's absolute nonsense, of course, but I know I won't get a minute's peace from them if I didn't come."

Bainbridge continued to study her face. "I have to agree with your friends, Miss Davereaux," he said. "You do bear an uncanny resemblance to the missing girl's sister."

Catherine flung back her head defiantly. "My father is Jon-Pierre Davereaux. Perhaps you're familiar with the name? He owns one of the largest vineyards in northern France."

Bainbridge shook his head. "No, I'm afraid not."

Catherine shrugged. "My parents are on safari for the next three weeks. I'm sure they will sort out this nonsense on their return."

"Where are they, exactly?"

She waved her arm in the air. "God only knows. Somewhere in Africa, Kenya, I think. I wasn't particularly interested in their travel plans, to be honest."

Cooper approached the table and sat next to Bainbridge. "Were you adopted, Miss Davereaux?" she asked.

Catherine scowled. "Of course, I wasn't adopted. That's ridiculous."

"I take it you live in France?" Cooper said.

"France mostly," Catherine said. "We have a chateau in the Rohan Valley and a house on the Devon coast. I spend my time between the two."

Bainbridge took out a pen and notebook from his pocket. "Miss Davereaux," he said, "it's getting late. Could you give me an address where I might contact you tomorrow so we can continue our chat? I will arrange for a DNA test to be carried out."

Catherine tutted. "Is that really necessary? This whole thing is a dreadful mistake. They say everyone has a doppelganger somewhere in the world. This girl... Daisy, wasn't it? She's obviously mine."

Bainbridge gave a faint smile. "Perhaps, Miss Davereaux, but I'd like to be certain."

Catherine stood. "All right, if you want to carry on with this nonsense. I'm staying at the Grand Hotel in Saltburn, room 201."

"Thank you," Bainbridge said, writing it in his notebook.

She sighed and walked towards the door. "You really are wasting your time, Detective Chief Superintendent," she said. "My parents will tell you that when they get back."

Cooper opened the door for Catherine. "I'll see you out," she said. "By the way, Miss Davereaux, is your mother French?"

Catherine frowned and shook her head. "No, she's not French. My mother is English."

"May I ask her name?"

Catherine inhaled deeply. "Why do you want to know that?"

"Just for our records," Cooper said.

She huffed. "Well, if you must know, my mother's name is Claudia. Claudia Davereaux."

After Catherine left the room, Bainbridge turned to Cooper. "Well? What do you think?"

"She certainly has a look of Daisy," she said, "especially the eyes."

"It's the fancy clothes and makeup that make her look different," Bainbridge said. "That girl is the missing Poppy Lee. I'll stake my career on it." He sank back into his chair, rubbing his chin. "Wasn't Bobby's mother called Claudia? I'm sure that's what Eddie said."

Cooper nodded. "You're right, but surely it can't be the same woman? Why on earth would she steal another woman's child after abandoning her own?"

"Tomorrow, I'm going back to the Lee's house and see if Eddie has a photograph of Claudia."

"He'll want to know why."

"Mm… I'll think of something."

The desk telephone rang. "Who the hell can that be at this

time of night?" He picked up the receiver. "Bainbridge…" he said. "… No, I'm sorry, I can't comment on that… Like I said, I have nothing to say at this time." He put down the receiver with a bang. "Damn it. That was the local rag. They want to know if it's true Poppy Lee has made contact."

"How the hell did they know so soon?"

He frowned. "It's probably one of that lot out there," he said, nodding in the direction of the incident room. "If I find out who's been talking, I'll…"

"It doesn't matter. It was bound to come out sooner or later."

Bainbridge walked over to the door. "I'm going for a quick pint. Do you fancy joining me?"

"Why not," she said. "I think we've earned a drink."

31

It was eight-thirty the following morning when Bainbridge pulled up at Hudson Gardens. Rosie and Eddie Lee hurried up the path to meet him.

"Is it true?" Eddie said. "Has Poppy turned up?"

Tears streamed down Rosie's face as she grabbed Bainbridge's arm. "Please tell us. Have you found our baby?"

"Let's go inside," he said, guiding the tearful Rosie back into the house and into the lounge.

Daisy sat on the couch, nervously twisting her fingers on her lap.

"Well?" Eddie demanded. "Is it true what that reporter told us?"

"What exactly did the reporter tell you?" Bainbridge said.

"He said that our Poppy had been to the police station."

"Daisy, I could murder a coffee," Bainbridge said. "Could you get me one? I bet your mam and dad could do with a drink as well."

Daisy remained silent as she hurried through into the kitchen and closed the door. Bainbridge turned to face Rosie and Eddie. "Last night, a young woman came to the police station. I'm carrying out a DNA test later to establish if she is indeed your missing daughter, Poppy."

Eddie gasped. "What happened to her? Where has she been?"

"Do you think she is Poppy?" Rosie said.

"I honestly don't know. She does have a remarkable resemblance to Daisy. She has been brought up mostly in France."

"There you go," Eddie said. "Didn't that bloke Wray say there were French euros near the car that took her? That proves it."

Bainbridge shook his head. "It proves nothing. The girl's father is a well-respected businessman. Not the sort of person to creep along a beach and take a child from its mother."

Eddie folded his arms across his chest. "Can we see this girl? We'll know if she's ours."

"Let's wait until I've conducted the DNA test first, shall we? I want to do a test on Daisy as well, for comparison."

Daisy came back into the lounge carrying a laden tea tray. "What do you want me to do?" she said, placing the drinks on the low table.

He explained the procedure as he took out the kit. "It doesn't hurt, Daisy. I just need to take a mouth swab."

After he had finished, he turned to Eddie. "There is one more thing," he said.

"What's that?"

"Do you have a photograph of Claudia, Bobby's mother?"

Eddie scowled. "Claudia? What the hell for? What's that bitch got to do with it?"

"Probably nothing."

"I have a picture," Rosie said, rushing over to the dresser and rummaging in one of the drawers. "It's in here." She removed a leather-bound photograph album. "There's a photograph of Claudia and Eddie somewhere." She began turning the pages.

Eddie looked on. "Why on earth would you keep a photograph of that bitch after what she did?"

Rosie lifted her head sharply. "Claudia's still Bobby's mother. One day, Bobby might... Oh, here it is." She removed a photograph from the album and handed it to Bainbridge. "She was a striking woman, wasn't she?" Rosie said. "I can see her likeness in Bobby."

Bainbridge took the photograph. "Thank you, I'll see it's returned to you."

Eddie snorted. "Don't bother. If I'd known it was there, it would have been on the fire years ago. Why do you want it, anyway? You can't think Claudia's involved?"

"Just routine. Can I ask you not to say anything to the press about what we've discussed this morning? We should wait until we know for certain what we're dealing with."

Daisy walked over to Bainbridge and sat next to him on the couch. "If it is Poppy, what happens then?"

"One step at a time, eh, Daisy?" He got up and walked to the hall door. "I'll be in touch as soon as I get the results."

He left the house and climbed into his car, aware that almost every house in the street had its front curtains pulled to one side.

32

Bainbridge called at the station before visiting The Royal Hotel. The incident room buzzed with activity. "What's going on?" he said, addressing Sergeant Brown.

"There's been another one, sir," the sergeant said.

"Another what?"

"Another young woman reported missing. DI Cooper is dealing with it."

"When was this reported?"

"About fifteen minutes ago. We didn't think anything about it when she didn't come to work yesterday. We assumed she was sick, although, by rights, she should have telephoned in."

"What are you talking about, man?"

"The missing girl, sir. It's young Sally, the office typist. Her mam telephoned the station to report her missing. In a right state, she was."

Bainbridge narrowed his eyes. "I have some urgent business in Saltburn this morning, and I need a female officer with me. But I need to be kept informed of progress," he said, walking through to his office. He placed the DNA sample he had taken from Daisy Lee into the drawer of his desk. This would be sent to the lab once he had taken the DNA of the young woman he was about to visit in Saltburn.

Bainbridge and the officer arrived at the Royal Hotel just before eleven. They went straight up to room 201 and knocked on the door. It was opened immediately by Catherine Davereaux.

She was dressed casually in blue leggings and a blue and white striped top. Her hair fell loose on her shoulders, and her flawless complexion bore no makeup.

"Come in," she greeted. "Please, take a seat." She indicated two grey velvet wingback armchairs in front of the large bay window overlooking the sea. "Beautiful view, isn't it?" she said. "I've never been further north than London before."

Bainbridge and the officer sat. "Miss Davereaux," he began.

She smiled. "Oh, please, call me Catherine. What should I call you? Detective Chief Superintendent is rather a mouthful, don't you think?"

"Andy," he said. "My name's Andy."

"Well, Andy, I suppose we'd better get this nonsense over with. You'll want a mouth swab, I presume?"

Bainbridge removed the kit from his briefcase and handed it to his colleague. "Yes. It will only take a minute."

She quickly completed the task and placed the swab into the plastic tube provided.

"Have you managed to contact your parents?" he asked.

Catherine shook her head. "No, I'm afraid not. Like I said, they're in the middle of nowhere at the moment. They'll ring me though when they're on their way back." She flung herself onto the velvet couch. "May I offer you a drink? Tea or coffee, perhaps?"

He shook his head. "No thanks. We must get back to Redcar, but I do need to ask you some questions first."

Catherine stretched out her long, elegant legs. "Ask anything you like, Andy," she said, "but I can assure you, you're wasting your time."

"Firstly, do you have a birthmark behind your right ear?"

She frowned. "What a strange question. Do I?" She turned to the side and pulled up her hair, allowing Bainbridge to examine behind her ear. "Well?" she said. "What can you see?"

Bainbridge squinted as he examined the skin behind her right ear. "There's definitely a birthmark there. It's faint, but it is there."

Catherine let her hair fall onto her shoulders. "I never knew that. Nobody ever told me I had a birthmark behind my ear."

"It's in the shape of a question mark," he continued, "just

like Daisy's."

She sat bolt upright. "Coincidence. It has to be a coincidence."

"We'll soon know once we get the DNA results. Tell me about your parents."

"What do you want to know?"

"What sort of man is Jon-Pierre?"

"He's kind," she said, "and rich. Disgustingly rich. Dad had been married three times before he met my mother." She laughed. "That's not so unusual. He is French, after all."

"I take it Jon-Pierre is older than your mother?"

"Yes, over thirty years, but I can assure you, they are devoted to each other."

"I daresay. Does your father have children from his previous marriages?"

Catherine shook her head. "No, just me. He always said I am his special child, a gift from God."

"Tell me about your mother?"

"What can I say? She's my mother."

"Where did she meet your dad?"

Catherine shrugged. "She was a model working in London. She met my father at some function, and apparently, it was love at first sight."

"Catherine, can you tell me if you recognise this woman in the photograph?" He removed the picture he had been given by Rosie and handed it to her. Catherine stared at the photograph, then at Bainbridge. "That's my mother," she said quietly. "Where did you get this? And who's that man with her?"

"If I'm right," he said, "that man is your father."

She pulled away from him, a look of shock and defiance on her face. "No, you're wrong. Jon-Pierre Davereaux is my father." Catherine began to wind her fingers nervously on her lap.

Bainbridge studied her as he recalled Daisy making exactly the same gesture earlier that day.

"Once I contact my parents, I'm sure they'll put things right," she said. "This is all some terrible mistake." She got up and walked over to the window. "Tell me about the people you think are my real family."

"If I'm right, and all the evidence so far says I am right, your birth mother is Rosie Lee."

Catherine began to chuckle. "Rosie Lee? You have to be joking?"

"No, her name is Rosie Lee. Her husband, your father, is Eddie Lee."

"What sort of people are they?"

"Decent, respectable people," he said. "Eddie works on the market stalls around the northeast selling women's and children's clothing. He has done for years."

"You're telling me my father is a market trader?"

Bainbridge nodded. "He thinks the world of his children. He took care of his son, Bobby, when Claudia, his mother, abandoned them both."

Catherine turned sharply to face him. "She did what? I don't believe you."

"Bobby was seven when Claudia left, leaving Eddie to take care of the child on his own. That's when he met Rosie, your birth mother."

Catherine lowered her head into her hands and inhaled deeply. "If you don't mind, Andy," she said, "I think I would like to be alone now."

Bainbridge and the officer stood and walked towards the door. "Will you be staying here?" he said, "at least until we get the results through?"

"Yes, of course. I'll stay here as long as it takes to get this mess sorted."

"I'll be in touch soon. And please, promise me that you won't talk to any reporters if they manage to track you down."

Catherine nodded. "Okay. But, Andy?"

"Yes?"

"Do you think you could get me a copy of that

photograph?"

Bainbridge smiled. "Leave it with me. I'll see what I can do."

33

16 Greta Street was a Victorian mid-terrace house in Dormanstown, just outside Redcar. Cooper parked her Metro outside the house and knocked on the door.

Christine Lomax, Sally's mother, opened the door. She was a plump, middle-aged woman with greying hair styled in a bun on the top of her head. Cooper introduced herself and followed Mrs Lomax into the spacious living room.

"Please, take a seat," she said, indicating for her to sit on the brown leather couch. "Can I get you a cup of tea or something?"

Cooper shook her head as she perched on the couch. "No, thank you, Mrs Lomax."

"It's not like our Sally to go off all night without letting us know," she said, wringing her hands, "and then not turning up at work – well, I don't know what to think."

Cooper took out her notebook. "When was the last time you saw your daughter?"

She produced a tissue from her pocket and blew her nose loudly. "Tuesday night, it would be, about seven o'clock. Sally said she was going out to see a friend and... well you can't watch them all the time, can you? Sally's old enough, after all."

"Do you know which friend she was visiting?"

"No, she didn't say. She has so many friends."

"Weren't you worried when she didn't come home on Tuesday night?"

She leant forward, nervously twisting the tissue between her fingers. "I didn't know she hadn't come home. I go to bed early, you see. I got up about nine on Wednesday morning and assumed Sally had gone to work. She does love working at the police station. She talked about joining the police when she's older, but her dad won't hear of it."

"What about your husband? Didn't he notice Sally hadn't been home?"

"Alfred works nights at the foundry. He goes out at seven

o'clock in the evening and doesn't get back until six the following morning." She dabbed her eyes. "He's out there now looking for her. He's out of his mind with worry."

"Are there any relatives she could have gone to? Grandparents or cousins, perhaps?"

"Both sets of grandparents are dead," she said. "Me and Alfred are both only ones, so there's nobody, really."

Cooper continued to make notes. "Has Sally been upset about anything recently, Mrs Lomax?"

She screwed up her face and frowned. "She was upset about Janette Walsh going missing. They used to be good friends at school."

"Used to be?"

"Me and Alfred discouraged her mixing with Janette, to be honest. These last couple of years, Janette's turned into a real handful for her parents. Have you seen the way she dresses and those dreadful tattoos? We didn't want her influencing our Sally."

"So, the girls didn't socialise?"

She put her hands to her temple. "Not as much as they used to. But like I said, Sally is old enough to make up her own mind. We can't make her do what we say." She stood up and walked to the window. "I was nearly forty when I had Sally. She's our only child. I know I'm not as up to date with modern trends as I should be, but I do try and give Sally her freedom. She's a good girl."

"So, you can think of no reason why she should disappear?"

"No, none. Something's happened to her. I know it has. Something bad."

Cooper put the notebook into her bag and stood up. "Do you mind if I look around Sally's room? There may be something there that may help."

"Help yourself," she said wearily. "Her room's the first left at the top of the stairs. I won't come up if you don't mind, dear. Sally doesn't like me going into her room. You know what teenage girls are like?"

Cooper made her way into the bedroom. A small bookshelf containing a number of romantic fiction paperbacks was next to the bed, and a small, pink-coloured laptop was on the dressing table. She picked up the laptop to take back to the station. Apart from half a dozen pairs of jeans and a couple of hoodies, the wardrobe contained skirts and tops that she had seen Sally wearing for work. Cooper frowned. Everything in the wardrobe was for casual wear. It would seem that Sally did not own any formal clothing. Leaning down, she retrieved a small red-tartan rucksack from the bottom of the wardrobe and placed it carefully on the bed. She pulled back the zip fastening and, reaching inside, removed a black and silver sequined mini dress. The dress bore the label Ashley Drake, a designer who had taken the fashion industry by storm last season. A pair of black patent stiletto shoes were also in the bag, together with a quantity of black lacy underwear and several pairs of stockings. Also in the rucksack was a small gold-coloured toiletry bag. She pulled back the zip and saw it contained cosmetics, together with a bundle of twenty-pound notes, held together with an elastic band. Cooper counted seven hundred pounds before replacing the items into the rucksack.

When Cooper returned to the lounge, Mrs Lomax stood in front of the window, gazing out. "I've made you a coffee, dear," she said, indicating a mug on the coffee table. "I didn't know if you took sugar."

Cooper smiled and sat on the armchair in front of the table. "No, I don't. Thank you."

"Well, did you find anything helpful?"

"I'm taking Sally's computer in for analysis," she said. "You'll get it back in the next few days. By the way, does this belong to Sally?" Cooper held up the rucksack. "It was at the bottom of her wardrobe."

"No, it belongs to Janette. She asked Sally if she could leave it here a few weeks ago."

"Why did she do that?"

Mrs Lomax hunched her shoulders. "I think there was something in it she didn't want her mother to see. From what Sally told me, Elizabeth Walsh is a bit of a nosey-parker."

"Have you looked inside the bag?"

"No, I most certainly have not," she said, "and I don't want to. Everyone's allowed some privacy, or at least they should be. If Janette didn't want her mother to know her business, that's all right with me."

"I'm going to have to take the rucksack with me," Cooper said.

"All right, if you think it will help," she said.

Cooper sipped her coffee. "At this stage, everything has to be looked at. You don't know what's important and what isn't." she reached into her bag and removed her notebook again. "Can you tell me more about your daughter? What did Sally do in her spare time, for instance?"

Mrs Lomax fidgeted with the gold chain around her neck. "She's a quiet girl, really, I suppose. She liked to read, mostly Mills & Boon. She has dozens of their books in her room."

"Yes, I saw them. Anything else?"

"She went out to eat with her friends sometimes. McDonald's usually, and she liked to go to the cinema."

"What about clubs? Do you know if Sally went to any clubs?"

"Oh, no," she said. "Sally wasn't interested in that sort of thing. I know because I heard her arguing with Janette about it one time."

"Oh?"

"Janette wanted Sally to go with her to a party in some club, but Sally said no. Janette got angry and flounced out of the house."

"When exactly did this argument take place?"

"It would be about a week before Janette disappeared, but they made up soon afterwards. Girls do fall out sometimes, don't they?"

"Did you ever hear parties mentioned again?"

Mrs Lomax frowned and shook her head. "No, but I don't go listening at keyholes. Sally's a bright girl. She wouldn't get involved in anything bad."

Cooper leant over. "I'm sure she wouldn't," she said. "By the way, has Janette stayed over recently?"

Mrs Lomax shook her head. "No, she hasn't. Not for months. She used to stay regularly when they were at the Comprehensive, but since Sally started work and Janette went to college, all that stopped."

Cooper replaced her notebook and pen. "Well, I think that's all for now," she said, walking towards the door. "If you do hear from Sally, you will let me know straight away, won't you?"

"You think something has happened to Sally, don't you?" she said, her eyes brimming with tears.

"Try not to worry," Cooper said. "We're doing everything we can to find her."

As soon as she returned to the office, DI Cooper arranged for the rucksack's contents and computer to be sent to Forensics before typing her notes into her computer. She was startled by PC Lisa Walker's sharp rap on her door.

"Ma'am," she said. "I wonder if I might have a word?"

Cooper nodded. "Yes, of course. Please, take a seat." She had barely spoken half a dozen words to the probationer since her arrival at the police station two weeks previously.

PC Walker perched on the edge of the chair, nervously touching the lapels on her jacket. Her face was flushed.

"What is it?" Cooper asked. "Is something the matter?"

Walker lifted her head and sniffed. "It... it's about Sally, ma'am."

"What about Sally?"

"I... I saw her the night she went missing. I spoke with her."

Cooper sat bolt upright. "Where was this?"

"In the high street, near the pet shop. Sally was trying to get a taxi."

"Where was she going?"

"I asked her. She said that she was going to speak to someone who would know where Janette might be."

"Janette Walsh?"

Walker nodded.

"Why didn't you stop her?"

She lowered her head and continued giving her jacket lapel more attention. "I… I was with someone. We were going out for a drink, so—"

"So, you let a vulnerable young girl get involved with god only knows what?" Cooper said, clasping her hands. "You do realise Sally's been missing over forty-eight hours?"

"Yes, ma'am. I'm… I'm sorry. I know I should have done something, but—"

"Did you see Sally get into a taxi?"

"No, ma'am," she said. "Sally tried ringing, but her phone was out of charge."

"So, what happened?"

"I offered her my phone, but she said it didn't matter. She would walk. It wasn't that far."

"And you've no idea where she was going?"

"No, ma'am. The last time I saw her, she was heading towards the coast road."

34

As probationary officer Walker rushed from Cooper's office, she almost collided with Bainbridge, who was entering.

"Leave whatever you're doing, Jilly," he said. "Sally Lomax has been found."

Cooper put her hands to her face and gasped. "Oh, thank god for that. Where is she?"

"She's at the hospital. She's been involved in a motor accident."

"Is she badly hurt?"

Bainbridge shrugged. "I only spoke briefly to the doctor. They were taking her down to theatre. I'm going to the hospital, and I'd like you to come along." Cooper nodded and followed him to his car.

The journey to the hospital took fifteen minutes. Bainbridge went straight to reception but returned to Cooper a couple of minutes later. "A doctor is coming down to speak to us," he said. "Let's wait over there." He walked over to a small booth with two plastic chairs and a low table in front. "Fancy a coffee?" Not waiting for an answer, he walked over to the vending machine and returned to the booth a few minutes later, carrying two paper cups. He handed one of the cups to Cooper. Sipping it, he wrinkled his nose. "I requested coffee. I'm not quite sure that's what we've got."

She took the cup and sniffed at the muddy liquid. "I don't think Starbucks have anything to worry about," she said and sipped her drink.

Five minutes later, the officers were joined by a doctor. "DCS Bainbridge?" he said, holding out his hand. "I'm the doctor looking after Sally Lomax."

Bainbridge shook the doctor's hand. "How's Sally doing? Is she going to be all right?"

He frowned. "The young lady has sustained a fracture to her left femur, and several ribs are broken."

Cooper's posture stiffened. "But Sally will be all right,

won't she? She will recover?"

He sighed. "She also has a head injury. It's too early to say how this will affect her."

"You mean she could be brain damaged?" Bainbridge said.

"It's possible, yes, but let's not jump to conclusions just yet. She is young and strong. That has to be in her favour."

Bainbridge thrust his hands into his pockets. "When will I be able to speak with her?"

"Not for some time, I'm afraid. She should be out of theatre in the next hour."

"I need to find out where she's been for the past forty-eight hours," Bainbridge said.

The doctor walked towards the lift and then half-turned to face the officers. "I don't know where the young lady has been, but I do know what she's been doing."

Bainbridge frowned. "What do you mean by that?"

He walked back towards them. "There are drugs in her system."

Cooper shook her head in disbelief. "No, that can't be right. Sally was not the sort of girl to get mixed up in drugs."

The doctor leant close and spoke in a hushed tone. "Ms Lomax had a substantial quantity of lysergic acid diethylamide in her system. That's a hallucinogenic commonly known as LSD." The doctor's beeper began to buzz. "I'm sorry, but I'm needed on the ward."

Both police officers watched open-mouthed as he walked over to the lift.

Bainbridge huffed. "I don't care what the doctor said. Sally Lomax would no sooner take drugs than I would."

Cooper was about to reply when she saw Sally's parents entering the hospital concourse. She turned to Bainbridge. "Should I go and talk to them?"

He shook his head. "No, leave them," he said, placing his hand on her arm. "We'll speak to them later." He walked towards the exit. "Let's talk to the traffic boys. I want to know exactly what happened to Sally Lomax."

The Traffic Division of Cleveland Police was in a separate location from the main police station. Bainbridge had telephoned ahead of his arrival. He was met at the front desk by Chief Inspector Harry Denton.

"Let's go to my office," Denton said, opening the swing doors leading to a long corridor. "I'm just along here." Both officers followed Denton to the last room on the left. "It's a bit of a squeeze, I'm afraid," Denton said, opening the door. "We don't get many visitors."

The room was small and airless, with a tiny window high up on the wall. Denton scooped up several files off the two chairs, placing them on his already cluttered desk. "Take a seat," he said, going around to the far side of the desk. "I'd offer you a coffee, but the machine's bust."

"We're fine, thanks," Bainbridge said. "I need information on the RTA involving a young woman on the A174 earlier today."

Denton raised his eyebrows. "Oh, her? She's lucky to be alive."

"Have you been able to establish what happened?"

"A hit and run. The poor kid had been seen staggering along the road minutes before the accident," he said. "Witnesses said she looked out of it."

"No one stopped to help her?"

Denton shook his head.

"Did anyone witness the accident?"

"No."

Bainbridge slammed his fist onto the desk. "Christ, I don't believe this." He inhaled deeply. "Do you have any idea what type of vehicle was involved?"

"Not really," Denton said. "But someone thought they saw a Nissan speeding away further up the road." DI Denton put his elbows on the desk and steepled his fingers. "What we do know is this was no accident."

Bainbridge sat bolt upright. "What do you mean?"

"The car involved reversed and deliberately ran over the

girl a second time."

"Are you sure about that?" Bainbridge said. "There's no mistake?"

Denton inhaled sharply. "I've been doing this job for over fifteen years," he said. "This was no accident. I'll bet my pension on it."

35

"If we hurry, we should be able to get something to eat at Duffy's before they stop serving lunch," Bainbridge said as he drove back into Redcar.

Cooper smiled weakly. "Okay, but we'll have to be quick. I've got a lot to get on with this afternoon."

He parked the car at the back of The Coppers Inn, and they made their way to a table by the window. Bainbridge ordered them a sandwich and a coke.

"You spoke to Sally's parents this morning, didn't you?" he said. "How did you get on?"

Cooper relayed the conversation she had with Sally's mother and finding the red-tartan rucksack in the wardrobe. "According to Mrs Lomax, the bag and contents belonged to Janette Walsh."

Bainbridge stroked his chin. "It seems you were right about Janette having a secret life."

"I bet Sally knew all about it, though. Let's hope we can talk to her soon and find out what Janette was in to."

"That could be the reason Sally got attacked," Bainbridge said. "If she knew who…"

"Andy, there's something you should know." She quickly relayed the conversation she had earlier with Lisa Walker.

"When we get back to the office, we'll check all CCTV along the coast road. We may find out exactly where Sally went that night, and—"

Duffy bounded towards their table and pulled up a chair. "Andy, great to see you again," he said. "You too, Jilly."

Bainbridge smiled weakly and nodded by way of acknowledgement.

"Is anything the matter?" Duffy said. "You look like you've lost a pound and found a penny."

"Just work," he said.

Duffy grinned. "Yeah, it can really get to you sometimes, can't it? I'm glad I'm out of it. There's far too much stress, being a policeman."

Bainbridge shrugged. "I'm beginning to think you're right."

"Andy, if there's anything I can do to help," Duffy said.

Daisy arrived at the table with the food.

"Is everything all right, Daisy?" Cooper asked.

Daisy briefly looked away. "What's happening about Poppy? Nobody's telling us anything. Mum and Dad are out of their minds with worry."

"I'll be in touch as soon as we have the DNA results," Bainbridge said. "The samples went to the lab this morning, so we should hear in a couple of days."

Daisy pursed her lips. "I want to see her. Why won't you let me see her? I'll know straight away if she's my sister. It's not right the way you're treating my family." Tears trickled down Daisy's cheeks. She quickly wiped them away with the sleeve of her top, turned and scurried behind the bar into the pub's kitchen.

Duffy sighed and got up from the table. "I'd better go and see she's all right," he said, standing. "She's been like this ever since that damned programme."

It was three o'clock the following afternoon when Leo Cutts, the forensics officer, arrived at Cooper's office with Sally Lomax's computer under his arm.

Cooper pushed the file she was reading to one side. "Well? Did you find anything useful?"

"Good afternoon to you too." He pulled up a chair, placing the laptop on the desk, a faint smile on his pale, angular face. "I don't suppose there's a cup of tea on offer?"

Cooper fidgeted with impatience. "Leo, stop pissing about and tell me something useful."

He opened the laptop and pressed a couple of keys. "An extremely dull girl, young Sally Lomax," he said as he began scanning the screen. "She didn't seem to have much of a life, just a lot of chit chat with a group of empty-headed young girls in the main. What's been on the telly, which celeb is dating who? That sort of nonsense."

Cooper sighed. "I'm only interested in any contact she had with Janette Walsh. What have you got?"

Cutts turned the laptop at an angle that Cooper could easily read. "She sent a couple of emails to Janette a month ago," he said, bringing them up on the screen. "There's been nothing else since then."

Cooper scanned the computer. The first email had been sent to Janette's account three days before she had disappeared.

'Don't worry,' it said. *'I've put your stuff in a safe place like you asked, but I still think you're making a mistake agreeing to go there again. Please change your mind and tell him you're not going to his posh house anymore. It's dangerous, and there are more important things in life than money.'*

Cooper read and re-read the email several times. She then opened the second email, sent on the morning of Janette's disappearance.

'I'm glad you've seen sense,' it said. *'Never mind what he says. There's nothing he can do to make you go to that place again. Just give him the clothes back. Let him give them to some other silly girl to wear at one of his parties. Come around to mine tomorrow night, and we'll have a pizza and watch a film. That new Johnny Depp film is on. Please stop worrying. You've done the right thing.'*

Cutts leant back in the chair, placing his hands around the back of his head. "Looks like Janette Walsh was a bit of a wild child."

Cooper made no reply as she continued to stare at the screen.

He began to chuckle. "I wonder where these parties are being held. I wouldn't mind checking it out myself."

Cooper slammed the computer lid down and glared at him. "Grow up. Sally has been attacked, and her friend... well, who knows?"

Cutts sat bolt upright. His face flushed as he pushed a

strand of hair from his eyes. "Sorry. That was in bad taste."

"What about the rucksack and its contents? Any joy there?"

"Yes and no," he said.

"What does that mean?"

"The DNA we got from the dress definitely confirms that it was worn by Janette, as do the shoes, but…"

"But what?"

"Well, that's all we got. There's no other DNA, so it doesn't tell us much really."

Cooper narrowed her eyes. "Keep trying. There's got to be traces of someone else."

He shrugged. "Okay, if that's what you want, but you do know the cost of each forensic test we do? Are you sure the budget's up to it?"

Cooper glared at Cutts. "Just do it. The dress is an Ashley Drake original. It costs a small fortune. I'm sure we can trace who bought it. You can bet it wasn't Janette Walsh."

He cocked his head to one side as he headed towards the door. "That's your department. I'll let you know what further tests tell us." He thrust his hands into his trouser pockets and walked along the corridor, whistling to himself.

Cooper exhaled and walked over to the door. "Twat," she muttered, slamming the door shut.

36

Three days later, Bainbridge drove to the Grand Hotel in Saltburn. He knocked lightly on the door of room 201, and it was opened by Catherine Davereaux.

"You're an early bird," she said. "It's barely eight o'clock."

He entered the room, closed the door quietly behind him, walked over to the armchair near the window and sat down.

"I take it the DNA results are back?" she said, perching on the edge of the couch.

"The results were conclusive, Catherine," he said. "You are the daughter of Rosie and Eddie Lee."

She flung back her head and exhaled softly. "So, what happens now?"

"I'll need to speak with your… with the Davereauxs," Bainbridge said, rubbing his chin. "Have you managed to contact them?"

"Like I said, they're on safari somewhere. They should be back any time, but who knows?"

"It might be best if I speak with them before we proceed any further," Bainbridge said. "I need to get the full picture of exactly what happened."

Catherine stood up. "I want to meet the Lee family as soon as possible. I need to meet them. Surely you can understand that?"

"Catherine, you have to be patient." He rose from the chair and headed for the door. "This has been a shock for you and for the Lee's."

"But—"

"I'll call you later," he said as he opened the door. "In the meantime, keep trying to contact the Davereaux's. Unfortunately, we're not having much success tracing them."

"Jon-Pierre likes his privacy," Catherine said. "But don't worry. They'll ring me as soon as they're on their way home." She put her hands on her slender hips and shook her head slowly. "I don't understand why they would do such a wicked thing. It doesn't make sense."

Bainbridge reached into his inside jacket pocket. "Oh, I almost forgot. I had a copy made of the photograph of Claudia and Eddie."

"Thank you." She reached out and took the picture before slowly walking back towards the couch.

Bainbridge went straight to Hudson Gardens after leaving Catherine at the hotel.

Rosie opened the door. "Any news yet? Is it our girl?"

"Yes, Rosie," he said. "I'm pleased to tell you the DNA results confirm that the young lady is your missing daughter, Poppy."

Rosie squealed with delight as she lunged forward and hugged Bainbridge tightly. "When can I see her?"

"There are certain formalities to be dealt with first. Are Eddie and Daisy around?"

"They're both at work. Eddie's on Redcar Market today. I can get him home now if you like."

"No, that's not necessary," he said. "There are still things to arrange. I'll bring Poppy to the house tomorrow evening if that's all right?"

Rosie picked up the telephone. "I'll ring Bobby and let him know the news. He'll want to be here too."

Bainbridge turned to leave. "I'll see you all tomorrow at about seven."

Rosie stepped towards him. "Andy," she whispered. "Thank you. Thank you for not giving up on finding my girl."

Bainbridge entered the car park of James Cook Hospital as his mobile rang. It was Catherine Davereaux. "I was about to ring you," he said. "I've arranged for you to meet Rosie and the rest of the family tomorrow night at their house. If that's convenient?"

"Yes, that's fine... My mother's been in touch. She's back in England."

"Where is she? I need to speak to her and Jon-Pierre as soon as possible."

"Dad had to go straight to France. Mum says he's unwell."

"What about Claudia? I'm about to issue a warrant for her arrest. You do know that?"

"Please, there's no need for that. She's on her way to Redcar to meet you and explain what happened."

"Tell her to be at my office by three-thirty this afternoon."

"All right, I'll tell her."

"I'll see you tomorrow," he said. "I'll pick you up at six-thirty."

37

Sally Lomax had been placed in a single-occupancy side room at the hospital. The doctor stood by her bed studying her chart when Bainbridge arrived. "How's she doing, Doctor?" he asked. "Any change?"

The doctor put down the clipboard and sighed. "The patient is in an induced coma. We will be bringing her out of it later today."

"Will I be able to speak to her then?"

He shook his head. "I'll be surprised if this young lady can tell you anything, at least not for the next few days. Like I told you before, she's been through quite an ordeal."

"But she will be all right, won't she? I mean, Sally will get better?"

"I have done all I can," the doctor said wearily. "It's up to her now."

"There's no permanent brain damage, though, is there?"

The doctor sighed. "Like I told the other male officer yesterday, I am hopeful that this young lady will make a full recovery. The damage to her head was not as severe as I first thought."

Bainbridge arched an eyebrow. "You say another officer was here? What was his name?"

The doctor shrugged. "I don't think he gave a name. He just asked how she was doing and if she would be able to remember what happened."

"What did he look like?"

"I didn't pay much attention," he said, scratching his head. "I was more concerned with my patient."

"Doctor, I am going to arrange for a uniformed officer to be placed outside Sally's room from now on."

He scowled. "That's most irregular. Why do you want to do that?"

"Sally was deliberately attacked. I think whoever attacked her came here, claiming to be a police officer."

"Do you think he intended to harm her?"

Bainbridge shrugged. "Maybe," he said. "Or frighten her into keeping quiet. Either way, I don't want anyone having access to this room other than medical staff."

"And her parents, of course?"

"Only her parents. No uncles or cousins."

The doctor began shaking his head slowly as he walked towards the door. "The world is becoming a dangerous place. A very dangerous place indeed."

38

The clock struck eleven-thirty as Harriet Johnstone readjusted her hat in the hall mirror. "Are you sure you don't want to come along, darling?" she asked and began to reapply her vibrant red lipstick. "Claudia would love to see you again."

Nigel strolled into the hall to stand behind his wife. "Far too busy at the office," he said, encircling his wife's waist and nuzzling her neck. "Melanie is still on maternity leave, and Jonathan broke his ankle falling off that damned bicycle of his. Things are tough at the moment." He squeezed his wife affectionately around her waist, grinning mischievously. "I might have to ask you to come back to work to help out."

Harriet shook her head vigorously. "Not likely. I was a solicitor for nearly thirty years. That was long enough. I'm enjoying my retirement too much to go back, thank you." Satisfied with her appearance, she put the lipstick back into her handbag and turned to face her husband. "When we moved to Whitby, I thought we were both going to retire. Instead, you seem to be working harder than ever."

Nigel winked. "Old habits. When did Claudia and Jon-Pierre get back from Kenya? I thought they were staying until the end of the month."

"So did I, but Jon-Pierre isn't well. He's gone straight to France for more chemo."

Nigel frowned. "I would have thought Claudia would have gone with him instead of coming to England. I wonder what's going on."

Harriet shrugged. "I have no idea. Claudia telephoned me this morning to invite me to lunch in Saltburn. She seemed upset about something."

His frown deepened. "What's she doing in Saltburn of all places?"

"I've no idea, darling. All I know is Claudia wants to speak to me urgently. To be honest, she did seem a little... desperate."

He scoffed. "Desperate? Claudia? That's a first. I wouldn't have thought she had a care in the world."

"Well, whatever it is, she wants to discuss it with me as a matter of urgency."

"I'm sorry I can't join you," he said. "Give her my love." The sound of a car horn caused him to stop. "Oh, there's your taxi. Let me know how you get on."

She kissed her husband lightly on the cheek and hurried to the door. "Will do," she said as she made her way to the waiting vehicle. "I shouldn't be late back."

She gave her husband a quick wave as the taxi sped off in the direction of Saltburn.

He closed the front door and hurried to his study. He picked up the telephone and rang a familiar number. "Any news?"

"She's not dead," the voice said. "Not yet."

"If she opens her mouth, we're fucked," Nigel said. "You'd better make damned sure—"

"Leave it to me. She won't be talking to anyone."

He took a cigarette from his desk drawer and lit it, something he hadn't done in over three months. "She'd better not."

"Stop worrying," the voice said. "I've told you, I'll deal with her." The line went silent for a few seconds. "By the way, when is the next party? I've already got six punters lined up."

He growled. "Are you mad? We have to keep a low profile, thanks to your incompetence."

"Keep your wig on, your Honour," the voice said. "I've told you, there's nothing to tie her to us. By the way, I have two new girls ready to party."

Nigel drew hard on his cigarette. "I'll think about it. But if I decide to hold back, that's the end of it. Understand?"

"Sure. You're the boss. But you'll be disappointing a lot of punters."

"I'll let you know when I've decided," he said. "Just make sure you deal with that nosey little bitch once and for all. I don't understand how she found out what was going on in the first place."

The voice tutted. "I've told you I'll take care of it."

"You'd better," he said. "Now, tell me about the girls."

39

Harriet sat across from Claudia in the restaurant. "I really think Jon-Pierre should be here too," she said thoughtfully. "You need to get your stories straight. Otherwise, the police will tear your account to pieces."

"Jon-Pierre had to go back to France. He has cancer, and he's having a relapse. Anyway, it was my idea to take the girl, not his. I'm the guilty one."

"What about Catherine? Have you seen her yet?"

Claudia shook her head. "No. I spoke to her on the phone this morning, and she told me what's been going on. That's why I came straight to see you."

"I'm glad you did. You do know that what you did was kidnapping?" she said. "That's a serious offence. You could go to jail."

Claudia took out a handkerchief from her bag and blew her nose. "I don't care," she said. "I would do it again. It was the right thing to do."

"If what you told me is true, you should have gone to the police years ago and told them everything that happened."

Claudia turned sharply to face her friend. "Do you think the police would have believed me? That anyone would have believed me?"

"But to take another woman's child…" Harriet sighed deeply. "What part did Jon-Pierre play in all this?"

She shrugged. "My husband is a good man. When I told him the circumstances, he agreed to help me. He had connections, so it was easy for him to get forged papers for Catherine."

Harriet raised her hand. "For goodness sake, don't tell the police that, or there will be more charges brought."

She lowered her head into her hands. "I never thought Catherine would be traced. It's been over sixteen years since I took her from the beach."

Harriet removed her phone from her bag. "I think Nigel

should join us. He has far more experience in criminal law than I do."

She leant forward and grabbed her friend's wrist. "No, not Nigel. I want you to represent me. I trust you. Please, Harriet."

"Of course I'll help you, Claudia, but you must realise that I specialised in civil law."

She inhaled deeply. "Harriet, I'm begging you. I want you to represent me this afternoon when I meet with the police. Please say you will."

"All right," she said, "but I think you're making a mistake."

The waiter came over to the table and began to clear the plates. "Will there be anything else, ladies?" he said. "Coffee, perhaps?"

"Brandy," Harriet said. "A large one."

40

Cooper identified two stockists of the Ashley Drake dress in the area, *The First Lady*, an elite boutique based in Yarm, and *Elegance by Design*, a company in Newcastle. She picked up the phone and dialled the Yarm number. It was answered immediately.

"Good morning, I'm Detective Inspector Cooper from Redcar Police."

"Oh?" a voice said. "What's wrong? What's happened?"

"There's nothing wrong," Cooper said. "I just need to ask you some questions. May I have your name, please?"

"Elkin," the woman answered with slight hesitation. "Jane Elkin. I'm the proprietor."

"Ms Elkin, I understand you are stockists for a range of Ashley Drake dresses?"

"Yes, that's right," she said. "We have three of their designs."

"It's the Valentino I'm interested in," Cooper said. "How many of those have you sold, say, in the last eighteen months?"

"I'll have to check, but not many. We never stock more than three of the same design. I'll just be a moment."

Cooper listened to the rustling of papers.

"I was right. Only one Valentino has been sold. The dress costs almost three hundred pounds, so it's out of reach for a lot of people."

"Who bought the dress?"

"That's confidential. I can't give out information about our clients."

"Ms Elkin... Jane," Cooper said, "I can get a warrant to search your records by this afternoon. Is that really what you want me to do?"

"But—"

"It's important I know who bought that dress. I can't tell you why at this stage, it is part of an ongoing enquiry. Now, please give me the name."

There was a pause. "It was Clare," she said. "Clare Osmond."

"I'll need her address."

"She's not in the country at the moment. She's on honeymoon, somewhere in America, I believe."

"Oh?"

"Clare got married last week. The dress was part of her trousseau."

"I see," Cooper said, "but I'll still need her address."

"I don't know where she'll be living when she gets back. I can give you her parent's address." Cooper listened as more papers were shuffled. "Her mother is Jocelyn Osmond. She was the mayor of Middlesbrough last year, and her father is the manager of one of the banks on the High Street. They're a respectable family. I can't understand what—"

"Thank you for your co-operation," Cooper said. "You've been most helpful." She hung up the receiver just as Bainbridge came into the room.

"I'm going for an early bite at The Coppers Inn," he said. "Fancy joining me?"

She sighed as she picked up the telephone. "Sorry. I'm chasing up on who bought Janette's dress."

He walked over to her. Then, leaning over the desk, he took the telephone from her grasp. "That can wait," he said as he replaced the receiver. "You've still got to eat. Besides, I've got some exciting news."

41

It wasn't until they were seated at a table in The Coppers Inn that Bainbridge told Cooper about the DNA positively identifying Catherine Davereaux as the missing Poppy Lee.

"Andy, that's wonderful," she said, leaning over and squeezing his arm. "It's hard to believe Poppy's alive after all this time."

"She's very much alive."

"You say she had no idea that Claudia wasn't her real mother?"

Bainbridge shook his head. "No. She didn't have a clue. If it hadn't been pressure from her friends after the television appeal... They saw the resemblance to Daisy straight away."

"So, what happens now?"

"I've arranged to pick Catherine up at six-thirty tomorrow evening. I'm taking her over to meet Rosie and Eddie at their house."

"What about Claudia and Jon-Pierre?"

"Jon-Pierre is in France. He's receiving urgent medical treatment, but I'm interviewing Claudia later this afternoon at the station. It'll be interesting to see what she has to say for herself."

"There's a warrant out for Jon-Pierre, isn't there? You could always get him extradited."

Bainbridge raised an eyebrow. "I could, but he's a powerful man with a lot of influence. Their solicitor, Ms Johnstone, telephoned me earlier. She gave me her assurance that Claudia Davereaux will be at the station at three-thirty this afternoon."

"Even so—"

"Oh, look," Bainbridge interrupted. "It's Duffy coming over with a bottle of bubbly."

Duffy bounded towards their table, a bottle of champagne in one hand and three glasses in the other. "Well done, mate," he said. He placed them down on the table and drew up a chair. "Daisy's told me the news. Who'd have thought after all this time? I felt sure Poppy had been swept out to sea that day."

"You've heard then?" Bainbridge said.

"Half of Redcar has heard," Duffy said. "A bloody miracle, that's what it is."

Bainbridge raised his hand as Duffy was about to open the bottle. "Sorry, mate, we're still working. We only came in for a sandwich and a coke."

Duffy shrugged his disappointment. "Okay. I'll put it on ice for later." He signalled to the waiter. "Quick as you can, Harry. Two cokes and two ham and cheese." He turned to Bainbridge. "That's right, isn't it? Well, if you can't have the champagne, at least have lunch on me," he said. "I've heard Poppy has been living the high life in France. Rich as Croesus, somebody was saying."

Bainbridge smiled and shook his head. "I really can't comment on that. You know that, Duffy."

"I suppose Daisy won't want to work here, now that she has a rich sister?"

"The girls haven't seen each other in sixteen years," Bainbridge said. "Who knows how they'll get on?"

Duffy stood and shrugged his broad shoulders before turning and walking through into the kitchen.

"He's got a point," Cooper said when Duffy had gone. "Things could be awkward between the girls."

Bainbridge placed his elbows on the table and steepled his fingers. "Mm, maybe, but there's nothing we can do about that. Things are where they are. By the way, how are you getting on with tracking down the dresses?"

"I'm not getting very far. There are only two stockists in the area. I spoke to the first outlet this morning. I'll contact the second one when I get back to the office, but if Janette bought it herself, I'm struggling."

"No other leads?" Bainbridge asked as the young waiter placed the sandwiches and two glasses of coke on the table and left.

"No. I'm just hoping Sally recovers and can tell us more."

"Let's hope so," he said. "By the way, I've arranged for a guard on Sally's room."

"Really?"

"According to the doctor looking after, someone was asking questions about her. He was claiming to be a police officer."

"Oh, my god. You don't think…?"

Bainbridge shrugged. "It's just a precaution, that's all, but it's best to be safe."

"Can I sit in on the interview with Claudia? I'm curious to know why a woman would do what she did. She must be heartless."

"Let's not jump to conclusions," Bainbridge said as he picked up his coke. "She's not a stupid woman by any means. However, I can't help thinking there's a lot more to this than we realise."

They finished their lunch and walked towards the exit. Duffy stood in the doorway smoking a cigarette. "How's that lass from the station doing?" he asked. "The one that got knocked down."

"She's not good," Bainbridge said. "Sally's not recovered consciousness yet."

"I was thinking of taking her some flowers if that's all right."

"Sorry, Duffy. There's no visiting allowed at the moment. Besides, I don't think you can take flowers to the hospital these days."

Duffy shrugged. "Never mind. It was just a thought."

Cooper was back at her desk by two o'clock. She picked up the telephone and rang the second shop which stocked the dress found at Sally's house.

"Elegance by Design," answered a woman with a southern accent. "How may I help you?"

Cooper introduced herself. Unlike Jane Elkin, Diane

Simms was more than willing to co-operate.

"Yes, we stock the Valentino," she said, "but I'm afraid we don't have any in stock at the moment."

"How many dresses did you have?" Cooper asked.

"Three. One black, one silver and one scarlet."

"Do you have a record of who purchased them?"

"Yes, of course. All of them were purchased by the proprietor herself. Two last year and one a few months ago."

Cooper frowned. "That's a little unusual, isn't it? Why would she want all three dresses?"

"She said they were presents for her nieces."

"Is the proprietor there now? I'd like to speak with her."

"She's not here at the moment. Cheryl spends a lot of time in France. She stays at the most marvellous chateau over there."

"Is she in France now?"

"Yes, but she's coming back to Newcastle tomorrow for a few days. It's our monthly stock check."

"Do you have a contact number for her?"

"Yes, of course. May I ask what this is all about?"

"I'm sorry, I'm not at liberty to say at the moment," Cooper answered. "By the way, what is Cheryl's surname? Just for my records."

"Lewis. Cheryl Lewis."

42

It was three-thirty-five when Claudia Davereaux arrived at Redcar Police Station accompanied by her solicitor, Harriet Johnstone. They were taken to interview room one.

Bainbridge walked down the corridor and tapped lightly on Cooper's door. "She's here," he said, poking his head into the room. "Do you want to sit in on the interview?"

Cooper shook her head. "Sorry, Andy, I have to go to the hospital. The doctor telephoned to say Sally was beginning to regain consciousness."

"Good," he said. "Let's hope she can tell us what happened. Make sure to let me know straight away what she has to say."

"I will," Cooper answered. "By the way—"

But he had already entered the interview room and closed the door behind him.

Claudia Davereaux was standing by the window when Bainbridge entered. Tall and slim, with glossy black hair styled in a short bob, Claudia was dressed in a dark grey tailored suit and pink silk blouse. Her porcelain skin bore little makeup, and her eyes were the colour of burnt amber underneath her long black lashes.

She turned sharply to face him. "Well?" she demanded, crossing her arms and tilting back her head. "What's this all about?"

"Please sit down, Mrs Davereaux," Bainbridge said, indicating the chair on the opposite side of the table. Claudia's posture stiffened, and she pursed her lips.

Standing by her side, Harriet gently took her upper arm and guided her to the wooden chair. "Sit down, Claudia," she said softly. "The sooner we get this sorted, the sooner we can get out of here." Harriet delved into her briefcase and removed a single sheet of paper which she handed to Bainbridge. "My client has provided a written statement.

Claudia has no further comment to make at this time."

Claudia flung back her head. "Catherine tells me you have taken a DNA sample from her. Is that right?"

"Yes."

Her hands formed into fists on her lap. "How dare you? You had no right to do that. Catherine is my daughter."

Bainbridge arched an eyebrow. "Is she? The DNA results say differently."

She narrowed her eyes. "I don't know what you're implying. Catherine belongs to me. I'm the one who takes care of her. Who protects her."

"Protects her from what?"

Harriet lifted her head, glaring at him. "Do you have any idea who Claudia Davereaux is?" she said. "Her husband—"

"I am perfectly aware of Mrs Davereaux's position," Bainbridge said, leaning back into his chair.

There was a loud commotion outside the room, and the door flung open. Eddie Lee burst into the room with Sergeant Brown in close pursuit. His face contorted with anger as he barrelled towards Claudia. "You fucking bitch," he screamed. "Why did you take my daughter?"

The Sergeant lunged forward and forced Eddie's right arm behind his back while Bainbridge got between Eddie and Claudia.

"Let go of me," he said as he struggled to release the officer's grip. "I'll kill the evil bitch."

Two more officers rushed into the room and manhandled Eddie against the wall. "That's enough, Eddie," Bainbridge said. He turned to the officers. "Put him in a cell. I'll deal with him later."

Still cursing and struggling violently, Eddie was frogmarched out of the interview room towards the cells.

Claudia had fled to the back wall, her body trembling uncontrollably.

"Are you all right?" Bainbridge asked. "You're not hurt?"

Harriet put her arm protectively around Claudia's

shoulders. "Does she look all right?" she said. "That maniac tried to kill her."

Claudia sobbed as she dabbed her eyes with a tissue. "May I… Could I have some water, please?" she asked quietly. "I don't feel well."

"Yes, of course," Bainbridge said, indicating for the officer at the door to fetch a drink. He soon returned with a paper cup containing water from the dispenser.

"I think it would be best if I speak to my client privately for a few minutes," Harriet said. "You can see how upset she is."

"Fifteen minutes," Bainbridge said. "When I return, I will be expecting answers."

Bainbridge returned to his office and took out the note given to him by Harriet. It was hand-written on crisp, white paper. It read:

'I Claudia Davereaux confirm that I am the mother of Catherine Davereaux. My daughter came to me at the age of two and has been looked after with the greatest of care. She is happy, healthy and above all, she is safe. I do not intend to give further details at this time other than to say I love her with all my heart, and I believe Catherine feels the same way towards me.'

Bainbridge stroked his chin as he read and re-read the note. "The arrogance of the woman," he murmured as he placed the note in his desk drawer.

There was a sharp rap on the door, and Sergeant Brown came into the office. "What do you want me to do with Eddie Lee?" he said. "The bloke's carrying on like a madman in the cells."

Bainbridge got up from his desk and walked towards the door. "I'll have a word."

The sergeant frowned. "You can't blame him, I suppose. I know if somebody took one of my kids, I'd—"

"That's enough, sergeant," Bainbridge said. "We don't have all the facts of what happened yet."

"I would have thought it straightforward enough, sir," the sergeant continued. "That Davereaux woman took the poor little mite away from her family. Just because she has money doesn't mean—"

"I said that's enough. Get back to work and leave Eddie Lee to me."

The sergeant left the office and returned to the incident room, muttering softly to himself.

Eddie Lee paced the small cell as Bainbridge unlocked the door. His face was pale and haggard, his eyes moist and puffy.

"Eddie, what the hell do you think you're playing at carrying on like that?"

Fists clenched, nostrils flared, Eddie lunged forward towards him. "Let me out of here," he screamed. "I want to know why she took my little girl, the evil bitch."

Bainbridge grabbed Eddie by his arms and pushed him further into the cell. "I'm warning you," he said. "Calm down, or I will arrest you. You don't want Poppy seeing her dad locked up, do you?"

"Arrest me? It's that cow you should be arresting. She's the one who—"

"Eddie, please stop this and let me do my job."

He dropped onto the wooden bench, both hands clenched tightly into fists. "All right," he said. "Have it your way, but if she doesn't give some answers, I swear to god I'll…"

Bainbridge put his hand on Eddie's shoulder. "Come on, mate. Go home and get some rest. You'll be meeting your daughter tomorrow."

He stood and wiped his eyes with the back of his hand. "Okay, Andy, I suppose you're right." He walked towards the cell door and then turned back. "I don't suppose Claudia said why?"

Bainbridge shook his head. "I've only just started the interview. Don't worry. We'll sort this mess out."

When Bainbridge returned to the interview room, both

women sat quietly at the desk. Harriet stood and walked towards him. "Detective Chief Superintendent. My client is in no fit state to continue with this interview at present. I want you to release her into my care." She handed Bainbridge her card. "This is my address. We will return here at your convenience when she will make a full statement of the events leading up to… up to this unfortunate scenario."

He took the card. "I see you live in Whitby?"

"Yes. My husband is Nigel Johnstone. He's a solicitor. Perhaps you've heard of him?"

He nodded. "By reputation, but we've never actually met."

"I assure you Claudia will remain under our supervision until her return here," Harriet said. "We must find out exactly what led to this unfortunate event."

"All right," he said. "I'll get you the necessary documents to sign, but…" he turned to face Harriet. "I want Mrs Davereaux back here first thing in the morning. Is that understood?"

She nodded and smiled. "Perfectly. Come on, Claudia. Let's go home."

"One more thing," Bainbridge said. "I do not want her to make any kind of contact with Catherine. Is that understood?"

Claudia nodded as she walked towards the door, arm-in-arm with Harriet, and then turned to face Bainbridge. "When you see Catherine, please tell her…"

"Tell her what?"

"Tell her that I love her, and I will explain everything that happened very soon."

"I'll make sure she gets the message," Bainbridge said.

43

Cooper got to the hospital just after four o'clock. An officer stood by the door, and the doctor was inside Sally's room when she arrived.

"How is she?" Cooper asked as she joined the doctor. "Is she able to speak yet?"

He shook his head. "Patience," he said. "These things take time. My patient has opened her eyes a couple of times momentarily, but she's not ready to wake up yet."

"I'll wait," Cooper said. "I want to be here when…"

"It will be some time before she is fully conscious," he said. "Perhaps you would be better trying to find out who did this to her? I will let you know when she can speak, but I warn you, it could be some time yet."

Cooper pulled the blue vinyl chair close to the bed and settled into it. She reached out and gently took Sally's hand in hers. "When you're ready, Sally," she said softly. "I'll be here." Sally's eyelids flickered for a moment. Cooper leant closer. "You're safe now," she whispered. "No one can hurt you."

"I understand this young lady is a colleague of yours?" the doctor said.

Cooper nodded.

"Her mother telephoned earlier. She's on her way. I can only allow one person here at a time. You do understand that?"

"I'll leave when she gets here. I don't want Sally to be left alone."

The doctor walked over to the door. "Promise me you'll find the animal that did this."

"I promise I will do my best. You can count on that."

Cooper went straight to Bainbridge's office on her return to the station. He looked up from his desk. "How is Sally? Has she regained consciousness yet?"

She shook her head. "No, not really. She tried opening her

eyes a couple of times."

Bainbridge closed the file he had been reading and placed it in the top drawer of his desk. "How are you getting on with tracing Janette's dress?"

Cooper told him of her enquiries with the two outlets of the dress. "I'm telephoning the second one tomorrow afternoon when Cheryl Lewis arrives. She's flying into Newcastle Airport."

"You said her name's Cheryl Lewis? Isn't that the name of Rosie's friend who she met that day on the beach?"

Cooper gasped, putting her hand to her mouth. "Of course. I thought the name was familiar. It was such a long time ago. Do you think it's the same person?"

He nodded. "I want her picked up at the airport tomorrow and brought here straight away."

"Leave it with me. I'll make the arrangements. By the way, how did you get on with Claudia Davereaux?"

He gently rubbed the back of his neck and sighed. "I'm interviewing her at length tomorrow. She was too upset to co-operate properly. She's staying with her solicitor in Whitby at the moment."

"Do you think that's wise? She could abscond."

He smiled and shook his head. "I have someone watching the house. If Claudia attempts to leave, I'll know about it."

"What did you think of her? What sort of woman is she?"

He stroked his chin. "I think Claudia Davereaux is an attractive, articulate woman, but I think she's also a very frightened one."

"Frightened? You mean frightened of getting sent to prison?"

"I don't think it's that, not with her money and connections. No, there's something else. Something we don't know about yet."

Cooper walked towards the door. "Well, I don't know about you, but I've finished for today. A hot bath and an early night, I think."

He tilted his head and smiled. "Fancy a drink?"

She put on her coat before answering. "No, I don't think so. Another time, perhaps."

"I think we need to talk," he said. "I—"

"Andy, please. Not now," she said as she opened the office door. "I can't."

"I think you still have feelings for me. I know I still have for you."

She turned to face him. "That was a long time ago. We can't go back. It's not right."

Bainbridge stood and made his way across to the door. "Let me take you out to dinner at the weekend. There are things I want to say that can't wait any longer."

Cooper attempted to push past him, but he blocked the way. She sighed as his face neared hers, his warm breath on her face. "Saturday?" he whispered, leaning even closer. "Please, Jilly."

"All right," she said, gently pushing him away. "I'll meet you at seven, but no promises, okay?"

He smiled. "Seven o'clock it is."

44

It was nine-thirty the following morning when Claudia Davereaux and her solicitor, Harriet Johnstone, arrived at the police station. They were directed to interview room one. Bainbridge joined them immediately, accompanied by Sergeant Brown.

"Good morning, ladies," he greeted. "Firstly, can I get you something to drink? Tea or coffee, perhaps?"

"May I have a glass of water?" Claudia said, her voice quaking slightly. "It's rather warm in here."

The Sergeant left the room, returning a few minutes later with a paper cup containing water. She reached out and took the cup, nodding her gratitude at the sergeant.

Bainbridge cleared his throat. "Mrs Davereaux," he said, "this interview is being recorded. Before we begin, I must caution you." Bainbridge read Mrs Davereaux her rights. "At the conclusion of this interview, you may be charged with some serious offences. You do understand that?"

She flung back her head. "Yes. But I regret nothing. On the contrary, I would do everything exactly the same. Do you understand that, Detective Chief Superintendent?"

"That's enough, Claudia," Harriet said. "Remember what we discussed?"

"I'm sorry, but it's true. I've been holding too many secrets for all these years. It's time people knew what really happened."

Bainbridge leant back into his chair. His hands clasped on the table. "Mrs Davereaux," he began, "perhaps we can—"

"Please, call me Claudia," she said. "I hate this formality."

He nodded. "Claudia, did you abduct, or cause to be abducted, two-year-old Poppy Lee from the beach in Redcar on the tenth of August 2002?"

She gave out a shrill laugh. "Abduct? Of course I didn't abduct her. I saved that little girl."

He frowned. "Saved her? What exactly do you mean by

that?"

"I think what my client means is—"

"I know exactly what I mean, Harriet," she said. "I saved her."

Bainbridge leant forward. "Are you saying that Poppy Lee was in some kind of danger?"

"Yes. That's exactly what I am saying.

"What kind of danger exactly, and from whom?" Bainbridge said.

"The danger to that little girl began years earlier," she said, "when I was living with Eddie."

"I understand you left your home, leaving Eddie to take care of your seven-year-old son, Bobby. Is that correct?"

It was several moments before she spoke. "Eddie and I..." she said, "we should never have got together. It was wrong from the start."

"What do you mean by that?"

"We were young. Far too young."

"What happened, Claudia? Tell me about the events that led you to abandon your family?"

She took a sip of water and lowered her head. "I was modelling in London. It was exciting and glamorous, but then I met Eddie, and soon afterwards, I found I was pregnant. Eddie worked for the same agency doing odd jobs, deliveries, that sort of thing." She lifted her head again, her eyes brimming with tears. "We rented a small flat in Peckham, and for a time, we were happy. I loved my life back then. Then Eddie's mother died and left him a house in Middlesbrough. He insisted we leave London and move to the northeast."

"You found it hard to settle?"

"I was lonely. I had no friends, no job. Eddie began working the markets, and I was left on my own a lot of the time."

Bainbridge frowned. "I can understand a woman leaving her husband for whatever reason, but to leave her child? That I don't understand."

She scraped back her chair and, standing up, began to pace the room. "You make me sound like a heartless monster. You have no idea... no idea."

"Then tell me," Bainbridge said. "Tell me what makes a woman abandon her seven-year-old son and then go on to steal another woman's child?"

She removed a handkerchief from her bag and began to mop her brow. "It's warm in here. Can you open the window, please? I... I can't breathe."

Bainbridge signalled for the sergeant to open the window. "Are you all right? Do you need a doctor?"

"I'm fine," she said, returning to her seat.

Harriet leant forward. "Claudia, you have to tell the officer exactly what you told me."

"There's something you should know from the beginning," she said, her voice little more than a whisper. "Eddie Lee is not Bobby's father."

45

Rosie was dusting in the dining room when Bobby arrived at half-past twelve. He rushed straight to his mother's side and kissed her on the cheek. "So," he said, "when can we expect to meet the long-lost Poppy Lee?"

Rosie could barely contain her excitement as she hugged her son. "She's coming here about seven. The DCS is bringing her."

"Do we know anything else about where she's been all this time?"

She took Bobby's hand. "Of course, you won't have heard, will you?"

He frowned. "Heard what?"

"It was Claudia who took Poppy. She's had her all the time. They've been living in France."

He flopped onto a dining chair and rubbed his face. "Claudia took her? Why the hell would she do that?"

Rosie put her arm around him and kissed the top of his head. "Who knows? She's being interviewed at the police station today. They'll be throwing the book at her."

He jumped to his feet, pushing Rosie away. "Where's Dad and Daisy?"

"Your dad's gone to get his hair cut, and Daisy has gone to the florist. I want to make the house look nice when Poppy gets here."

He strode over to the window. "There's no doubt that this girl is who she says she is?"

"Of course there isn't. Bainbridge said the DNA test he carried out proves it." She put down her duster, joined her son by the window and put her arm through his. "Is everything all right, Bobby? You don't seem excited to be meeting your long-lost sister."

He pulled away from his mother, shaking his head. "I don't understand why she would take Poppy, that's all. I'm her son, her flesh and blood. If she was going to take a child, why not take me?"

"Does it matter now, after all this time?" she said. "What's done is done. I'm just happy that I'll soon have all my children back under one roof, just like it should be."

He pushed past his mother. "I'm going for a walk. I need some air. Tell Daisy I'll meet her at The Coppers Inn."

"But I'm going to make lunch shortly. We can—"

The front door closed with a bang as Bobby hurried down the road in the direction of the town.

Bobby was on his third pint of lager when Daisy arrived. She rushed over to her brother, a look of concern on her face. "Is everything all right?" she said, pulling out a stool from underneath the table. "Mother said you were upset."

He scowled. "I'm not upset. I'm bloody angry. You know Poppy was taken by Claudia, my real mother?"

She nodded.

He sneered. "Why would she do that? I don't understand."

Daisy reached out and took Bobby's hand in hers. "Don't worry about Claudia. Just concentrate on our sister coming home at last. I wonder what she'll be like."

He huffed. "She'll look just like you, I suppose. That's how she was recognised, isn't it?"

"Of course, she'll look like me. But I wonder if she'll be like me in other ways. Whether she'll like the same food, or like listening to the same music, or—"

Bobby flung his head back and drained his glass. "I'm getting another drink. Do you want one?"

Daisy screwed up her nose. "No, I promised to give Mum a hand. I just came to make sure you're okay."

"Why shouldn't I be?"

"I spoke with Karen the other day," she said. "She told me what's been going on."

Bobby growled. "You'd no business sticking your nose into my affairs. It's nothing to do with you, with any of you."

"But Bobby—"

"Karen and me, we're finished. That's the end of it."

"Are you going to tell Mum and Dad?"

"No, I'm not," he said, grabbing Daisy by the wrist. "And neither are you."

Daisy struggled to free herself from his grip. "Bobby, let go. You're hurting me,"

His nostrils flared as he stared defiantly at his sister. It was a few seconds before he released his grip. He lowered his head. "Sorry. It's just that I don't like people interfering in my life."

"I'm not people," she said, rubbing her wrist. "I'm your sister, and I'm worried about you."

He grunted. "What the hell for?"

"Well, you're drinking for one thing. The last time you were here, you said you didn't drink alcohol. What happened?"

He banged his fist on the table. "I'll tell you what happened." A trace of spittle ran down the side of his mouth. "My mother abandoned me when I was a kid, and then she goes and helps herself to someone else's. I'm expected to carry on as if it doesn't matter, but it does matter. It matters very much."

"I don't understand. This has nothing to do with Poppy. She didn't ask to be taken."

His eyes narrowed. "Didn't she? Sweet, innocent little Poppy, with her golden curls and big blue eyes. She had all the attention. You both did. Nobody noticed me. I was just the big brother." He wiped his mouth with the back of his hand. "It didn't matter that I was the one with the brains, the one who won a scholarship."

Daisy stood and took a step back from him. "What's the matter with you? Are you crazy? Why are you saying these things?"

Bobby staggered to his feet, glared at his sister and then headed over to the bar. He placed the glass on the counter with a loud thump. "Another," he slurred.

Daisy walked over to her brother's side. "Don't you think you've had enough? You don't want to be drunk when you meet Poppy, do you?"

He threw some coins onto the bar. "Don't I?"

She reached for his arm, but he turned and pushed her away, causing her to fall against the vending machine on the wall. Duffy, who was behind the bar and had witnessed the incident, rushed over and, taking Daisy gently by the arm, guided her to a chair. "Are you all right, Daisy?" he said, pushing back a strand of hair from her face. "Are you hurt?"

She shook her head. "I'm fine, Duffy. I... I slipped, that's all."

He turned to face Bobby. "I think you've had enough to drink, don't you, son? It's time you went home." He grabbed Bobby's arm and propelled him towards the door. "Getting hammered is the last thing your family need today. Now piss off and sober up."

The ambulance arrived at the police station less than ten minutes after the call was made. Two paramedics were attending to Claudia as she lay unconscious on the ground.

"She just held her chest and keeled over," Bainbridge said to one of the attendants. "She complained of being too warm."

"She has angina," Harriet said. "She's had a couple of attacks like this before."

The medics carefully placed Claudia onto a stretcher and headed for the ambulance.

"I'll go with her to the hospital," Harriet said as the ambulance doors were closed and the vehicle pulled away, its sirens blaring, its blue light flashing.

46

The plane from Paris, with Cheryl Lewis on board, arrived in Newcastle at two-fifteen. A police car was waiting at the airport to take her to Redcar Police Station.

Cooper was in the incident room when she arrived. "PC Walker," she said, "I want you to sit in on the interview. It will be good experience."

"Yes, ma'am," answered the young police officer. The two women walked up the corridor to interview room two.

"Would anyone care to tell me what the hell this is about?" Cheryl said when the two officers entered the room. "I've been dragged here as if I were a common criminal. Am I under arrest?"

"No, you're not under arrest. You are helping with our enquiries. Sit down, please," Cooper said, placing a buff-coloured folder on the desk. "The sooner we get certain matters cleared up, the sooner you can leave."

Cheryl flounced down on the chair, crossing her long slender legs. "What matters? I've done nothing wrong."

"I understand you no longer work for Chic Fashions and that you own a dress shop in Newcastle?"

"It's not a dress shop. It's a boutique," she said. "There is a difference."

Cooper opened the folder and took out a photograph of the dress found at Sally's house. "Do you recognise this dress?" she asked, pushing the photograph across the table.

She gave it a cursory glance. "Should I?"

"It's an Ashley Drake," Cooper said.

"I can see that. What of it?"

"I understand that over the last eighteen months, you have purchased three Ashley Drake dresses from your own stock. The Valentino designs. Who were the dresses for?"

"That is none of your damned business," she said. "Why do you want to know about them anyway?"

"Just answer my questions," Cooper said. "Who were the

dresses for?"

She leant back in the chair and exhaled. "They were presents."

Cooper arched an eyebrow. "Expensive presents. They cost three hundred pounds each, or so I'm reliably informed."

"That's the retail," she said. "Anyway, what's it got to do with you who I buy presents for? It's still a free country, isn't it?"

"One of those dresses was found amongst the possessions of a missing girl. I need to know how she came by it."

Cheryl Lewis pursed her lips. "I'm not the only supplier of Ashley Drake. There are other outlets."

"Not in the northeast," Cooper replied.

Cheryl casually glanced at the photo of the dress again. "What was the girl's name who had the dress?"

"Janette Walsh," Cooper said, pushing a photograph of Janette towards her. "She lives here in Redcar."

"I don't know her," she said, pushing the picture back towards Cooper. She scraped back the chair and stood up. "Now, if you don't mind, I have business to attend to."

PC Walker, standing by the door, placed herself in front of it, blocking her path. Cheryl Lewis turned sharply to face Cooper. "What the hell's going on? You can't keep me here."

"Sit down," Cooper said. "We haven't finished."

She strolled back to the desk and flung herself into the chair. "I want a solicitor," she said. "I want to speak to Nigel Johnstone. His practice is in Whitby."

Cooper frowned. "I know Mr Johnstone."

"Then kindly inform him that I wish him to represent me. I'm not saying another word until I've spoken with him."

"Why do you think you need a solicitor? Do you have something to hide?"

"Of course not."

"I understand from the assistant at your shop… your boutique… that you spend a lot of time in France."

"I have friends who have a chateau. I stay with them. It's

not a crime, is it?"

"No, that's not a crime," Cooper said. "What is your friend's name?"

"That's none of your damned business," she said. "I have nothing more to say. Not until I have spoken to Nigel Johnstone."

47

"It's PC O'Connor, sir," the young officer said. "I'm at the hospital with Mrs Davereaux."

"How's she doing, constable?" Bainbridge asked. "Is there any news?"

"Her condition has improved, sir, but she will be staying here overnight under observation."

Bainbridge sighed. "Thank god for that. I want you to stay outside her room until your relief arrives at ten o'clock. Is that understood?"

"Yes, sir," he replied. "By the way, sir, do you know PC Porter is on duty across the corridor outside Sally Lomax's room?"

Bainbridge ran his hand through his hair. "If the two patients' rooms are so close, there's no point in you both being there," he said. "You'd better come back to the station. Tell Porter to keep an eye on Mrs Davereaux as well as Sally. If she attempts to discharge herself from the hospital before tomorrow morning, I want to know about it."

"Yes, sir. I'll speak with PC Porter right away."

Bainbridge left the police station just after six and drove to The Grand Hotel in Saltburn. He hurried along the corridor and knocked on Catherine's hotel room door.

"Ready," she said as she opened the door and bounded out, a broad smile on her face. She wore a pale pink floral dress with a white cardigan draped over her slender shoulders. Her hair was tied back in a ponytail.

"I'm sorry about your mother... about Claudia," he said. "The hospital said her condition isn't serious, and she should be released tomorrow."

Catherine flicked back a stray strand of hair. "I heard. Someone from your office rang me. But that woman is not my mother, is she? She's the one who stole me." They made their way down and into the car. "Tell me about my sister,"

174

she said after they had been driving for a few minutes. "Do you know Daisy well?"

Bainbridge smiled. "I've met her a few times. She still lives with your parents and works in one of the local pubs in Redcar."

"Are you saying my sister, my twin sister, is a barmaid?"

"What's wrong with that? Daisy is a lovely girl."

"And my brother? Is he lovely too?"

Bainbridge glanced over at Catherine. "They're all good people," he said. "Rosie never stopped looking for you, did you know that? It was her idea to do the appeal on television."

Catherine scoffed. "Good for Rosie. Let's hope she won't be disappointed when she finally gets to meet me."

"Why should she be disappointed? I don't understand."

Catherine put her hand to her mouth and leant forward. "Stop the car. I feel sick."

He pulled into a layby, and she got out of the car and rushed to the hedgerow. After a few minutes, she joined him back in the car.

"Are you all right?" he asked, "you look really pale. Do you want a few minutes to recover?"

She shook her head. "I'm fine now, thanks. I think it's just nerves."

"Don't worry. Everything will work out, you'll see."

"But what if they don't like me?" Catherine said.

"Of course, they'll like you. They've been waiting for this day for sixteen years."

He started the engine again, and they drove in silence for a few minutes.

It was Catherine who spoke first. "What's going to happen to Claudia and Jon-Pierre? Will they go to prison?"

"That's for the courts to decide. Don't upset yourself about them. Just concentrate on meeting your new family."

"They did take good care of me, you know," Catherine said. "I had everything I wanted. I suppose they over-indulged me sometimes."

"I'm sure they did," he said. "By the way, I never did ask you, what is it you do for a living?"

She shrugged. "Nothing exciting. A bit of admin in Dad's office, and I sometimes accompany him on trips around Europe promoting his wine."

"That sounds interesting."

"You think so? I hated it most of the time." She stared out of the window and sighed. "I really wanted to work in fashion. Mum's friend, Cheryl, owns a chain of boutiques. I wanted to work for her, but Mum said no."

"Cheryl? Is that Cheryl Lewis?"

She turned to face him. "Yes, that's right. Cheryl is my mother's best friend. She stays at our chateau most summers. Do you know her?"

Bainbridge exhaled deeply. "We've met," he said, steering the car onto the drive of no 14 Hudson Gardens. He turned off the engine. "Here we are. Let's go inside and meet your family."

48

Rosie and Eddie stood by the open door as Bainbridge and Catherine got out of the car.

Rosie rushed forward, arms outstretched. "Poppy. Is it really you?" She embraced the girl tightly, kissing her on the cheek. "I thought I'd never see you again. I've missed you so much."

Eddie moved forward and put his hands on his wife's shoulders. "Let the girl breathe, Rosie," he said.

Rosie released her hold and, stepping back, took Catherine's hands in hers. "Oh, you look so much like your sister. Let's go inside and meet her."

Catherine walked slowly towards the house, Rosie and Eddie's arms wrapped protectively around her shoulders.

"Welcome home, lass," Eddie said softly, kissing Catherine on her cheek. They entered the lounge where Daisy and Bobby sat. "She's here," Eddie said. "Our Poppy has come back to us."

Daisy used the back of her hand to wipe away the tears running down her cheeks as she slowly approached her sister. The two girls stared at each other in silence before Catherine leant forward and tightly hugged her. "Don't cry. I'm back now. Everything's going to be all right, you'll see."

"I… I can't believe it's really you," Daisy sobbed. "We all thought you were dead, that you'd drowned."

"No, I wasn't drowned, as you can see," Catherine said. She smiled and took hold of her sister's hand. "I'm very much alive."

Eddie clapped his hands together. "Get that champagne, Rosie," he said. "We need to celebrate."

Rosie rushed into the kitchen.

Catherine turned to face Bobby, who was sitting motionless on the couch. "You must be my big brother," she said.

Smiling, Bobby stood up and put his arms around

177

Catherine, kissing her lightly on the cheek. "Welcome home, little sister," he said, then, releasing his hold, he sat back on the couch.

Rosie came back into the lounge carrying a tray containing a bottle of champagne and several glasses. She put the tray on the table. "You will join us, won't you, Andy?" she said as she began to pour. "After all, it's down to you that Poppy is back where she belongs."

Bainbridge, who had been hovering in the lounge doorway, put up his hand. "No, sorry. I have to get back to the station. There's still work to be done."

"Have you locked that bitch up yet?" Eddie said. "You should throw away the key."

"Eddie, that's enough," Rosie said. "What Claudia did was wrong, and she should be punished, but she did look after Poppy. You can see that."

Bainbridge walked into the hall. "I'll call in tomorrow afternoon, and we can have a proper chat then. Will you be staying here, or…?"

Catherine shook her head. "No, all my things are back at the hotel. I'll be going back later tonight."

"I'll drive you over when you're ready," Bobby said.

"No, you don't have to do that," Catherine said. "I can get a taxi."

Bobby shrugged. "It's up to you. Now come and have some champagne. We have a lot of catching up to do."

Catherine laughed. "All right, big brother. Let's do that."

49

It was nine o'clock when Bainbridge got back to the station. He paused as he spotted Cooper still in her office. "Don't you have a home to go to?" he asked.

She looked up from the papers on her desk. "How did the reunion go?"

"Great. I thought Rosie was going to burst with excitement," he said. "When I left, they had just cracked open a bottle of champagne."

Cooper began putting the documents into a buff-coloured folder. "Andy, I need to talk to you about Cheryl Lewis."

He raised an eyebrow. "What about her?"

"I interviewed her earlier today. She refused to discuss the dresses until she speaks with her solicitor. I've arranged an interview for tomorrow morning, but… there's something else."

"You mean her association with Claudia and Jon-Pierre Davereaux?"

"You know about that?"

"Catherine told me. It seems Cheryl is a frequent visitor to their chateau in France."

"That means she must have been involved with Poppy's abduction or at least knew about the Davereaux's part in it."

"It's certainly looking that way," Bainbridge said. "What time are you interviewing Cheryl Lewis tomorrow?"

"She'll be here at three with her solicitor, Nigel Johnstone."

"Nigel Johnstone? That's the husband of Claudia's solicitor, Harriet."

"How is Claudia? I heard she had a funny turn."

"She's staying in hospital tonight for observation, but I'll be interviewing her some time tomorrow. Do you want to sit in?"

"I'd love to."

He leant on the door jamb with his hands thrust deep in his pockets. "I'm going for a drink. Do you fancy joining me?"

Cooper smiled as she placed the files into the cabinet. "Give me five minutes. I'll just freshen up."

The Coppers Inn was busy when they arrived.

Bainbridge looked around. "No Duffy tonight?" he said, addressing a pale, spotty-faced youth behind the bar.

"Nah," he said. "It's the boss's night off."

"I'm glad somebody gets a night off." He ordered the drinks and, after paying for them, turned to face Cooper, who was straining to see beyond the crowd to the other side of the bar.

"Isn't that Daisy and Bobby Lee?" she said, nodding in their direction. "Over there by the window."

"I think you're right. Let's go and join them."

Daisy smiled as they approached. "Andy. Isn't it wonderful, having Poppy back?"

"Where is she? I thought she'd be out with you two."

Bobby drained his glass and turned to his sister. "Fancy another?" Daisy nodded, and Bobby made his way to the bar.

"Poppy had to go back to the hotel," she said. "She'll be coming back tomorrow, though."

Bainbridge smiled. "Will she be staying at Hudson Gardens?"

"Nothing's been decided yet, but I hope so. I can't see her wanting to go back to France after what's happened."

"How does it feel to meet your sister after all this time?" Cooper asked. "You must be excited."

Daisy clasped her hands. "Oh, I am. Catherine seems so nice. It'll be fun getting to know her."

"What about Bobby? How's he coping with having another sister?"

Daisy sighed. "I think he's having trouble getting his head around that woman taking Poppy after abandoning him. After all, Claudia is his real mother."

"Hopefully, we'll get some answers," Bainbridge said. "I'm interviewing Claudia at the police station tomorrow." His mobile rang out its shrill tone. "Sorry," he said, turning and walking towards the door. "I must take this."

Cooper sipped her wine and watched as he spoke on the phone. "If you'll excuse me," she said, "I think work is beckoning."

She walked over to Bainbridge just as Bobby returned with the drinks. "What's up with those two?" Bobby asked.

Daisy shrugged as she took the wine glass from Bobby. "Something to do with work, I think."

"Well, let them get on with it. I don't like them hanging around us all the time."

Daisy gave her brother a darting glance but said nothing.

Cooper joined Bainbridge as he left the pub and waved her over to him. They headed towards his car. "What's wrong?" she said, hurrying to catch up.

"Some bastard has tried to smother Sally at the hospital. They've kicked the shit out of PC Porter."

Cooper gasped. "How's Sally? She's not…?"

"No, but it was a close thing. The doctors are with her now. I'm going to the hospital."

He unlocked his car, and Cooper slid into the front passenger seat beside him. "I'll come with you."

50

Bainbridge and Cooper arrived at the hospital twenty minutes later. They made their way up to Sally's room, where the doctor was at the washbasin rinsing his hands.

"How is she?" Bainbridge said, rushing to the side of Sally's bed. "What did that bastard do to her?"

The doctor turned to face him. "She's going to be all right. Someone put a pillow over the girl's face. Fortunately, a nurse was passing and saw what was happening. She raised the alarm."

"Can she describe the man?"

He shook his head. "No, not in any detail. He wore a white medical coat with a mask over his mouth. The nurse is outside making a statement to one of your officers."

Leo Cutts approached Bainbridge. "I've taken swabs, sir," he said, "but it looks like whoever attacked Sally wore gloves."

Bainbridge sighed and nodded. "Do what you can. Where's PC Porter?"

"He's in x-ray," the doctor said. "He sustained a bang on the head, but I don't think his condition is serious."

"I'll need to speak with him," Bainbridge said. He turned to Cooper. "Stay here with Sally. Let me know if she wakes up."

The x-ray department was on the floor above. Bainbridge quickly ascended the stairs to find PC Porter sitting on a bench in the corridor drinking a cup of tea. A pretty blonde nurse was seated beside him. At the sight of the DCS, Porter sprang to his feet.

Bainbridge growled. "How the hell did this happen?" he said as he approached the young officer. "You were supposed to be watching Sally."

"I... I don't know, sir," Porter said. "I looked in on the Davereaux woman. She was asleep, and when I came out of the room... I was hit from behind. I didn't see a thing."

"Did you see anybody hanging around the corridor before you checked on Mrs Davereaux?"

The officer shook his head. "No, sir, only medical staff occasionally."

"Who exactly?"

Porter smiled and nodded towards the nurse. "Nurse Brough brought me a cup of tea about half-past eight," he said. "Then a doctor went into the room next to Mrs Davereaux."

"Did you see the doctor come out?"

He screwed up his face in concentration. "I... I can't remember."

Nurse Brough tilted her head and frowned. "Why would a doctor go into that room? That patient was discharged this morning."

Bainbridge turned and raced to the stairs, descending two at a time. "Cutts," he shouted. "Cutts, where the hell are you?"

Cutts, who had been on his hands and knees at the far side of Sally's bed, got to his feet. "Where's the fire?"

"I want you to do a sweep on the room across the corridor," Bainbridge said. "The room next to Claudia Davereaux's."

He frowned. "Okay. You're the boss." He picked up his bag and left the room.

"What's going on?" Cooper asked when he had gone. "Why that room?"

"I believe that's where the assailant hid until the coast was clear," Bainbridge said. "The crafty buggar disguised himself as a member of staff." He turned to the doctor. "I'll need to look at the CCTV for this corridor. Can you arrange that?"

He shook his head. "Sorry. The system is being overhauled. It won't be back in action for a couple more days."

Bainbridge clenched his fists and grimaced.

"Let's go, Andy," she said. "There's nothing more we can do here tonight. There's a guard inside Sally's room, and officers are taking statements from the staff."

Bainbridge exhaled heavily. "Okay, I suppose you're right. Let's hope we get some answers tomorrow."

They got into the car and drove back to Redcar in silence.

51

It was early the following morning when Bainbridge arrived at the station. He went straight to his office and took out the notes from his previous interview with Claudia Davereaux. He was still re-reading them when Sergeant Brown entered the room. "They're here, sir," he said. "Mrs Davereaux and her brief."

Bainbridge glanced at his watch. "Show them to interview room one," he said as he began collecting the various papers and placing them in a file. "I'll be along in a moment."

Five minutes later, he walked down the corridor to the interview room.

Cooper stood outside the door. "You said I could join you?"

Bainbridge smiled. "Sure. You're more familiar with the case than anyone."

Claudia Davereaux stood by the table, nervously twisting her fingers. When the two officers entered the room, Harriet Johnstone, sitting at the table rummaging through documents in her briefcase, looked up. She stopped, smiled, and held out her hand. "Good morning, Detective Chief Superintendent," she said.

Bainbridge shook her hand before taking his seat with Cooper by his side.

"Good morning, ladies," he said. "Are you sure you're feeling well enough to continue, Mrs Davereaux... Claudia?"

She nodded. "I'm perfectly well, thank you." She pulled a chair from beneath the table and sat. "Let's just get this over with."

Bainbridge turned on the tape. "I must remind you that you are still under caution and that this interview is being recorded."

"Yes, I know all that. Harriet explained earlier."

"Good," Bainbridge said as he shuffled papers in front of him. "Perhaps we can start with the statement you made at our last interview concerning Eddie Lee not being Bobby's father. Was that statement true?"

"Yes. I was pregnant before I met Eddie."

"But you let him think he was Bobby's father?"

She clasped her fingers and stretched her arms across the table. "You have to understand, back then, my life was chaotic. Lots of drink, lots of drugs and there was the sex too, of course. It was just one party after another."

"I take it you got pregnant at one of these parties?"

"Clients from Milan had come over," she said. "All the models were expected to... to entertain." She lowered her head and ran her fingers through her hair. "I know it was stupid, but I was young and foolish. I didn't think twice when I was invited onto the client's yacht."

"Is this really necessary," Harriet asked. "I don't see how—"

"It's all right, Harriet," Claudia said. "It's best the police know everything."

"Go on," Bainbridge encouraged.

"I realised I was pregnant just after I started seeing Eddie," she said. "Back then, Eddie was so handsome and charming."

"So, you let him think he was Bobby's father?"

Claudia sighed. "He could have been," she said. "We started sleeping together soon after we met."

"But now you're sure he isn't?"

"I had to know the truth," she said. "That's why I did a DNA test on Bobby. Eddie didn't know anything about it."

"And the test came back negative?"

She nodded. "That's right. It confirmed what I already knew. Bobby's father was one of the Italian clients that had been on the yacht."

Bainbridge took a deep breath and leant forward, steepling his fingers. "Why did you abandon your son, Claudia?"

"Detective Chief Superintendent," Harriet said, "I must protest. My client is here to talk about Catherine, not Bobby."

Bainbridge turned abruptly to face the solicitor. "Your

client is here to answer whatever questions I put to her," he said. "Now, Claudia, please answer my question. What happened to make you abandon your child?"

She began to rock backwards and forwards, slowly at first, then a little faster. Harriet put her hand on Claudia's arm. "Take your time, dear," she said. "Don't get yourself into a state."

Claudia picked up the glass of water in front of her and took a sip. "The three of us were living in Middlesbrough, the house that had belonged to Eddie's mother," she said. "It was a decent house with a big garden at the back."

"So, what happened?"

Claudia looked away from the officers.

"Claudia, what happened?" he coaxed.

She exhaled. "Bobby was a quiet, studious child," she said. "He didn't mix with other children. When he didn't have his nose in a book, he spent most of his time tramping around the garden. There were a lot of trees at the bottom end, and he loved to play amongst them."

"It sounds idyllic for a young boy," Bainbridge said.

Claudia took another sip of water. "My cat, Smokey, went missing," she said. "He was a beautiful cat. He'd sit on my lap purring away for hours."

Bainbridge frowned. "I don't understand. What's the cat going missing got to do with Bobby?"

"It was the end of September. I'd decided to plant some spring bulbs underneath the trees." Claudia gave an involuntary shudder. "I began to dig down. That's when... when I found him."

"You found the cat?"

She nodded. "I knew it was Smokey. He still had his blue collar with the brass bell. I bought the bell so he wouldn't be able to creep up on the birds without being heard."

Bainbridge's frown deepened. "You think Bobby was responsible?"

Claudia lifted her head, her eyes glistening with tears. "Of course, he was responsible. Bobby was always hanging about at the bottom of the garden." Claudia gulped and took another sip of water. "There were other animal carcasses there too."

"What did you do?"

"I challenged him about it when he came home from school. He… he just smirked."

"Did you tell Eddie what he'd been up to?"

Claudia shook her head. "Eddie was away that night. He was working markets up in Northumberland."

"So, what did you do?"

"What could I do? I gave Bobby his tea and sent him up to his room. I told him I'd be telling his dad when he got home the following day."

"And did you tell Eddie?"

She shook her head. "I didn't get the chance. That night, it must have been about three o'clock in the morning, I woke up. I had an uneasy feeling something was wrong." She clasped her hands and gave another involuntary shudder.

"Take your time, Claudia," Bainbridge said. "Tell me what happened?"

"The curtains had been drawn back, and the streetlight was shining into the bedroom," she said. "That's how I could see so clearly."

"What did you see?"

"I saw Bobby standing at the side of my bed, an evil sneer on his face. He was holding a knife above his head."

Bainbridge rubbed his chin. "You think Bobby was going to kill you?"

She nodded. "If I hadn't woken when I did… After that, I knew I had to leave, to get away as quickly as I could."

"Why didn't you wait and speak to Eddie?"

She huffed. "Eddie thought the sun shone out of Bobby. He wouldn't have heard a word said against him."

"But if you'd told him what had happened, about the knife and the cat…"

"I was too frightened," she said as tears trickled down her

cheek. "I was terrified of being alone with my seven-year-old son. Can you possibly begin to imagine how that felt?" She reached into her bag and, removing a tissue, dabbed her eyes. "I knew I had to get away, so the next day I left Bobby with a neighbour and went home and packed a bag. By lunchtime, I was on the train heading towards Kings Cross."

Bainbridge frowned. "So, Eddie had no idea what Bobby had done?"

Claudia shook her head. "None. A few months after I left him, I heard he had met someone else."

"Rosie?"

"Yes. She was pregnant within three months."

"How did you know about that if you were in London?"

Claudia shrugged. "I got told."

"I presume it was Cheryl Lewis that told you about the twins?"

"I... I need a rest," she said. "I'm feeling tired."

Harriet took Claudia's hand and squeezed it. She turned to Bainbridge. "I insist we take a break. You can see my client is still unwell."

"Does she need a doctor?" he asked. "I can—"

Claudia raised her hand. "No, I don't want a doctor. I'll be all right if I have a short rest."

"Half an hour," Bainbridge said as he collected his papers together. "If you're not fit to continue by then, I'm calling a doctor."

"I'll be fine," Claudia said. "Perhaps I could have some tea?"

"Of course," Bainbridge said as he made to leave the room.

Bainbridge arranged for tea to be taken into the interview room. He returned to his office, accompanied by Cooper. "Well," he said, "what do you make of that?"

She flopped down on a chair and shook her head. "What Claudia was describing were the actions of a psychopath. If she's to be believed, Bobby Lee is an extremely dangerous young man."

Bainbridge frowned. "We don't really know a great deal about him, do we? Of course, he was only seven."

Cooper nodded. "Yes, I suppose he was, but we know this type of behaviour usually starts at a young age."

Bainbridge sighed. "I'm going up to the canteen for a coffee and a quick bite," he said. "I have a feeling we could be in for a long day."

52

Bainbridge and Cooper returned to the interview room thirty minutes later.

"Are you all right to resume, Claudia?" Bainbridge asked.

She smiled weakly and nodded. "Yes. Let's get this over with."

Bainbridge took his seat at the table and opened the folder as Cooper remained near the door. "Before we get on to Poppy's abduction," he said. "I want you to tell me what happened when you left Eddie and went to London."

Claudia tilted her head. "I went back to my old haunts. I couldn't work as a model anymore, but I knew the business."

"So, you went to work for the fashion houses?"

"That's right. I had studied design at college, so I got a job easily enough."

"Is that where you met Cheryl Lewis?"

"Yes, she was a trainee buyer. We became friends."

"I presume she told you about Eddie marrying Rosie?" he said.

"That's right. Cheryl had been to school with Rosie. It came up once in conversation."

"So, she kept you informed of Eddie and your son?"

Claudia nodded. "She visited Redcar every so often and took photographs of Bobby. After all, he was still my son."

"That's understandable," Bainbridge said.

"It was when she told me about the accidents to the girls that I started to get worried."

"What accidents?"

"Poppy had treatment in hospital after falling off her swing. It seems the front bar came loose. Shortly afterwards, Daisy fell off her tricycle and got hurt, then she was splashed with boiling water after a pan fell off the hob."

"You thought the girls were in danger from Bobby?"

Claudia nodded again. "Of course, I did. I told you, Bobby frightened me." Claudia gave another involuntary shudder.

"Cheryl telephoned me on the Wednesday. She was upset. She had seen Bobby place the girls in an inflatable and push it out to sea. It was only by luck that a man saw them and brought them back to shore." She took a sip of water. "I knew then that the girls were not safe near Bobby. That's when... when I decided to take them."

"A witness said that on the day of the abduction, there were two seats in your car. Were you planning on taking both girls?"

"Yes, but when Rosie went to get the kids an ice cream, she took Daisy with her."

"I take it Cheryl Lewis was going to help you with the second child?" Bainbridge said.

"She was standing down the beach ready to take one of the girls."

"What was your plan once you had stolen the children?"

Claudia inhaled deeply. "I don't think I'd thought that far at the time. All I knew was that the girls must be saved."

Bainbridge frowned. "Tell me what happened once you had Poppy in your car. Where did you go?"

"I went back to London. I had a small flat there."

Bainbridge leant forward. "But surely someone would become suspicious of you with a small child?"

Claudia glared at him. "I didn't care. All I was bothered about was keeping the child safe. I was devastated I only got Poppy, but then I heard Bobby had received a scholarship and would be away from Redcar most of the year. So I knew Daisy would be safe."

"How did Jon-Pierre Davereaux become involved?" Bainbridge said. "Did he have any part in the abduction?"

"No. He knew nothing about it until he came round to my flat that night and saw Poppy."

"How did he react?" he asked.

"He was shocked at first, but after I'd explained why I'd taken her, he agreed to help me." She took another sip of the water. "He asked me to marry him, and the three of us moved to France. Jon-Pierre had no children, but he loved Catherine as if she were his own."

"You raised Poppy... or Catherine as you call her, in France?" Bainbridge said.

"Not entirely. We also own a house on the coast in Devon. We spent half the year in England."

Bainbridge rubbed his chin. "I take it Jon-Pierre sorted out the false documentation, birth certificates, passports, that sort of thing?"

Harriet leant forward. "My client does not have to answer that."

Bainbridge frowned. "I will need to speak to your husband at some point, Claudia."

"That's impossible. My husband is a sick man. He's dying. He doesn't have much time left."

"I'm sorry to hear that," Bainbridge said. "Didn't either of you ever consider telling Catherine the truth?"

"Absolutely not," Claudia said. "Catherine is my daughter. I have taken care of her since she was two years old."

"You do know she's been reunited with her real family?"

Claudia huffed. "I can give that girl much more than they can. She'll soon realise that."

Bainbridge collected together the papers on the table and placed them in the file. "Claudia Davereaux, I'm going to postpone the interview at this point. You will be bailed to return here in one week when you may be officially charged. In the meantime, I need you to surrender your passport."

"But I have to go to my husband. I've told you. He's dying."

"I'm sorry," Bainbridge said. "That's a matter for the court to decide."

"Claudia can stay with Nigel and me in Whitby," Harriet said. She turned to her friend. "Hand over your passport, Claudia, and then we can get out of here."

53

After the interview, Bainbridge and Cooper went to the canteen. He grimaced after biting into the chicken sandwich. "This is bloody awful. How's the tuna?"

"Not much better," Cooper said.

"What did you make of Claudia? Do you think she's as wicked as she's been made out?"

Cooper shrugged. "I suppose I can understand her concern, but to take the child like she did, that's not right." She took another bite of the offending sandwich. "What I don't understand is why she didn't seek help when she realised what Bobby was up to with the girls?"

"Probably the same reason she didn't do anything about it when she was with Eddie. The woman was terrified of him."

"Do you think Bobby is still a danger to the girls?"

Bainbridge shrugged. "I don't know. It might have been juvenile jealousy. Something he's grown out of. On the other hand…"

Cooper picked up her cup and took a sip. "Oh." She winced. "This is awful."

He sniffed at his drink. "I think that's tea. This is coffee." He pushed the cup across the table towards her. "What time are you expecting Cheryl Lewis?"

"Three-thirty," she said. "She has got a lot of explaining to do."

"I'm going back to Hudson Drive," Bainbridge said. "I want a word with Bobby. What about you? What are your plans before your interview with Cheryl?"

"I'm going to the hospital as soon as I've finished this gourmet meal," she said. "The doctor seemed hopeful that Sally would start to come round properly today."

"Let's hope so," he said. "By the way, are we still on for dinner tomorrow night?"

Cooper lowered her head. "Sure, I'm looking forward to it."

Bainbridge arrived at Hudson Gardens just after two o'clock. Before he could knock on the door, Rosie opened it.

"How's things?" he greeted as he followed Rosie into the lounge. "Where is everybody? I thought you'd have a full house today."

"Eddie's working Redcar Market," Rosie said. "Bobby has driven the three of them over to the Marina at Hartlepool." She began to plump up the already plumped cushions on the couch. "Poppy has a motorboat in France, but she's considering bringing it over and mooring it at the marina."

Bainbridge perched on the arm of the couch. "How do Daisy and Poppy get along?"

Rosie's face creased into smiles. "It's wonderful to see them, Andy. They didn't stop chatting this morning."

"And Bobby? How does he get on with Poppy?"

Rosie tilted her head. "What do you mean? Poppy is his sister. Of course, he gets on with her."

"Sit down, Rosie. I need to speak with you about Bobby."

She scowled. "What about him?" she said, flinging herself into an armchair.

"Did you ever witness any hostility from Bobby towards the girls when they were tiny?"

Her posture stiffened, and she inhaled deeply. "What do you mean hostility?"

"Before Poppy was taken, the girls did have quite a few accidents. Did you ever suspect Bobby was responsible?"

She jumped to her feet and glared at him. "I don't know what you're talking about. Bobby was... is a good boy. He would never hurt his sisters."

"A few days before Poppy disappeared, the girls were found floating out to sea in an inflatable. Do you remember that?"

Rosie snorted.

"I've recently been informed that it was Bobby who put the girls into the inflatable and pushed them into the water."

She turned away. "I don't believe you. Bobby would never

do anything so wicked."

"He was seen, Rosie. I have a witness who saw him do exactly that."

She slowly shook her head and turned back to face him. "Please tell me that isn't true. Bobby's my son. He would never... he could never hurt his sisters."

"What time are you expecting them back?"

She wiped her eyes with a tissue. "They promised they'd be back when Eddie gets home, about six. We're all going out for dinner at The Coppers Inn later."

"I will need to speak with Bobby. It may have been a silly childish prank, but I have to make sure your daughters are safe with him. You do understand that?"

She sneered. "Has this nonsense come from Claudia? I bet it has."

He shook his head. "I'm sorry, I can't comment on that."

"You were interviewing her this morning, weren't you? Have you locked the evil bitch up yet?"

He sighed as he walked towards the hall door. "It's not that straightforward, I'm afraid. Investigations are still continuing."

"I think you'd better leave." She walked into the kitchen and closed the door behind her.

54

Twenty minutes after leaving the station, Cooper arrived at the hospital. There was no sign of the doctor. Instead, a young police officer lounged in a chair next to the bed, engrossed in that day's edition of the Gazette.

On seeing her, the PC pushed the newspaper aside and stood to attention.

"Everything all right, constable?" Cooper asked. "No sign of Sally regaining consciousness yet?"

"She did open her eyes, ma'am. Just for a minute or so."

"Did she speak?"

"No, ma'am. I shouted for the doctor, but by the time he got here, she'd closed them again."

"Have you had your lunch yet?" she asked.

"No, ma'am," he answered. "I'm going to be relieved at three."

She opened her purse and took out some coins. "Get yourself a cup of tea from the canteen and get me a coffee while you're there."

"Yes, ma'am," he said. He reached out and retrieved the money. "I won't be long."

Left alone with Sally, Cooper perched on the edge of the bed. She took Sally's hand in hers. "Come on, Sally," she whispered. "It's time to wake up." There was no response. "Sally, open your eyes. That's a good girl," she persisted. Still silence. Cooper stood and walked over to the window. "I really need to know about that dress I found in your bedroom. I want to know how your friend Janette came to have it."

There was a muffled, murmuring sound. Cooper strained her ears. Had she imagined it? No, there it was again. She turned sharply. Sally's eyes fluttered, and her lips twitched. Cooper rushed over to the side of the bed. "Sally, it's me, Jilly Cooper. You're going to be all right, love. Just take your time and breathe slowly. That's a good girl."

The PC returned, carrying a cup of coffee in each hand.

"Quick," Cooper ordered. "Find a doctor. I think Sally's coming round."

55

The dark-blue Aston Martin, driven by Nigel Johnstone, raced along the A174 from Whitby in the direction of Redcar. Beside him sat Cheryl Lewis.

"Why the hell did you drag me into this?" he said through gritted teeth. "How many times have I told you to keep a low profile?"

"I had no choice, Nigel. Those bastards had one of the dresses. That cop wanted to know who I gave it to."

"You'll just have to deny it," he said. "After all, you can't be the only person to stock that design."

"It's pretty exclusive. It seems I'm the only one in the area with sales unaccounted for."

He took a deep breath. "How many did you provide altogether?"

"Three," she said. "I don't know why you insisted on giving them such expensive clothes. I could have got something from Primark for them to wear. It would have been a lot cheaper."

"I needed the girls to have style," he said, "a little panache. They might be scrubbers, but I wanted my clients to think they were high-class escorts. They can't do that in a frock from Primark."

She huffed. "From what I've heard about the damned parties, the girls didn't keep the dresses on long enough to give any impression."

He scoffed, "We've all been on a good earner with the parties, so don't start getting haughty with me. Now, tell me exactly what the police said about this missing girl."

"Her name's Janette. She's the girl with the tattoos and piercings. You thought she'd be a novelty for the clients, remember?"

"So how did the police find out about the dress?"

"She'd left it with a friend for safekeeping."

"Why would she do that?"

She shrugged. "She lived at home. I suppose she didn't want her mother to see it."

"So, she left the dress with a friend."

"I think so, Nigel. You don't know anything about the girl's disappearance, do you? I mean…"

He pulled the car into a layby and, raising his arm, slapped Cheryl across the face with the back of his hand. His eyes narrowed, and he pushed his face closer to hers. "What the fuck are you saying?" He grabbed her shoulders and shook her violently, causing her to bang her head on the side window. "The girl's done a runner, that's all. It is nothing to do with me, so I suggest you keep your fat mouth shut."

Cheryl struggled to get free. "Stop, you're hurting me." She tried to push him away, but he kept a firm grip.

"You're in this up to your neck, Cheryl," he said, placing his face even closer to hers. "When you lost your job at that fashion house, it was me that provided the capital for you to start up the boutiques. You'd be nothing without my help. Don't you forget it."

She nodded weakly. "You're right," she whispered. "Please, let me go."

Nigel grunted before releasing his grip. He lit a cigarette before turning on the engine and joining the line of traffic. "When we get to the station," he said, "this is what I want you to say…"

56

"Stay with Sally," Bainbridge instructed Cooper when she informed him of the situation at the hospital. "I'll conduct the interview with Cheryl Lewis."

When Cheryl Lewis and Nigel Johnstone arrived, Bainbridge and Sergeant Brown were already in the interview room.

Johnstone removed his dark-blue lamb's wool coat, and after carefully folding it, placed it on a chair to the side of the room. He was a small man, no more than five-foot-six, with sandy-coloured hair and shrewd pale-blue eyes. Dressed in a navy-blue suit and crisp white shirt, he oozed confidence.

Johnstone took his place at the table and put his briefcase on the desk. "Good afternoon, Detective Chief Superintendent Bainbridge. I've heard a lot about you from Owen… Owen Davies, that is, the Chief Constable." He opened the briefcase and removed a notebook and pen. "Owen and I play golf most Sunday mornings, work commitments permitting, of course." He gave an insincere little laugh. "You must join us one of these days." He smiled.

Bainbridge mused for a moment, staring at the perfect white teeth of Johnstone grinning at him. He took an instant dislike to the solicitor. "Thank you, I'm not really a golfer."

"Right," Johnstone said and cleared his throat. "I understand from my client that you wish to speak with her about the whereabouts of three dresses. Is that correct?"

Bainbridge's dislike of the solicitor increased at the realisation that Johnstone was attempting to conduct the interview. He leant forward, steepling his fingers on the table. "When we spoke last, Ms Lewis, you informed me that over a period of eighteen months, you had purchased three Ashley Drake dresses to give as presents. Is that correct?"

Johnstone furrowed his brow. "In the interest of clarity, Detective Chief Superintendent, what is the police's interest in these garments?"

"One of the dresses was found amongst the possessions of a missing girl. I need to know how she came by it."

"That may well be, but I fail to understand what this has to do with my client."

"We believe the girl could be in danger," Bainbridge said as he turned to face Cheryl. "Now, tell me the whereabouts of the other two dresses."

She sat motionless, her hands resting in her lap. She leant forward and was about to speak when Nigel reached across, placing his hand on hers. "My client is unable to help you in this matter. The dresses were stolen from the boot of her car."

Bainbridge raised an eyebrow. "Both of them?"

"So I understand."

"Were the thefts reported to the police?"

Cheryl shook her head. "No. What's the point? I'd put them in the boot of my car, and I hadn't locked it. It was my fault the dresses were stolen."

Bainbridge frowned. "But you would have to report the theft to make a claim against your insurance?"

"My client decided to accept the loss," Johnstone said. "Like she said, she rather foolishly left the car unattended with an unlocked boot."

"Are you saying you're prepared to lose six hundred pounds? Was CCTV in the area checked?"

"Detective Chief Superintendent," Johnstone said, "my client has told you what happened. If she is prepared to accept the loss, that is down to her. It is not a police matter." He began to gather his papers into a neat pile. "Now, if there's nothing else?"

Bainbridge inhaled. "Actually, there is another matter," he said. He turned to face Cheryl again. "I want you to explain to me your part in the abduction of Poppy Lee on the tenth of August 2002." Bainbridge proceeded to caution her.

Johnstone jumped to his feet. "This is outrageous. My client came here to answer questions about missing clothing, not about an alleged abduction."

"I have recently learnt that Ms Lewis was present when Claudia Davereaux took Poppy Lee from Redcar beach," he said. "As a frequent visitor to the Davereaux's chateau in France, she must have been aware that her friends, Claudia and Jon-Pierre, had the little girl."

Johnstone sat down heavily on the chair. "I need to confer with my client."

"Ms Lewis," Bainbridge said. "Tell me what happened that day."

"Don't say another word, Cheryl," Johnstone said.

"It's all right, Nigel," she whispered. "It has to come out sooner or later."

Johnstone frowned. "But we haven't discussed this. I need to advise you that—"

Cheryl raised her hand. "That's not necessary," she said, turning towards the DCS. "What exactly do you want to know?"

Bainbridge eased back into his chair and opened the folder in front of him. "Firstly, tell me of your relationship with Rosie Lee. Did you keep in touch with her after Poppy's abduction?"

Cheryl shook her head. "No, I only saw her once."

"Why was that?"

"I didn't see the point. I knew Poppy was safe. I visited Redcar occasionally at the request of Claudia to take photographs of Bobby. She still wanted to make sure her son was all right. Then, one time, quite by chance, I met Eddie in the pub. We had a couple of drinks."

"You and Eddie had an affair?"

"Is this relevant?" Johnstone said, fanning out his fingers on the desk. "I don't see how my client's love-life bears any relevance to the matter in hand."

"It's all right, Nigel," Cheryl said. She turned to face Bainbridge. "Yes, Eddie and I had an affair. Not my finest hour, I admit, but that's what happened."

"How long did the affair last?"

"Not long," she said. "A few weeks, that's all. It was while I was seeing Eddie that I heard about the girls having accidents."

"I understand you were aware Bobby tried to hurt his sisters?"

She nodded. "I saw him. I told Claudia, and she got into a state. She was worried sick. She said Bobby was dangerous, and she had to get the girls away from him as quickly as possible."

"What did you think about that?"

"At first, I thought she was crazy. You can't just take somebody else's child, can you?"

"So, what happened to change your mind and help her?" Bainbridge said.

"I'd gone over to Redcar to check out the hotel where my company were having their meeting. I was walking along the beach on Wednesday afternoon when I saw Rosie and the children."

"Did you approach them?"

"No. Rosie was asleep in the deckchair, and Bobby and the girls played close by with an inflatable. I saw Bobby drag the inflatable to the shoreline and lift both girls into it."

Bainbridge leant forward. "You actually saw him do that?"

"Yes. He lifted them into the thing and then pushed it into the water. Then, before I could do anything, a bloke saw the girls floating out to sea and ran into the water and dragged it back to the beach."

"Didn't you think to tell Rosie what you had seen?"

"No. The bloke was giving her a mouthful of abuse about being negligent, so I just turned and walked away."

"And then you rang Claudia?"

Cheryl nodded. "That's right. She said she was coming up to Redcar to sort things out."

"What do you think she meant by that?" Bainbridge said.

"I don't know. I didn't think she would kidnap the girls if that's what you mean."

"But later you did agree to help her take the children?"

"My client has no comment to make," Johnstone said, putting his hand on Cheryl's arm.

"Cheryl Lewis, I'm bailing you to return here in one week," Bainbridge said. "At which time you may be charged with a series of offences. I will need you to surrender your passport."

Nigel Johnstone huffed. "Is this really necessary? My client did not take that child. She's told you that."

"In the meantime," Bainbridge continued, "Sergeant Brown will take your statement." He collected together his papers and placed them back in the file. "One week," he said as he turned and left the room.

57

As instructed, Cooper waited in the corridor outside Sally's room while the doctor and several nurses attended to the patient. Twenty minutes had passed before the doctor left the room and came into the corridor. "Sally's awake now," he said. "You may speak with her for a few minutes."

"Thank you, doctor," Cooper said as she hurried past him into Sally's room.

Sally looked pale and fragile as she lay in the hospital bed, propped up by three pillows. Cooper approached her slowly. "Welcome back, Sally," she said softly, taking a seat next to the bed. "You've given everyone quite a scare."

Sally blinked then slowly turned her head to the side where the water decanter was on the bedside cabinet.

"I'll pour you a drink," Cooper said, leaning over and pouring her a glass of water. She bent over and gently put the glass to Sally's lips. She leant forward and sipped the water tentatively before sinking back into the pillows.

"Where am I?" she whispered.

"You're in hospital," Cooper said. "You had an accident."

Sally closed her eyes. When she opened them a few seconds later, she looked straight at the police officer. "Who are you?"

Cooper reached over and gently took her hand. "I'm DI Cooper. Do you remember me?"

Sally frowned. "I… I don't think so."

"Things are bound to be a bit hazy at first," Cooper said. "Can you remember anything at all about what happened?"

She closed her eyes and shook her head slowly.

"Do you remember Janette Walsh?" Cooper said.

Sally turned to Cooper, a blank expression on her pale face.

"It's all right, Sally. You lay back and rest. You'll soon start to remember."

Sally looked around the room and opened her mouth as if to speak.

"What is it, love?" Cooper asked.

"Where am I?"

When Cooper left the room, the doctor was waiting for her in the corridor. "Don't be alarmed," he said, holding his clipboard close to his chest. "It's common for patients who have suffered trauma not to remember the details straight away. She'll be confused for a while yet, but her memory will return. You just have to be patient."

Cooper sighed. "I hope you're right. I really do need to speak to her as a matter of urgency."

"I presume the police will still be remaining outside her door?"

She nodded. "Yes, just as a precaution."

"Very well," he said. "Now, if you'll excuse me, I have other patients."

"Of course. You will let me know if…?"

The doctor nodded. "Certainly," he said, and turning, hurried down the corridor.

58

On Saturday evening, Cooper chose a black and white silk shift dress for her date at the Spa Hotel. Her auburn hair hung loose on her shoulders, and her make-up was lightly applied but effective.

"I'm not late, am I?" she said, joining Bainbridge in the bar.

He grinned and shook his head. "No, I've only just arrived myself," he said and kissed her lightly on the cheek. "You look lovely." He linked his arm through hers and led the way to the table by the window.

"Would you care to see the wine list?" the waiter asked, handing them a red, leather-bound menu.

"What do you fancy, Jilly?" he said. "I see they have your favourite Chardonnay."

She smiled. "Perfect."

Bainbridge ordered a bottle of wine and leant back into the plush seat, content with the companionable silence between them.

It was Cooper who spoke first. "You seem lost in thought tonight. What are you thinking about?"

He ran his hand through his hair, his eyes half-closed. "Retirement. It's getting ever closer."

She leant forward and touched his arm. "You don't have to retire. Not if you don't want to. A chief super can stay on another five years if they choose."

He shrugged. "Extended service is an option, I suppose."

"What are you planning to do with your time if you do leave the Service? Have you decided?"

"I was planning to travel," he said, "the Greek Islands, perhaps."

"What's stopping you?"

He reached forward and took her hand in his. "You," he said. "You're stopping me."

She tried to pull away from him, but he held firm.

"Why don't you put your ticket in too and come with me? Things could be like they used to be. Better. We could—"

"Andy, stop," Cooper said. "This is crazy talk."

"Can you deny you don't still have feelings for me?" He lifted her hand to his lips and kissed it gently. "I know you still care for me. I can see it in your eyes."

"I... I don't know how I feel," she whispered. "After what happened last time, the way you spoke to me... I just don't know, Andy."

"I've told you why I had to end our affair. My wife was going to destroy you. I couldn't let that happen."

"But..."

The waiter came to the table with the chilled wine bucket.

"I'll pour, thanks," Bainbridge said as the waiter began to lift the bottle.

"Very well, sir," the waiter said. "I'll bring you the menu." He disappeared in the direction of the bar, returning a few minutes later with two leather-bound menus.

Bainbridge nodded his thanks and then turned to face Cooper. "I've booked a room here for tonight. Will you spend the night with me? Let me show you how much I love you. Please say you will."

Her eyes glistened as she reached over and gently stroked his face. "I... I don't know. This is all happening so fast."

"We'll go at whatever pace you want. I just need you in my life again."

She blushed. "I'll think about it, but do you know what I really want right now?"

"What's that?" he said.

"A glass of wine."

"Coming right up," he said and began to pour. "I've heard the ribeye steaks they serve here are the best in the area."

She took a sip of wine. "Sounds good."

Bainbridge turned around to attract the waiter when he saw two familiar figures sitting at a table at the far side of the restaurant. "Christ, I don't believe it," he said, more to himself than his companion.

"What is it, Andy?"

He motioned in the direction of the table. "Over there. It's Nigel Johnstone."

"What's surprising about that? He lives at Whitby. That's not far away from here."

"No, it's not that," he said. "It's who he's having dinner with."

Cooper began to chuckle. "Don't tell me the randy bugger's got a girlfriend on the side?"

"I don't think it's a girlfriend, not by their body language," he said. "Nigel looks like he's about to throttle her."

Intrigued, Cooper turned around to look. "Oh, isn't that Cheryl Lewis? I wonder what she's done to upset him."

59

Bainbridge was in his office on Monday morning when the desk sergeant entered. "Sir, Bobby Lee is at the front desk. He wants to speak with you. He seems agitated."

"Show him through," Bainbridge said.

Bobby Lee bounded into the office, a thunderous look on his face. "What the hell have you been saying to my mother?" he demanded. "She thinks I'm responsible for hurting my sisters."

"Sit down," Bainbridge said.

He snarled. "I don't want to bloody sit down. Why would you say those things?"

"Are you denying it's true?"

His eyes bulged, and his lips curled. "Of course I'm denying it. Who accused me of doing that? I'll bloody kill them."

Bainbridge got up from behind his desk and walked towards Bobby. "Calm down," he said, taking him by the arm and steering him to a chair. "Sit down, and then we can talk."

Bobby flopped into the chair. Bainbridge propped himself on the corner of his desk, and reaching for the telephone, rang through to the sergeant. "Arrange for two teas to be brought in," he said. He turned to Bobby. "I intended coming to see you. I wanted to speak to you about certain allegations which have been made concerning your conduct."

"By whom?"

"That doesn't matter for now," Bainbridge said. "Bobby, do you remember the day your sisters were blown out to sea in an inflatable?"

He scowled. "Yes, it was a pink unicorn, but that had nothing to do with me."

"I have received information that you were responsible for putting the girls into that contraption and deliberately pushing it out to sea."

Bobby banged his fists on the chair arm. "That isn't true. I never did that. I left them and went off with my mates leaving them playing with it on the beach. They were nowhere near the sea. I swear they weren't."

"Tell me how Daisy came to fall off her trike? Weren't you supposed to be looking after her?"

He shook his head. "I don't know what happened. One minute, she was riding the thing along the drive, and the next, the trike was on its side. The trike wasn't very stable."

"You didn't push her over?"

"Of course I bloody didn't."

"There were other accidents too. Didn't Daisy get scalded when a pan fell off the hob?"

"That had nothing to do with me. Rosie hadn't put the pan on straight. She was always doing stupid things."

"Tell me about your mother. Claudia, I mean. I heard you terrorised her when you were a child?"

Bobby lowered his head and inhaled deeply. "You mean the knife?"

"Yes, Bobby. I mean the knife."

"Is... is that why she left, because of what I did?"

"Give me your side of the story," Bainbridge said.

There was a tap on the door, and PC Beaumont entered with two mugs of tea.

"Thanks," Bainbridge said. "Put them on my desk."

When the constable left the room, Bainbridge turned to Bobby. "When you stood over her with a knife in your hand, did you intend to hurt her?"

He lowered his head into his hands. "I... I was angry with her. I didn't know what to do after she accused me of killing the cat. I was scared she'd tell Dad."

"You admit you killed the cat?"

Bobby nodded. "Back then, I was in a bad place. Everything was mixed up in my head. I can't explain why I did it. I'm ashamed, really I am." He sniffed loudly before reaching into his pocket and taking out a tissue. "I can only put it down to home circumstances and the pressure I was under."

"What do you mean by that?"

"Well, Claudia and Dad argued all the time. She was always threatening to leave Dad and take me with her."

"How did that make you feel?"

"There was no way I would have gone away with her. I loved my dad. I could never leave him."

"You mentioned you were under pressure? What did you mean?"

He reached out and took the mug of tea from the desk. "I wasn't like other kids my age," he said. "I'd been recognised as gifted when I was four years old. You can't imagine the attention I got." He sipped the tea. "I'd been offered a scholarship in London at a prestigious school. It was a fantastic opportunity. Everybody had such high expectations."

"Yes, I heard about that. Rosie and Eddie were very proud."

Bobby leant back into his chair. "Once I started at the school, everything changed. I was happy. I was mixing with students who were the same as me, intellectually, I mean." He blew his nose loudly on the tissue. "I had a few sessions with a child psychologist and felt much better after that."

"I hear you did well for yourself. What are you doing now?"

He took another sip of tea. "I had so much promise back then," he said. "A golden future, that's what everyone said." He placed his half-empty mug on the desk. "It didn't quite work like that, I'm afraid. I'm more a gold-plated failure these days."

"Oh? What went wrong?"

Bobby's shoulders sagged. "Where do you want me to begin? I married too young for a start. I worked for the wrong company. I made the wrong choices. Take your pick."

"It can't be that bad, surely?" Bainbridge said. "Rosie was telling me how well you were doing in London."

He shook his head and smiled weakly. "Rosie believes everything I tell her. She's very trusting." He tilted his head to face Bainbridge. "The truth is my life is in a spiral. My wife's left me, I walked out on my boring job, I drink too much… but I give you my word, I never hurt my sisters. I would never do that."

"Tell me about the day Poppy was taken."

"I told the police everything. I left her to be with my mates, you know that."

"Bobby, is there anything you're not telling me?"

"What do you mean?"

"You're a bright lad. I would have thought you might have seen something that day?"

He leant back into the chair. His eyes fixed on the far wall. "All right. I did see Claudia. I saw her lift Poppy off the sand and take her away."

"Why the hell didn't you tell anyone?"

He shrugged. "I suppose I was glad Poppy had gone. I was jealous of the twins with all the attention they got."

"Did Claudia know you'd seen her take Poppy?"

Bobby nodded. "Oh yes. She put her finger to her lips like this." He made the same gesture. "And then she was gone."

"Do you realise the pain, the anxiety your parents went through thinking Poppy had been drowned?"

He shrugged again. "Like I said before, I'm not a nice person."

60

Sally was sat up in bed, eating a bowl of muesli, when Cooper arrived on Monday morning. Her hair had been brushed, and she was wearing a crisp blue nightdress.

Cooper turned off her mobile and walked briskly up to the bed. "You're looking better," she said. "How are you feeling?"

Sally put down her spoon and pushed the dish away, screwing up her nose. "I hate muesli. I prefer porridge."

Cooper reached over and took Sally's hand in hers. "Are you up to answering some questions for me?"

"I'll try," she said weakly, "but I can't remember much."

"Tell me what you can remember," Cooper said.

She closed her eyes for a moment. "I remember a car. I remember it coming towards me, and I was scared, but…"

"But what, Sally? What is it?"

"I'm not sure. I think it was driven at me deliberately." She gave a slight shudder.

"Do you remember what happened before the car? Where you went? Who you saw?"

She furrowed her brow. "I… I don't know," she said quietly. "It's all a bit fuzzy."

Cooper squeezed Sally's hand. "I think it was something to do with Janette Walsh," Cooper said. "You told Lisa Walker you were going to speak to someone who might be able to tell you where Janette was. Can you remember who that was?"

She looked at Cooper and furrowed her brow. "I said that?"

Cooper nodded. "Where were you before the accident, Sally? Can you tell me anything about that?"

She put her hands on either side of her head and began to rock slowly backwards and forwards. "I'm not sure."

"Apart from the car, what is the last thing you do remember?"

"I was in a room," she said, "no… no, it wasn't a room. It was a cellar." She sat upright. "I was in a cellar of some kind."

"Can you describe the cellar?"

"It was dark and damp. I could hear voices in the distance."

"Could you hear traffic?"

She shook her head. "I don't think so. There were people in the distance laughing and talking."

"Do you know how you got into the cellar?"

"I remember feeling strange and woozy," she said. "Everything seemed to be spinning and…" She sank back into her pillow. "I can't remember anything else. I just remember feeling dizzy and waking up in a cellar."

The door opened, and the doctor strode into the room. "That's enough. My patient needs to rest."

"But doctor, I—" Cooper said.

"I know you have a job to do," he said, "but so do I, and right now, my job has priority over yours." He leant over the bed. "You must rest now, Miss Lomax. The questions can wait."

61

After his meeting with Bobby, Bainbridge picked up the files of the three missing girls and placed them in his briefcase. He glanced at the wall clock. It was ten-thirty. He straightened his tie and put on his jacket before walking through to the incident room. Sergeant Brown was at the front desk.

"Is Cooper around?" he asked the sergeant.

"No, sir. She's gone to the hospital to interview Sally Lomax. Can I give her a message when she gets back?"

Bainbridge strode towards the outer door. "No, I'll speak to her later. I have a meeting with the Chief Constable."

Brown scratched his chin and turned to the young officer standing next to him. "I wonder why he's going to see the old man? Something must be up."

Chief Constable Owen Davies was a tall, heavily built Welshman in his early fifties. His deep tanned complexion was testament to his frequent visits to his Spanish villa.

"Good morning, sir," Bainbridge said, standing to attention in front of the Chief Constable's impressive oak desk.

"Good morning, Andy," the Chief Constable said. "Do take a seat."

Bainbridge sat back in the grey upholstered chair and placed his briefcase on his knee.

"These young women who've gone missing in Redcar." Davies said, "do you suspect foul play?"

Bainbridge sighed. "To be frank, sir, we really don't know. None of the women has been in contact with their friends and family. But on the other hand, we haven't found any bodies either."

"Have you spoken to the girl who was attacked? Sally something?"

"Sally Lomax, sir. DI Cooper is with her at the hospital now."

"Well, let's hope she gets us something to work with." The Chief Constable picked up the internal phone. "Bring in two coffees, please, Cynthia," he said. He placed the receiver back on its cradle. "DI Cooper mentioned something about women's frocks. What do you know about that?"

"All three of the missing women were in possession of an Ashley Drake dress," Bainbridge said. "It seems the supplier of these dresses was a woman called Cheryl Lewis. She is on police bail at the moment in connection with another matter."

"The missing kid?"

"Yes, that's right, sir. She was present when Poppy Lee was taken. She was in cohorts with the Davereaux's who took the child."

"You need to tread carefully with the Davereaux's," Davies said. "Jon-Pierre has a good deal of power and influence."

"Yes, sir, I'm aware of that," Bainbridge said. "He's seriously ill in France. His condition is terminal, according to his wife."

There was a tap on the door and a smartly dressed, middle-aged woman, bristling with efficiency, entered the room carrying a tray with the coffee paraphernalia.

"Thank you, Cynthia," Davies said. "Leave the tray. I'll pour."

"Yes, sir," Cynthia said as she quickly turned and left the room, closing the door quietly behind her.

Bainbridge opened his briefcase and removed the three files, placing them on the desk. "Sir," he said, "I think it's prudent to proceed as if this were more than a missing person's enquiry."

Davies picked up the coffee pot and began to pour. "I hear what you're saying, Andy," he said, "but I think we might be jumping the gun a bit here. After all, there's nothing to indicate that any of these young women didn't leave under their own volition, is there?"

"There was no reason for them to leave, though,"

Bainbridge persisted as he opened Deborah Jenkins' file. "Deborah was starting to get her life in order. According to her friend, Maria McGuire, she had found lucrative employment and—"

"Yes," Davies interrupted, "but doing what? No-one seems to have the least idea how Deborah was making her money." The Chief Constable arched an eyebrow. "Do you think she could have been on the game?"

Bainbridge shook his head. "I think it was something much more sinister, sir."

"Like what?"

"All I know is she mysteriously went off the radar a couple of evenings every month dressed up to the nines. When she returned, she had a bundle of notes. Whatever Deborah was up to was organised, not random."

Davies filled a cup and handed the coffee to Bainbridge. "What about the second girl, Suzie Graham?"

Bainbridge took out the second file from his briefcase. "Suzie came to Redcar from Edinburgh to be with her boyfriend. She went out to walk the dog one night and never came back."

Davies furrowed his brow. "From what I've read, this young woman was in the habit of taking off when it suited her. It's more than likely she went back to Scotland."

"I don't know, sir. Everything that girl owned was left behind in the flat."

"But there wasn't much to leave by all accounts," Davies said. "If she'd found a way of earning big money... I think we should keep an open mind on her disappearance." He sipped his coffee. "Was the boyfriend ever in the frame? He doesn't seem to have much of an alibi."

"I'm sure Sam Carter had nothing to do with it," Bainbridge said. "He was questioned at the station at the time Suzie disappeared, and again recently by DI Cooper."

"Well, keep digging. If she has been murdered, it's usually the husband or boyfriend who's responsible." Davies sipped his coffee. "Now tell me about this third girl, Janette Walsh. I understand she was a friend of Sally Lomax?"

"Yes, sir. They were at school together."

"I see from your notes that Sally was aware of Janette's activities."

Bainbridge nodded. "It would appear so. She mentions the dress and the parties in an email she sent shortly before Janette disappeared."

"But Sally never mentioned anything to her colleagues at the station about what her friend was into?"

"No, sir," Bainbridge said.

"Tell me, Andy, what's your gut feeling about all this? Do you think a serial killer is roaming the streets of Redcar?"

Bainbridge huffed. "It's the attack on Sally Lomax that makes me think there is more going on than we realise. It's possible the attack is not related to the missing women, of course. We won't know that until Sally is able to tell us what happened."

Davies frowned and stroked his chin. "It won't do the town's reputation any good if we start talking about serial killers. You do know that?"

"Yes, sir."

"I'll tell you what we'll do," Davies said before taking another sip of his coffee. "We'll wait until we get Sally Lomax's story. You say DI Cooper's with her now?"

Bainbridge nodded.

"Good. We'll see what she has to say before we launch a murder investigation."

Bainbridge gathered the files and began putting them in his briefcase. "Very well, sir. If that's the way you want to proceed."

Davies smiled. "It is. By the way, I hear you're about to retire next month. Are you sure you can't be persuaded to stay on a few more years?"

He shook his head. "No, sir. I think thirty years is long enough, don't you?"

Davies sighed. "Retirement can be lonely. If I hadn't got my work after my wife died…"

Bainbridge tilted his head and smiled. "What makes you think I'll be alone?"

"Oh, I see. May I ask who?"

Bainbridge smiled. "Early days yet, sir."

"I hope it works out for you, Andy," he said, "but if you do change your mind about leaving us, the door's always open."

On returning to the office, DI Cooper was informed that Leo Cutts had rung, requesting that she give him a ring urgently. Taking out her mobile, Cooper realised it was still on silent and that she had three missed calls from Cutts.

"Oh damn," she said as she pressed his number. "Sorry about that, Leo," she said when he answered. "I've been visiting Sally in the hospital and forgot my phone was on silent."

"Never mind about that. I've got something that will knock your socks off."

"Tell me. I could do with some good news."

He laughed. "Good news? Well, firstly I'm going on my holidays tonight. Secondly, DNA has been found on the back of the dress you gave me."

Cooper plonked down heavily on her chair. "DNA? Are you sure?"

"Of course, I'm sure," Cutts said. "I am a professional, you know."

"I'm sorry. I thought you said there was nothing on the dress."

"That was the initial test results. But you authorised me to conduct a more thorough search, at a greater expense, I might add." He cleared his throat. "There's no doubt about it. A small trace of semen was present on the inside of the dress."

Cooper inhaled deeply. "Please say it's on our database."

"Yes, it most certainly is."

"Are you going to tell me who it belongs to, or do I have to guess?"

Cutts sniggered. "If I gave you one hundred guesses, you'd probably get it wrong."

63

The rain had started at midday. A light shower at first, but then the sky darkened, and the shower turned into a heavy downpour. By late afternoon, when Bainbridge got back to the station, it was a full-blown thunderstorm.

Bainbridge went straight to his office. Ten minutes later, Sergeant Brown entered carrying a mug of tea.

"Did it go all right with the boss?" he asked, handing the drink to Bainbridge. "I always think it's like going to the headmaster's office, being summoned by the old man."

"Oh, he's not so bad," Bainbridge said. "We've had worse chief constables."

"Mm… I suppose so," the sergeant said.

"Will you ask DI Cooper to pop in when you're passing her office? I need to know how she got on with Sally Lomax."

"She's not here, sir," the sergeant said. "She came back from the hospital, then left again about one o'clock."

"Did she say where she was going?"

Sergeant Brown shook his head. "Not to me, sir. I assumed she was going to lunch." He looked at his watch. "It's nearly four o'clock," he said. "My shift's over, but if there's anything I can do before I leave?"

"No, you get yourself off. I'll try her mobile."

It was eight-thirty. PC Porter was at the front desk when Bainbridge approached. "Still no word from Cooper?"

Porter shook his head. "No, sir. Maybe her phone's out of power."

Bainbridge frowned. One thing he did know about her was that her mobile was always fully charged. "Keep trying. By the way, did DI Cooper receive any calls when she got back from the hospital?"

"I don't know, sir. I've just come on duty."

The desk telephone gave a shrill ring. Both men looked at the phone expectantly. Porter picked up the receiver. "Redcar

Police Station," he said. After a few seconds, he turned to face Bainbridge. His face ashen, and his hands trembling.

"What is it?" Bainbridge demanded. "What's happened? Is it Jilly?"

"It's... it's her car, sir," Porter said. "It's been found at South Gare."

"South Gare? What about Cooper?"

Porter shook his head. "There's no sign. Traffic Division are there now."

Bainbridge rushed out of the station, and within minutes, he was speeding in the direction of South Gare.

The scene was chaotic when Bainbridge arrived at the Gare fifteen minutes later. Several police vehicles were parked alongside the muddy path. The dog patrol was searching amongst the rocks and surrounding waste ground. Cooper's dark-red Metro was on its roof, halfway down the concrete slope, water lapping against its side.

Bainbridge rushed down the embankment towards the up-turned vehicle where Chief Inspector Denton was directing operations.

"Any sign of the occupant?" Bainbridge asked, his voice barely audible against the noise of the driving rain.

Denton shook his head. "No, sir. It looks like the car was speeding when it hit the bollard up there." He indicated the top of the embankment. "It's a miracle the car wasn't washed away."

Bainbridge frowned. "Cooper is a first-class driver. She wouldn't do anything so reckless."

"If she had got caught in the storm..." He pulled up his coat collar as protection from the biting wind. "The lifeboat from Hartlepool is out searching, but there's no sign so far. The chances are she's been washed out to sea." He sighed heavily. "It's a lonely place to die, isn't it, sir?"

Bainbridge clenched his fists but said nothing. He scanned the dark, choppy water around him. Somewhere out there was the woman he loved, the woman who had agreed to spend the rest of her life with him. He turned to Denton. "I don't understand what she was doing out here," he said, shaking his head. "It doesn't make any sense."

Denton hunched his shoulders. "We're making enquiries over there," he said, nodding towards a group of green sheds used by local fishermen. "There aren't many people about because of the storm, but one of the fishermen said he saw a bloke on a pushbike riding like the clappers towards town."

"Not much to go on, is it?" Bainbridge said, walking back to his car. "I'm going back to the station. Keep me informed of progress."

"Yes, sir," Denton said, "but I've a gut feeling the news won't be good."

64

Bainbridge arrived at James Cook Hospital to find Beaumont on a wooden chair outside Sally's door reading The Gazette. He stood to attention as the DCS passed him and entered her room.

Sally was dressed and sat in an armchair at the side of her bed. Her left leg, in plaster, rested on a stool. "Hello, Sally. You're looking a lot better than last time I saw you."

She blushed. "I'm feeling better, sir. I still have a headache, and my ribs hurt a lot."

"Sally, was DI Cooper here earlier?"

"Yes, sir," she said. "She came this morning to ask me questions about… to see if I could remember anything about what happened. I wasn't much help, I'm afraid."

"Couldn't you tell her anything at all?"

She frowned. "Not really. I told her I remembered feeling woozy and faint. I vaguely remember being in some kind of cellar. Then I remember a car coming towards me, but nothing else."

Bainbridge plonked on the bed next to her chair. "Think, Sally. This is important."

She blinked rapidly. "I can't remember. I've tried but—"

"But what?"

Sally's brows knitted in concentration. "I remember hearing voices. Men's voices. They mentioned me by name."

"Didn't you recognise the voices?"

She shook her head. "It wasn't clear. They sounded distant, but I knew they were close."

"Can't you remember what the voices said?"

She leant back into the chair, her eyes half-closed. "One of the men said something about… about getting rid of me. I remember hearing that. Then the other one said it would cause more trouble. They began to argue."

Bainbridge leant forward. "You're doing brilliantly. Now, I want you to concentrate on the men's voices. Did they have an accent?"

"I'm sorry, but I really can't remember anything else."

"Did Cooper say anything about where she was going when she left here?"

She shook her head. "I think she was going back to the office. Why do you ask?"

Bainbridge stood and walked to the door. "It's nothing for you to worry about. You've been very brave. I want you to concentrate on getting better."

65

Bainbridge returned to his office and took out the bottle of whiskey he kept in his desk's bottom drawer. Not bothering to pour into a glass, he put the bottle to his lips and swallowed. He was about to take a third swig of the whisky when Sergeant Butler, the night sergeant, knocked on his door.

"Sir," he said. "A Mrs Turner telephoned earlier. She wants to speak with you as a matter of some urgency."

Bainbridge frowned. "Can't you deal with it, sergeant?"

He shook his head. "She insists on speaking with you, sir."

Bainbridge leant back in his chair and half-closed his eyes. "Does she indeed? What's Mrs Turner's problem?"

"It's her sister," he said. "She's gone missing."

Bainbridge sat bolt upright. "Oh god, not another one. How long has she been missing?"

"Five years, sir."

Bainbridge arched an eyebrow. "Five years, and she's only reporting it now?"

The sergeant shrugged. "What do you want me to do?"

"Ring her back and arrange a meeting for first thing tomorrow morning," he said. "I'm going back to South Gare. I can't sit here doing nothing."

It was eight-thirty the next morning. Sergeant Brown looked up in surprise at Bainbridge's dishevelled appearance when he entered his office. "Have you been here all night, sir?"

Bainbridge nodded. "There's still no news on DI Cooper. I can't understand what's happened."

The sergeant shrugged. "It's not like her to go out without telling anyone where she was going. By the way, sir, I... I have an electric razor in my drawer if you'd like to…"

"Thanks," Bainbridge said. "That would be useful."

The sergeant left the office, returning a few minutes later with the razor. "Mrs Turner is in reception. I'll bring her through in about ten minutes if that's all right?"

"Thank you, sergeant," Bainbridge said. "Perhaps you can rustle up some coffee?"

Moira Turner was in her early fifties, short and plump with short, curly auburn hair. She wore a green cotton dress and matching jacket and a pair of sensible brown leather shoes. Each of her chubby fingers bore gold rings, together with half-a-dozen gold bangles around both of her plump wrists.

"Good morning, Detective Chief Superintendent Bainbridge," she said in a strong Australian accent. "It's so good of you to agree to see me."

Bainbridge shook her hand. "Please, take a seat. I understand from my sergeant that you want to report your sister missing?"

"Yes, I do," she said. "I haven't heard from Helen in nearly five years." She wagged her finger at the policeman. "Something's wrong, I tell you. Something's very wrong."

"Your sister is Australian?"

Moira shook her head. "No, dear," she said, shaking her head. "Helen was born in Redcar. We both were. I emigrated with my late husband, Arthur, over twenty years ago, and Helen got involved with that brute. That was the cause of the argument and—"

Bainbridge raised his right hand. "Mrs Turner," he said, "perhaps if you start at the beginning?"

"Call me Moira," she said. "Everyone does." She opened her large black handbag and removed a photograph which she handed to him. "I have an old photograph of Helen and me together."

Bainbridge looked at the image of the two women and realized it was several years old. "Don't you have anything more... more recent?"

She shook her head. "I'm afraid not, Detective Chief—"

Bainbridge raised his hand again. "Please, call me Andy," he said. "My rank is a bit of a mouthful, isn't it?"

"Like I was saying, Andy," she said, "Helen and I had a disagreement a few years ago. It escalated, and... well you know how it is. We were as stubborn as each other." She took out a tissue from her bag and blew her nose loudly. "After Arthur died last year, I decided it was time to build bridges. I wrote Helen a letter, but I didn't get a reply."

"Perhaps she wasn't ready to make up," Bainbridge said. "Maybe she still held a grudge?"

"No, that's not like Helen. It's not like her at all. I wrote four letters in total, and I didn't receive one reply, so I decided to come over to England and sort things out face-to-face."

"What happened?"

"I tracked down her no-good husband. He was what all the trouble was about in the first place. He told me they had separated five years ago, and he didn't know where she had gone."

"Have you tried finding your sister through other means?"

"Yes, of course, I have, but there's no trace of her." Moira gritted her teeth. "Something's happened to Helen," she said. "I know it has, and her husband is responsible."

"What makes you say that?"

"Steven took control of Helen's inheritance," she said. "When Dad died, he left us both quite a bit of money. Poor Helen didn't see any of it. He made sure of that."

Bainbridge frowned. "What do you mean by that, Moira?"

"He spent it. Booze, women, cars... you name it. I begged her to leave him, but she said no. That's when we fell out."

"Where's her husband now?"

"He's still in Redcar. He's running a pub now, The Coppers Inn."

Bainbridge sat bolt upright. "Are you talking about Steven Duffy?"

"Yes, that's him. He used to be a policeman in Redcar before he bought the pub, paid for with Helen's money, I might add."

"Moira, leave this with me," he said. "I'll speak with Duffy myself."

"I'd appreciate that, Andy. I'm staying with friends in Marske." She passed him a piece of paper. "There's the address and phone number."

Bainbridge was about to leave the office when Sergeant Brown entered. "Sir," he said, "I've just remembered. That forensics bloke, Leo something, telephoned for DI Cooper yesterday while she was visiting the hospital."

"What did he want?"

The sergeant hunched his shoulders. "Not much, just that he needed to speak to her urgently."

Frowning, Bainbridge picked up the phone and rang the forensic laboratory. It was answered at once. "This is DCS Bainbridge," he said. "I want to speak with Leo Cutts."

"I'm sorry," a voice answered, "but Leo is on holiday. He won't be back for two weeks."

"Is he contactable?"

"No, I'm afraid not. He's on a walking holiday somewhere in Croatia."

Bainbridge huffed. "I understand he spoke with DI Cooper yesterday. I need to know what was said."

"Ah, that would have been about the DNA results he had run for her."

"Do you have a copy of those results?"

"No, I'm sorry. He hasn't printed off a copy. They're still on Leo's computer, and I'm afraid I don't have access."

Bainbridge clenched his fists. "Then get somebody who does have access. This is very important."

"I'll see what I can do," said the voice.

Bainbridge slammed the receiver onto its cradle. "That bloody useless sod," he said. "He's left the results on his computer and not produced a hard copy."

The sergeant shrugged and turned to leave the office.

"Before you go, sergeant," Bainbridge said, "tell me what you know about Steve Duffy."

"What do you want to know, sir?" he said. "Duffy was a colleague, that's all. We did our training together back in the day. I worked in Middlesbrough with him for a while. He moved about a lot. Then we both eventually arrived at Redcar."

"Did you know his wife?"

"Helen? Yes, sir. Lovely woman she was. Too good for Duffy, if you ask me."

"You've heard they'd separated?"

"Yes, sir. She went to live with her sister in Australia, I believe."

Bainbridge shook his head. "No, she didn't. Not according to her sister, Moira Turner. She hasn't seen Helen in years."

The sergeant's brow furrowed. "I… I don't understand. Duffy always said…"

"How well did you know Duffy personally?"

"Not well," Brown said. "Duffy was… is a queer sort of a bloke. He wasn't really one of the lads, if you know what I mean."

"In what way?"

"Well, sir, he had some strange ideas, especially regarding young women. Unhealthy ideas, really."

"Sit down, sergeant," Bainbridge said, indicating the chair opposite. "I want to hear everything you can tell me about Steve Duffy's unhealthy ideas."

66

Daisy linked arms with her sister as they walked along the beach. "I think Mam would like it if you called yourself Poppy and not Catherine," she said.

Catherine frowned. "I've always been known as Catherine. Poppy doesn't sound right somehow."

Daisy shrugged. "Well, it's your decision, I suppose. When are you going to France for Jon-Pierre's funeral?"

"Tomorrow," Catherine said. "Mother... I mean Claudia, has been given permission to leave the country to attend, but she will have a police escort, of course."

Daisy sighed. "It's all such a mess. I can't understand why she stole you in the first place."

Catherine exhaled deeply. "Who knows? I think they must have regretted it more than once."

"What do you mean?"

Catherine began to giggle. "When I was fourteen, I started experimenting with drugs. All the kids at the boarding school did. Jon-Pierre nearly had a fit when he found out. He dragged me out of the school and insisted I had private tuition at the chateau."

Daisy arched an eyebrow. "So, you were a bit of a rebel, eh?"

"It gets worse," Catherine said, a smirk spreading across her face. "When I was fifteen, I ran away with a man who worked for my father at the winery. We were gone for nearly two weeks before they found us."

Daisy sighed. "You seem to have had an exciting time. Nothing nearly as exciting has ever happened to me."

The girls walked towards the Stray. "Do you fancy a coffee?" Daisy asked as they got close to the café.

"Sure. It's nice enough to sit outside."

Daisy bought the drinks, and both girls sat at a wooden table facing the sea. "Have you decided what you're going to do?" Daisy asked. "I mean, are you going back to live in

France or staying here in Redcar with Mam and Dad?"

Catherine shrugged. "I haven't made up my mind. Now that Dad... now that Jon-Pierre has died, I'll be expected to get more involved in the winery. He always said the business would be mine one day."

"That's good. At least your future is secure."

Catherine clasped her hands together. "You don't understand. I'd hate it. I want to work in fashion, not wine."

"You could always sell the business."

"I suppose I could, but... well, there might be another option."

"Oh? What's that?"

Catherine smiled and tapped her nose with her finger. "Wait and see."

Rosie had just finished cleaning the kitchen after breakfast when she heard the knock on her front door. Opening it, she was greeted by Karen on the doorstep.

"Come in," she said, moving forward and hugging her. "It's lovely to see you again, Karen. It's been ages."

She followed Rosie into the lounge and sat on the couch.

"You know we got Poppy back, don't you?" Rosie asked.

She nodded. "Yes, it was all over the news. I'm so happy for you. I bet everyone is thrilled."

"I haven't stopped smiling," Rosie said. "I still can't quite believe my little girl has come back after all this time."

"Where is she now? I'd love to meet her."

Rosie began to laugh. "The girls have gone for a walk. I think they've gone to The Stray."

"Is Bobby with them?"

There was a slight hesitation. "No, he... he's gone for an interview in Middlesbrough. It's for the position of Assistant Manager at a bank."

Karen raised an eyebrow. "Working in a bank? Bobby will hate it."

Rosie perched on the arm of the couch and, reaching out,

took Karen's hand. "Look, love," she said softly. "I know it's none of my business what goes on between a husband and wife, but… well, if there's anything I can do?"

"There's nothing anyone can do, not now," Karen said. "It's too late."

Rosie got off the couch and walked towards the kitchen. "How about a cup of coffee? You're looking a bit peaky. Do you take sugar?"

Karen followed Rosie into the kitchen. "I had to see Bobby," she said, "to tell him I'm pregnant."

Rosie gasped and spun around, flinging her arms around Karen. "Oh, that's wonderful news. Bobby will be thrilled. The two of you need to sit down now and sort things out between you."

"That's… that's easier said than done. I can't—"

The front door opened. "Oh, here's Bobby now," Rosie said. "I'll leave you two to talk."

Bobby walked through from the hall, slinging his coat on the back of the couch. "Who're you talking to, Mum?" he said. "I—" He stopped abruptly at the sight of Karen. "What are you doing here? I thought we'd said all there was to say."

"Karen has something to tell you, dear," Rosie said. She picked up her bag. "I'm going into town to do some shopping. I won't be long."

Bobby frowned as Rosie rushed past him and out through the front door.

67

Bainbridge drove to the Copper's Inn. The only vehicle in the car park was the silver Audi owned by Steven Duffy. The main doors to the pub were closed, so he went round to the side door and knocked loudly. It was several minutes before the bolts were drawn back, and Duffy opened the door.

"You're keen," he said. "I'm not open for another hour."

Bainbridge walked into the building. "I'm not here for a drink, Duffy. I need to ask you some questions."

Duffy huffed as he closed the door shut. "Any news on Jilly?"

Bainbridge shook his head. "No, not yet."

"Well, if there's anything I can do, you let me know. She was a great girl."

"Was? We don't know she's dead yet."

"Of course not. I only meant—"

"I've come here about your wife, Helen."

He sighed and thrust his hands deep into his trouser pockets. "I take it you've been speaking to her bitch of a sister?"

"Moira Turner came to see me, yes. She's concerned as to Helen's whereabouts."

"Andy, I'll tell you what I told her and what I've told everybody else since that bitch left me. Helen has gone to Australia."

"Moira claims she never arrived. In fact, she hasn't heard from her at all in the last five years."

Duffy shrugged. "I don't know about that. As far as I was concerned, she went to Australia and Australia was welcome to her."

"Why did you split up?"

Duffy turned sharply to face him. "That's none of your bloody business."

"Look, this is serious. No one seems to have seen Helen in the last five years. Is there anywhere else you think she might have gone? You must have some idea?"

He shook his head.

"What about men? Was she seeing anyone that you knew of?"

Duffy took out a packet of cigarettes and a lighter from his pocket. He lit the cigarette before he answered. "Helen liked men," he said. "She liked flirting. When we got this place, she was in her element."

"Is that what caused the split?"

He drew heavily on the cigarette. "Like I said, Andy, that's my business. It's not a police matter." He walked over to the door and opened it. "Now, if you don't mind, I've got a pub to open up."

Bainbridge walked towards the door. "Enquiries will continue, I'm afraid," he said as he went into the car park. "An allegation has been made which can't be ignored. I will need to speak to you more formally at the station at some point."

Duffy muttered something unintelligible before slamming the door shut.

68

Bainbridge returned to the station deep in thought. As he walked into reception, a young woman rushed towards him.

"Are you the bloke in charge?" she said, pointing in the direction of Sergeant Brown. "I've got some information about Janette Walsh."

"I'm DCS Bainbridge. Who are you?"

"Alison Walsh," she said. "I'm Janette's cousin. There's stuff you should know about her."

He steered Alison towards his office. "Take a seat," he said, indicating the chair in front of his desk. He perched on the corner of his desk. "Now, what's this about Janette?"

She sank back into the chair, crossing her long, shapely legs as she did so. "Like I said, Janette's my cousin. More like a sister, really." Alison nervously twisted the chain of her pendant in her fingers. "It was Janette that first told me about the parties."

Bainbridge studied her. "What parties?"

"They were held every few weeks in a big house near Whitby. Janette said she earned loads of money just for flirting with a few old men."

"And you went to one of these parties?"

"Too right I did. A woman gave me a posh frock to wear and paid for my hair and makeup."

"And what did you have to do in return?"

She looked down at the floor and shrugged. "Just stuff," she said, the colour rising in her cheeks.

"What sort of stuff?"

"A bit of groping and kissing. That sort of thing."

"And sex? Did you have sex with any of these men?"

She gave a quick nod. "A couple of times, that's all. Nothing I hadn't done loads of times behind the Boardwalk for free."

"You've been to the Boardwalk Night Club? Did you know Debbie Jenkins?"

"Yes. Debbie went to the parties sometimes. In fact, it was Debbie that persuaded Janette."

Bainbridge frowned. "Was Janette happy to participate at these parties?"

"Of course she was," she said, "until that bloke hurt her."

"Which bloke?"

Alison shrugged. "I don't know his name. He was old. Janette went into a room with him, and then I heard her screaming. I tried to get in to help her, but the door was locked."

Bainbridge leant forward. "What happened?"

"I started banging on the door and shouting. I raised the bloody roof. Then the door opened, and she came out. She looked terrified."

"What did you do?"

"What do you think I did? I got her out of that place as quick as I could." She turned to Bainbridge. "My cousin was terrified of that bastard. I took her back to my flat, and she stayed there for a couple of nights."

Bainbridge banged his hand onto the desk. "Why didn't you report this to the police?"

"I wanted to, but Janette said no. The woman who gave me the frock came around and gave Janette a bonus to keep quiet."

"What did Janette say to this?"

"She agreed to keep quiet, as long as she didn't have to see the bloke again."

"Do you know the man's name?"

Alison shook her head. "No. All the men called themselves Joe."

Bainbridge raised an eyebrow. "Joe?" he repeated.

"I know it sounds crazy, but that's the way it was. I warned Janette they were dangerous people, but she... well, I think she liked earning the money. A couple of weeks later, Janette disappeared."

Bainbridge scowled. "And still you didn't think to come

forward?"

"Everyone said Janette had run off. She's done that before. She'd meet some lad and shack up with him for a few days, but she always came back."

"I'll need you to show me the house where the parties took place," Bainbridge said. "Do you think you can do that?"

"I've no idea where it is," she said. "On party nights, I was picked up at the Seagull pub in Whitby and driven to a big house. There were several other girls in the van. The van didn't have any windows, so I had no idea where the house was."

"How long were you in the van?"

"About twenty minutes, maybe less," she said. "We weren't far from the coast, though. You could hear the sea clearly."

Bainbridge frowned. "I'll need you to drive around with me and see if we can find the house."

She smiled. "No need. The woman rang me this morning and invited me to a party at the house this weekend."

After Alison made her statement, Bainbridge telephoned the Chief Constable and brought him up to speed on developments.

"You seriously think this has something to do with the three missing women?" the Chief Constable said.

"Yes, I do," Bainbridge said. "It can't be a coincidence that both Janette and Debbie visited these parties in Whitby."

"All right, Andy. Arrange observation outside the Seagull on Saturday."

"Thank you, sir," Bainbridge said. "In the meantime, I'll prep Alison on what to do."

69

It was Saturday afternoon. Harriet Johnstone picked up her small suitcase and turned to her companion. "You'll love the cottage, Claudia," she said. "It will be good for you to relax after Jon-Pierre's funeral."

Claudia smiled weakly as she placed clothes into her suitcase. "Are you sure I won't be intruding?"

"Nonsense. It will be lovely to have company for a couple of days. Besides, it will give us the opportunity to discuss your forthcoming interview with the police."

Claudia shuddered. "Oh please, don't remind me," she said, placing a beige sweater and matching cardigan into her case. "Doesn't Nigel ever go to the cottage with you?"

"No, he does not. The cottage is my little hideaway."

"What does he do when you're away? He must be lonely?"

"Don't worry about Nigel. He has friends come over, and they have a rare old time eating and drinking. I think they play poker too."

"It sounds like fun," Claudia said.

"Believe me, when Nigel and his friends get together, it's anything but fun. I just want to get as far away as I can."

"Well, if you're sure you don't mind? I'd love to come with you."

Harriet looked out the window. "You'd better hurry up with your packing. The taxi is just coming up the drive."

It was late afternoon. Nigel Johnstone, dressed in a black and white bathrobe, emerged from the en-suite and walked over to the bank of wardrobes in the adjoining dressing room. He opened one of the mirrored doors and, leaning in, removed a pale blue silk shirt. He held it against himself as he stood in front of the mirror. "Mm..." he murmured, squinting at his image. "Maybe not." He replaced the blue shirt and took out a dark red one. "That's better," he said, smiling to himself.

The telephone rang. "Damn," he muttered. "Who's that at

this time?" He walked over to the phone and checked the number. "Oh, it's you. Is something the matter?"

"No, of course not," answered the voice. "I'm just checking everything's all right for tonight."

"Why shouldn't it be?"

"No reason. That nosey copper came snooping yesterday and—"

"For fuck's sake, don't tell me you've killed her? I heard she was missing, but I thought... I hoped it was an accident."

"She said my DNA was on one of the bitch's frocks. I had to get rid of her. I had no choice."

Nigel was silent for a moment. "There's nothing we can do about it now," he said. "Just carry on as normal and hope they don't find the body."

"Don't worry, they won't. I've made sure of that."

It was seven-thirty when the first guests arrived. Simon and George Benson were regular visitors to the parties. They went through into the spacious lounge and sat on the couch.

"Usual tipple?" Nigel asked, handing them both a large whisky.

"What time are you expecting the girls?" Simon said as he took the glass and raised it to his lips.

Nigel grinned. "They'll be here about nine," he said. "That girl you took a shine to last month is definitely coming tonight."

George grimaced. "Simon, I don't know what you see in her."

Nigel put up his hand. "Gentlemen," he said. "May I remind you that once you enter this house, you become Joe."

"Sorry," George said. "I forgot. Tell me, Nige... I mean, Joe, how many girls have you got coming? I like a bit of variety."

Nigel laughed. "There's plenty, don't worry. Now, if we can get the money sorted first..."

At exactly eight-thirty, a dark blue Ford Transit pulled up

outside the Seagull Pub in Whitby. The driver pressed the horn, and three young women rushed out of the pub and climbed into the back of the vehicle. Alison Walsh was one of them.

"Get a trace on the registration," Bainbridge said.

"Yes, sir," answered PC Beaumont.

The van pulled away, and Bainbridge followed, a few yards behind. The vehicle came to a halt fifteen minutes later outside a large red-brick house.

"That registration number," Beaumont said. "The vehicle is owned by a company in Newcastle."

"What's the name of the company?"

"Elegance by Design, sir," the PC answered.

Bainbridge huffed as he radioed for other police vehicles to prepare for the raid. "Ten minutes, and we go in."

70

Had anyone in Bradley House been checking the CCTV, they would have seen the convoy of police vehicles silently snaking up the gravel drive. As they got closer, Bainbridge glanced up at the upstairs rooms, which were illuminated. Several vehicles, including the Ford Transit, used to transport the girls, were parked outside the house. Bainbridge frowned at the sight of a familiar silver Audi parked at the side of the house.

He jumped out of the vehicle and approached the property, then banged on the front door. "Police," he shouted. "Open up."

Raised voices could be heard from within, along with women screaming. Bainbridge banged on the door once more. Bolts were drawn back, and the door was eventually opened. Nigel Johnstone, arms folded across his chest, emerged from the house.

"What the hell's going on?" he yelled. "What's the meaning of this?"

Bainbridge held up a search warrant. "I have a warrant to search these premises," he said as officers began to push past and enter the building.

Scowling, Johnstone snatched the document off Bainbridge. "Suspicion of running a brothel? Ridiculous. This is a private party, and you've no right."

"Sir," shouted Sergeant Brown from inside. "Up here."

Bainbridge pushed past Johnstone and entered the hall. Several men scurried around the lounge in an attempt to get fully dressed while scantily clad girls cowered against the wall. He turned to one of the officers. "Nobody leaves," he said. "I want everyone's details and proof of identity."

"Yes, sir," the officer said.

Bainbridge rushed up the stairs to join Sergeant Brown. The sergeant was on the landing, comforting a young woman who was sobbing. She was fully dressed, but her face was red and swollen, and her bottom lip was bleeding.

Bainbridge moved forward. "Alison. Who did this?"

She pointed towards the bedroom door. "That bastard in there. He's the same bloke that hurt our Janette."

Bainbridge pushed the door open. Steven Duffy sat on the bottom of the bed with his head lowered into his hands. "Fair cop," he said. "Caught with my pants down, eh, Andy?"

"Steven Duffy, I'm arresting you for assault," Bainbridge said, grabbing Duffy's upper arm. "You don't have—"

Duffy pulled away. "Oh, spare me that horseshit. It was just a bit of fun that got out of hand. You know how these things happen. We're all men of the world, right?"

Bainbridge turned to Sergeant Brown. "Put Mr Duffy in the van."

"Yes, sir," he said, taking out a pair of handcuffs.

Duffy snarled. "For fuck's sake. There's no need for that."

Bainbridge nodded to the sergeant who placed the restraints on Duffy's wrists and led him downstairs to the waiting police van. He turned to Alison. "Are you all right?"

She nodded. "I am now," she said, wiping her eyes with a tissue. "Another few minutes and that pig would have…"

"My officer will take you to the medic," he said. "That lip looks painful."

She forced a smile and went down the stairs with PC Lisa Walker.

Nigel Johnstone was propped on a barstool in the lounge. By his side was Cheryl Lewis. "I'm going to sue," he said, pointing a finger at Bainbridge. "You've no right to—"

Bainbridge reached out and placed his hand on Johnstones's arm. "You're under arrest on suspicion of running a brothel."

Cheryl flung back her head. "This is ridiculous. Nigel was—"

"Cheryl Lewis, I'm arresting you on suspicion of helping to organise the said brothel." He turned to two officers standing close by. "Make sure you caution them both. Then put Ms Lewis in the van. Mr Johnstone can go in the car." Both officers took their prisoners outside to the waiting vehicles.

"That's a job well done, sir," Sergeant Brown said as they made their way back to the station. "I'd never trusted that smarmy solicitor. There was something about him."

"It's Duffy that's surprised me," Bainbridge said. "Tonight, it was like seeing him in a totally different light."

Sergeant Brown scratched his chin. "Like I said before, sir, Duffy had some strange ideas towards women. That party tonight would have been right up his street."

"What did you make of Cheryl Lewis?"

The sergeant frowned. "I was surprised she was there. I knew she supplied some of the fancy frocks for the girls, but to pick them up in her van like that and take them to the house…"

"Were any of them underage?"

He shook his head. "No, sir, and as far as we can tell, none were under duress. Arrangements have been made for all the men who attended to be at the station in the morning to make statements."

Bainbridge huffed. "Forensics should be at the house by now."

"If there's anything incriminating to find, sir, they'll find it," the sergeant said as their vehicle pulled into the police car park.

71

The following morning, officers began to take statements from everyone who had attended the brothel the previous evening.

It was nine-thirty when Sergeant Brown brought Nigel Johnstone from the cells to interview room one. Bainbridge sat behind the table.

The unshaven Johnstone plonked himself heavily onto the chair opposite Bainbridge. He lowered his head into his hands, staring vaguely at some spot on the floor.

"I must remind you that you are still under caution, Mr Johnstone," Bainbridge said. "I understand you do not want a solicitor present?"

He huffed. "That's right. I'm perfectly capable of representing myself."

"That's your decision, of course," Bainbridge said, opening the buff-coloured file on the table. "This interview is being recorded."

"Get on with it, man," he said. "I don't have all day."

"How often did you allow your home to be used for paid sex?"

Johnstone lifted his head and glared at Bainbridge but remained silent.

"A substantial amount of cash was found in your home, Mr Johnstone," he continued. "Would you care to elaborate how it came to be there?"

He sneered. "How do you think?"

"I think men paid you a great deal of money to attend your parties," Bainbridge said. "We are obtaining statements from all the men who were present last night. They're all saying the same thing."

Johnstone hunched his shoulders but remained silent.

"Tell me about the girls. How did you recruit them?"

"I advertised in the Gazette. How do you think?"

"I think the girls were recruited by your friends Cheryl

Lewis and Steven Duffy."

Johnstone yawned. "If you say so," he said, stretching his arms above his head. "What does it matter anyway? The girls came to the party of their own free will. Nobody forced them."

"What about Janette Walsh?"

"Who?"

"The young girl with the tattoos. She was at one of your parties about six weeks ago."

He shook his head. "Sorry, I don't remember."

"Janette was attacked by Duffy at your house. Do you remember now?"

Johnstone licked his lips. "Some of the girls like it rough. You can't blame a man if he goes too far."

"Janette has been missing for over a month. Do you know what happened to her?"

"No idea. She's probably working in some massage parlour. There are dozens of them in Middlesbrough, so I've heard."

"What about Deborah Jenkins? Deborah's been missing for eighteen months."

Johnstone rolled his eyes. "Sorry, I can't help you."

"What can you tell me about Suzie Graham? She mysteriously vanished. I understand she was a frequent visitor to your house. What can you tell me about her?"

"Like I've said, I don't know anything about these missing women. They come to my house to party, they get paid, and then they leave. That's it."

Bainbridge turned to PC Brooke, stood by the door. "Take Mr Johnstone back to his cell. I will resume this interview later today."

Johnstone got up and walked towards the door. "You're wasting your time asking me about missing girls. It's Duffy you want to be talking to. He's the psycho."

72

After postponing the interview with Nigel Johnstone, Bainbridge returned to his office just as the desk phone rang. It was Chief Inspector Harry Denton.

"Sir," he said, "it's been decided to call off the search for DI Cooper. The coastguard is convinced she's been washed out to sea. There's no chance of finding her body, I'm afraid."

Bainbridge took a deep breath and gritted his teeth. "Jilly could be injured somewhere," he said. "There's a lot of ground we haven't searched yet. She could be—"

"I'm so sorry, but Jilly's gone," Denton said. "She's been missing too long."

Bainbridge slowly put the phone back on its cradle, his eyes stinging with tears. Thirty seconds later, the phone gave out its shrill, familiar ring.

"Yes?" he said, wiping his eyes with the back of his hand.

"DCS Bainbridge?" asked a timid voice.

"Who's this?"

"It's Benton, sir. Lawrence Benton. I work with Leo Cutts. It's about those DNA tests Leo ran. I've managed to gain access to his computer."

"Well?" Bainbridge said.

"We have a definite DNA match with the semen stains on the inside of Janette Walsh's dress."

Bainbridge growled. "Well, man, whose DNA are we talking about?"

"Well, that's the thing, sir," Benton said. "The DNA belongs to a voluntary donor. We're not supposed to use it unless—"

"Never mind about that," Bainbridge said. "Whose DNA is it? This is a possible murder enquiry. I don't have time for niceties."

"No... no, sir, I understand that, but—"

"Well?" he demanded.

Benton cleared his throat before he spoke. "According to

the notes on Leo's computer, the DNA belongs to Steven Duffy. Seven years ago, Duffy provided a sample for elimination. He was a police officer at the time in Redcar."

Bainbridge banged the phone down hard on its cradle and hurried out of his office. Sergeant Brown was in the incident room, along with PC Beaumont. "Get that bastard Duffy to the interview room," he said. "And, sergeant, I want you in the interview room with me. You too, Beaumont."

Bainbridge rushed back to his office and collected the files of the three missing women, together with the statement from Moira Turner about her missing sister, Helen.

Duffy and the two police officers were already in the interview room when Bainbridge arrived. Duffy sat at the table opposite Sergeant Brown, and PC Beaumont stood by the door.

Dishevelled with heavy shadows beneath his eyes. He drummed his fingers impatiently on the table. "How long are you planning to keep me here?" he said as Bainbridge took his seat. "I'll put my hands up to assaulting that girl. Guilty as charged, but you can't keep me locked up for much longer." He grinned. "I know all about the law, don't forget."

"You're still under caution, Mr Duffy," Bainbridge said. "Do you want a solicitor to represent you?"

Duffy flung back his head and glared at him. "My brief is locked up in the next cell. If I can't have Nigel Johnstone, I don't want anybody."

Bainbridge raised an eyebrow. "That's up to you, of course, but I would suggest your interests are best served by having legal representation."

"No thanks," Duffy said, shaking his head. "Now, can we get this farce over with? I've got a pub to run."

Bainbridge placed the files on the table and leant back into his chair, steepling his fingers. "I want to speak to you about several matters."

Duffy narrowed his eyes and ran his tongue over his lips.

"What matters? I thought this was about that slapper last night."

Bainbridge opened the first file. "Tell me what you know about the disappearance of Janette Walsh?"

Duffy scowled. "Who the fuck's Janette Walsh?"

"She's the young woman you assaulted a couple of months ago at one of the parties."

"Who said I did?"

"There is a witness," Bainbridge said. "A reliable witness who saw the assault take place." He leant forward. "In addition, semen was found on the dress Janette had been wearing that night which matches your DNA."

Duffy breathed deeply, beads of sweat forming on his forehead. "No, mate, you've got this all wrong. She liked it rough. You know what these slags are like, Andy. They tease a bloke and then scream the place down when you respond."

"Janette is missing," Bainbridge said. "She's been missing for nearly two months."

Duffy shook his head. "Nothing to do with me. The last time I saw her, she was racing out of the house with her knickers in her handbag."

Bainbridge inhaled and opened a second file. "What can you tell me about Deborah Jenkins? She visited the parties regularly."

"So did loads of girls. Am I supposed to know all their names?"

"Deborah is missing too. So is Suzie Graham. She attended parties at the house."

Duffy shrugged. "The parties were just a harmless bit of fun. We both know the score, Andy. Blokes are prepared to pay for sex, and girls are happy to provide it, as long as they get paid, of course."

"You know the law as well as I do," Bainbridge said. "What you're describing is illegal."

Duffy snorted. "So is screwing a junior officer, but it didn't stop you and Jilly Cooper, did it? I knew your dirty little secret,

Andy, and I made sure your wife knew too."

Bainbridge narrowed his eyes. "We're not here to discuss my private life. We're here to discuss the disappearance of three young women from parties that you attended."

"I'm not saying another word," Duffy said. "If you want to charge me with shagging a few willing slags, go ahead."

"A warrant to search your premises has been issued," Bainbridge said. "Forensics are there right now. If you've anything to tell me, Duffy, now is the time."

He pursed his lips and turned his head to face the wall, folding his arms across his chest.

"Very well," Bainbridge said. "Interview postponed." He turned to PC Beaumont. "Take Mr Duffy back to his cell, officer."

Bainbridge was about to leave the interview room as PC Walker came hurrying up to him.

"Sir," she said. "The Chief Constable wants you to give him a call. He says it's urgent."

73

Bainbridge was in a glum mood as he parked his car outside The Coppers Inn thirty minutes later. The Forensic Science van was there, along with several police cars. Chief Constable Davies was standing in the doorway, his face ashen, his shoulders drooped.

Bainbridge rushed over to him. "I heard they've found bodies."

Davies stared blankly ahead. "Five. They're all in the back cellar."

Bainbridge attempted to push past him. "Oh, god." He gasped. "I have to see."

Davies put his hand on Bainbridge's shoulder. "One of the bodies is Jilly Cooper."

Bainbridge gulped and slumped against the door. "Are you sure? I must see her. I…" His legs crumpled beneath him, and Davies grabbed hold of him.

"We'll wait in my car," Davies said, guiding him towards his vehicle. "Let the forensic blokes do their job first."

Bainbridge climbed into the Chief Constable's car, his hands shaking uncontrollably on his lap. "Do they know how…? I mean, do they know if…"

"It's too early to say yet. All I know for certain is that there are five bodies in that cellar. All of them are female."

Bainbridge blew out hard. His body trembled as he slumped against the window. Davies opened the glove box on the dashboard and removed a silver hipflask containing whisky. "Drink this," he said, "you'll feel better."

Bainbridge took the vessel and, removing the cap, put it to his lips and drank some of the liquid.

"Have you begun interviewing Duffy yet?" Davies said.

Bainbridge nodded. "I've done a brief interview. He's not saying much, only that he attended the parties."

"What about that solicitor, Johnstone? Do you think he's involved in… in that?" he nodded in the direction of the pub.

"Yes, sir," Bainbridge said. "I think he's involved right up to his neck."

There was a sharp rap on the car window. It was Lawrence Benson, the forensics officer. He was dressed in a white bodysuit. Davies wound down the window.

"We've finished our preliminary examination, sir," Benson said. "You may go in now."

Both men got out of the car and entered the pub after putting on forensic suits.

"The entrance to the cellar is behind the bar," Benson said. "It's through here."

They followed him over to the open door at the back of the bar area, through the kitchen, and descended the steep steps. The cellar was brightly illuminated, with barrels stacked at one end, along with dozens of bottled beers, ciders and wines on metal shelving along another wall. A large table in the middle of the cellar held several boxes of different flavoured crisps.

"It's through here," Benson said, indicating a wooden door in the far corner of the cellar. "This was the ice room back in the day. Mind your head. The doorframe is very low."

All three entered the second cellar, a much smaller room than the first. This room was illuminated by police lighting. The air smelt pungent, and Benson handed both men a facemask. In a neat line at the back of the room lay five bundles, each wrapped in heavy-duty polythene and fastened with gaffer tape.

Bainbridge walked over to the first bundle, which had been carefully opened by the forensics officer. He gasped as he saw Cooper's lifeless face staring up at him.

Davies moved to his side, placing his hand on Bainbridge's shoulder. "Don't worry, Andy," he whispered. "We'll nail the bastard."

Bainbridge felt numb as he stood over the body, staring in disbelief.

"The next three bodies fit the description of the missing

girls, Janette Walsh, Deborah Jenkins and Suzie Graham," Benson said. "It's the end body that is baffling. She's much older and has been dead for some considerable time."

Bainbridge blinked rapidly. "I think you'll find that's the body of Helen," he said. "Duffy's missing wife."

74

Bainbridge and the Chief Constable drove back to the police station and went straight to Bainbridge's office.

"Are you sure you want to continue with interviewing Duffy?" Davies asked. "I can get Superintendent Barraclough to take over if you wish."

Bainbridge shook his head. "No, sir. This is the least I can do for Jilly."

Davies rested his hand on his arm. "All right, Andy, if you're sure, but get yourself a cup of tea and something to eat first. You look dreadful."

"I have to let the crew know what's happened," he said. "I don't want my officers finding out through the press."

"Leave that to me," Davies said. "I've assembled everyone in the incident room. I'll speak to them." He turned to leave the room. "Now remember what I said, a cup of tea and a bite to eat before anything else."

Bainbridge sat in the canteen staring at a half-eaten cheese and pickle sandwich when Sergeant Brown approached and slid into the seat opposite. "We've just heard, sir," he said, slowly shaking his head. "It's a terrible business about Jilly Cooper and those poor girls. Terrible."

Bainbridge sipped the cold tea in front of him. "Yes, it is, sergeant. And it's our job to put things right, isn't it?"

Brown bit into his bottom lip. "Some of the lads wanted to go to the cell and give the bastard a pasting."

Bainbridge scowled. "I hope you told them that was a bad idea, sergeant?"

"Yes, of course, sir, but you can understand feelings are running high. Cooper was well respected. Everyone liked her."

"Yes, they did," Bainbridge said quietly. He pushed the plate away and stood up. "Well, it's time we got this done. I want you and Beaumont back in the interview room."

Brown nodded. "It'll be a pleasure, sir," he said. "A real pleasure."

Steven Duffy sat in the interview room with his arms crossed behind his head as Bainbridge and the two officers entered. He leant back in his chair and grinned at them. "Well, I can tell you found them," he said, leaning forward and slowly clapping his hands. "I wondered how long it would take you."

"I must remind you that you are still under caution," Bainbridge said. "I will ask you once more, Mr Duffy, do you want a legal representative?"

"And I'll tell you for the last time, no, I bloody don't." He ran his fingers through his hair. "Just so you know, Andy, I didn't mean to kill Jilly. As God is my witness, that was an accident. I don't want you thinking I'm some kind of monster."

Bainbridge inhaled. "Tell me what happened?"

Duffy hunched his shoulders. "Jilly came to the pub about lunchtime. I could tell there was something up straight away."

"What happened?"

"We went through to the kitchen for some privacy, and then she started to caution me. She said I was being arrested, something about my DNA on a frock belonging to one of the girls that had gone missing." He closed his eyes and lowered his head. "The next thing, Jilly gets out her cuffs. I tried to laugh it off, but I could see she was serious." His hands curled into fists, and he drew them into his chest. "I tried to reason with her, but she wasn't listening. That's when I... I picked up the knife." He lifted his head and stared directly at Bainbridge. "I didn't mean to kill her. It just happened." Duffy reached out and took the paper cup of water from the desk, gulping the contents greedily. "The next thing, she was a crumpled heap on the floor. There was blood everywhere." He sipped more water. "At least it was quick. She didn't suffer."

"Why didn't you ring for an ambulance?"

Duffy scowled as he folded his arms across his chest. "Why? Jilly was dead. Any fool could see that. I took her down to the cellar straightaway and placed her next to the others."

"Then what happened?"

"I cleaned up the floor as best I could, then I changed my shirt and went back into the bar. I still had customers to serve after all."

Bainbridge clenched his fists under the table. "How did DI Cooper's car end up at South Gare?"

Duffy leant forward, spreading his fingers on the table. "I knew I had to get rid of the car, so I drove over to the Gare later that afternoon and pushed it over the edge into the sea. I thought the car would be swept away, and everyone would think Jilly had had an accident."

"I take it you were the person seen riding away on a pushbike?"

"I put the bike in the boot. The weather was foul that day." He took another sip of water. "There was no way I was walking all that way back to the pub in the rain."

"Tell me about the other bodies in the cellar," Bainbridge said. "Let's start with Helen."

Duffy snorted. "That bitch? She's been in the cellar about five years now."

"Why did you kill your wife?"

He began to chuckle. "She was threatening to divorce me and go to live with her sister in Australia."

Bainbridge tilted his head. "People divorce all the time. They don't kill each other."

He snarled. "I didn't give a damn about the divorce. Helen was past her sell-by date anyway. It was the money. She was going to take her inheritance. I couldn't let her do that. I needed that money to do the pub up."

"So, you killed Helen for her money?"

"Yeah," he said. "That's about it. Helen had been rabbiting on to everyone about going to Australia, so I just said she'd finally done it. Nobody questioned it." He tilted his head and grinned. "Isn't that right, Sergeant Brown?"

Sergeant Brown inhaled deeply. "Yes, that's right, Duffy," he said. "You fooled everyone."

Duffy leant back in his chair and placed his hands behind his head again. "Any chance of a cup of tea?" he asked. "I'm parched."

"I think we'll take a short break," Bainbridge said. He turned to Beaumont, stood by the door. "Get the prisoner a cup of tea."

"Milk, two sugars," Duffy said. "I don't suppose there are any biscuits?"

75

Brown stood outside the interview room, his legs planted wide apart, both hands curled into fists. "That bastard's mind is twisted. For two pins, I'll go in there and kick the shit out of him."

Bainbridge reached out and put his hand on the sergeant's arm. "You'll do no such thing. We have a job to do, sergeant."

The veins on Sergeant Brown's neck were pulsating, and beads of sweat ran down his face. "How can you be so calm? You heard what he did to Jilly, the murdering bastard."

"Losing your temper isn't going to help, though, is it?" Bainbridge said. "We have to let Duffy keep talking. We must find out about the three young women."

Brown scowled. "You do realise that sick bastard is enjoying this, don't you?"

"Just give him enough rope, sergeant," Bainbridge said, glancing at his watch. "He's had his break now. So, let's get this over with."

Bainbridge and Brown took their position at the table. Beaumont guarded the door. Duffy leant back into his chair and folded his arms across his chest.

"Are you all right, Andy? You're looking a bit peaky."

Bainbridge ignored Duffy's remark as he opened one of the files. "Deborah Jenkins," he said. "She hasn't been seen for nearly two years. Tell me about her."

Duffy frowned, tapping the corner of his mouth with his finger. "Ah, yes, Debbie," he said, a wide grin spreading across his face. "That was last Christmas, wasn't it? Oh, no, I stand corrected, the Christmas before." He leant forward, putting his elbows on the table. "Debbie was walking towards Marske. She was off her head, the stupid bitch. She liked popping pills."

"Did she take pills at Nigel's parties?"

Duffy nodded, his eyes shining with excitement. "Yes. All

of the time. That's why Nigel banned her. Punters had been complaining."

"So, what happened on Christmas Eve when you saw her on the roadside?"

Duffy began to chuckle. "I'd been to dinner at Nigel's in Whitby. My dear friend Harriet might be a shit-hot lawyer, but she's a lousy cook." He grimaced and shook his head. "I really can't recommend her beef wellington. Anyway, as I drove past the Stray, I saw Debbie staggering about. She recognised my car and flagged me down." Duffy ran his hand through his hair. "I pulled into the layby, and the next thing, she's jumped into the car beside me and starts giving me grief about being dumped. I told her to get out, but she refused to budge. She was shouting and making threats, so... so that's when I did it."

Bainbridge arched an eyebrow. "You did what?"

Duffy licked his lips. "I put my hands around her throat and squeezed like this." He gritted his teeth and formed his hands into a circle. "Do you know what I found surprising, Andy?" he said, tilting his head to one side. "It takes a lot longer to throttle someone than you would think, even a scrawny neck like hers. I thought it would take a couple of minutes, but it was nearer five."

"So, what did you do after you'd killed her?"

Duffy laughed. "I drove her to the pub to join Helen. I'm sure Helen would have appreciated having the company for Christmas."

Bainbridge's outward appearance gave no hint of the sickening disgust he was feeling towards Duffy. "Tell me about Suzie Graham," he said. "What happened there?"

Duffy screwed up his face. "Suzie Graham? Was that her name?"

"Why did you kill Suzie?"

Duffy shrugged his shoulders. "I guess you could say she was in the wrong place at the wrong time, but that's fate, isn't it?" He put his hands behind his head. "If she'd been on the street ten minutes later, or if she'd walked that dog of hers a different route, I might never have bumped into her, and she'd still be alive."

"Where exactly did you come across Suzie?"

"She was coming up the slipway off the beach. She'd been walking her dog."

"So, what happened?"

Duffy licked his lips again. "She was a pretty girl, wasn't she? I loved her long red hair. My mother had red hair like hers, did you know that, Andy?" He momentarily closed his eyes as if reliving the meeting. "I hadn't had the pleasure of Suzie at the party. I think she left early." He turned to Bainbridge. "I don't suppose there's a chance of another cup of tea?"

Bainbridge nodded to Beaumont, who left the room, returning with a paper cup containing tea a couple of minutes later.

"Thanks. Now, where was I?"

"You were about to tell me of your meeting with Suzie Graham."

"Ah, yes. Suzie Graham." He sipped his tea. "Like I said, I'd had designs on her at the party. Seeing her at the top of the slipway that night, well, it was as if I'd been given a second chance. I got out of my car and forced her back onto the beach behind the seawall." He scowled and shook his head. "Fucking on the sand is not ideal, but beggars can't be choosers, as they say." He began to laugh coarsely and then raised a finger. "I'll say this for Suzie. She fought like a tiger. I had the best shag I'd had in ages. After it was over, I did consider letting her go, but the silly cow became hysterical, shouting and screaming." He looked directly at Bainbridge. "She threatened to tell the police what I'd done. I had no choice. You do see that, don't you, Andy? I had to get rid of her."

"So, you strangled her too, just like you did Debbie?"

He leant forward. "It was a lot quicker the second time,"

he said. He began to chuckle. "Practice makes perfect, eh?"

"What happened next?"

Duffy inhaled deeply. "I brought the car up to the slipway and put her in the boot." He began to rock slowly in his seat. "I'll tell you a secret," he said, a broad grin spreading across his face. "On the way back to the pub, I had to stop the car and have a wank. Suzie had really got me going." He yawned and stretched out his arms above his head. "That bloody dog of hers bit me on the ankle. People shouldn't be allowed to keep dogs if they bite. Anyway, I gave it a swift kick in the ribs and off it went whining. After that, I drove back to the pub with Suzie so she could join the others."

Bainbridge frowned. "So, at this point, you had three bodies in the cellar? It was starting to get a little crowded, wasn't it?"

Duffy shook his head. "Oh, no. There was plenty of room for half a dozen more if I wanted," he said. "I kept the bodies in the old ice house beyond the main cellar, so they were quite all right. There's no ventilation in there." He tilted his head and frowned. "Mind you, I did have to buy more heavy-duty polythene once Suzie arrived."

Bainbridge leant back in his chair. "That leaves Janette Walsh," he said. "Tell me about her?"

At the mention of Janette, Duffy's whole persona changed. His eyes narrowed, and the muscles in his face tightened. "That girl was trouble," Duffy said through clenched teeth. "She caused a scene at the house one night. Nigel was furious."

"What happened to her?"

A malicious grin spread across Duffy's face. "That bitch was demanding more money to keep quiet about what had happened at the house. She'd already been paid a bonus." He tutted. "She was a very greedy girl. Anyway, I agreed to meet her in Locke Park."

"So, what happened?"

He laughed. "She got in my car expecting to get more cash.

You should have seen her face when I put my hands around her scrawny neck. It was priceless." He began to rock backwards and forwards more quickly this time. "I got her back to the cellar, and then... and then it made four in a bed." He began to chuckle. "Four in a bed, and the little one said... roll over... roll over."

Beaumont leant back on the wall. "Sir," he said, "I have to be excused. I—"

"That's all right," Bainbridge said. "Go and get yourself a cup of tea. Sergeant Brown and I can manage."

He hurried out of the interview room and headed straight to the men's toilets.

Duffy scratched his chin. "What's up with him? Is it something I've said?"

Bainbridge leant forward, fanning his fingers on the table. "Why did you attack Sally Lomax? She wasn't part of the sex parties."

"Sally came to the pub looking for her mate. Janette had told her all about the parties." Duffy frowned and slowly shook his head. "She was warned not to do that. Anyway, Sally turned up and threatened to go to the police if I didn't tell her where Janette was. The silly cow thought she'd been trafficked or something."

"So, what happened?"

"Nigel was in the pub that night. He gave Sally a drink laced with LSD that we use at the parties. She went out like a light. I was all for wringing her neck like the others, but Nigel said we should make it look like an accident."

"Whose car did you use?"

"There was a Nissan left round the back of the car park by one of the customers who got pissed. I used that."

"And the attack at the hospital? I take it that was you?"

Duffy scowled. "That kid must have rubber bones. I was sure I'd killed her with the car. When I found out she was still alive, I had to get rid of her. I had no choice."

"So, you went to the hospital and tried to smother her?"

Duffy huffed. "I needn't have bothered. From what I've heard, her brain's so scrambled she can't even remember her own name."

"Apart from the attempted murder of Sally Lomax, was Nigel Johnstone involved in the murders?"

Duffy grinned. "Nigel? Don't make me laugh. He hasn't got the balls for violence."

"But he did spike Sally's drink and encourage you to kill her?" Bainbridge said.

"Yeah, but he didn't attempt to kill her himself, did he?"

"Did he know you had murdered the three girls?"

Duffy shrugged. "I might have mentioned it to him. I can't remember."

PC Beaumont came back into the room, his face ashen.

Bainbridge placed the various documents into their folders. "Officer, take Mr Duffy back to the cells while I prepare the charge sheet."

"Yes, sir," Beaumont said, a slight quiver in his voice.

"I'll come with you," Sergeant Brown said, grabbing Duffy by the upper arm.

Duffy got to his feet. "Well, it's been nice chatting with you, Andy," he said, grinning, as Sergeant Brown steered him towards the door. "We really must do this more often."

76

Bainbridge returned to his office and telephoned the Chief Constable to inform him of progress.

"So, the bastard has admitted all five?" Davies said.

"Yes, sir, as well as the attempted murder of Sally Lomax."

"What about Nigel Johnstone? I can't believe I've played the occasional game of golf with him in the past."

"According to Duffy, he was involved in the attack on Sally, but not the murders. Duffy said he knew nothing about them."

"And you believe him?"

"Who knows? Superintendent Barraclough is interviewing him now, sir."

"What about this woman, Cheryl Lewis?"

"I'm seeing her shortly. I just need to clear my head of Duffy first."

"Yes, of course, Andy. Let me know how you get on."

Bainbridge went to the washroom to freshen up. When he returned to the interview room, Sergeant Brown had already brought Cheryl Lewis from the cells. She sat at the metal table where Duffy had been sitting, just an hour earlier.

"Good afternoon, Ms Lewis," he said. "Sorry to have kept you waiting."

"I don't care what excuse you have," Cheryl said. "I want to leave. You have no right keeping me here." She stood up and made towards the door.

"Sit down," Bainbridge said. "You have some questions to answer before you go anywhere."

Scowling, she returned to the table and sat heavily on the chair, her arms folded across her chest. "What is it you want to know?"

"Before we begin, I understand you have refused a solicitor to represent you?"

"That's right. I've done nothing wrong, so I don't see why

I should need a solicitor."

"Very well, if you're sure," Bainbridge said. "I want you to tell me what role you played in organising the parties at Nigel Johnstone's home?"

"Nigel asked me to get the girls some decent gear to wear, that's all. Each girl was given a dress and shoes, so they looked respectable for the clients."

"For which you got paid?"

Cheryl rolled her eyes. "Of course, I got paid. Very handsomely as it happens. Not that it's any of your business."

"You do know that three girls who attended these parties went missing and have subsequently been found murdered in the premises of Steven Duffy?"

Cheryl's posture stiffened and she inhaled deeply. "No, I didn't. But I really don't know what this has got to do with me. I had a business arrangement with Nigel. Like I said, I provided the clothes for the girls, and he helped me fund my boutique business. That's all."

"I take it Nigel paid for the dresses the girls wore for the parties?"

"Of course he did. Who else? They paid him back, one way or another."

"So, you're saying you knew nothing about Steven Duffy's involvement with the missing girls?"

"Duffy was Nigel's friend, not mine. To be honest, I found him to be a bit of a pest."

Bainbridge stroked his chin. "Moving on, tell me about your relationship with Claudia and Jon-Pierre Davereaux."

"Why do you want to know about them? They had nothing to do with this. Nothing at all."

"Please answer my question," Bainbridge said.

Cheryl shrugged. "Claudia and I were friends. We had been for nearly twenty years."

"So, you knew Claudia and Rosie Lee?"

"What exactly are you implying?" she asked.

"Did you tell Claudia that Rosie's children were being

mistreated by their brother, Bobby?"

Cheryl flung her head back, her eyes flashing in anger. "No, of course not. I don't know what you mean."

"I don't think for one minute that Bobby was hurting his sisters like you told Claudia. I think it was you poisoning her mind towards her son."

She stood up quickly, causing the chair to crash to the floor. "You're talking rubbish," she said, placing both hands flat on the table. "That boy was bad. He tried to kill his mother. Did you know that?"

Bainbridge nodded. "Bobby had his problems as a child," he said. "There's no denying that, but he would never have killed his mother."

"That's nonsense," Cheryl shrieked. "He—"

"Why do you hate Rosie so much? I thought she was supposed to be your friend."

She inhaled deeply but remained silent.

"It was you who put the girls into that inflatable, wasn't it? You tried to kill those little girls."

She shook her head vigorously. "No, it was Bobby. Bobby was the one."

"I don't believe you," Bainbridge said. "I think you wanted to punish Rosie. Eddie too, most likely."

Cheryl rushed towards the door. "No, no, you're wrong," she screamed. "It was Bobby." Sergeant Brown, who had been standing by the door, held Cheryl firmly by the arms and steered her back to the table, picking up the overturned chair and forcing her onto it.

"Now," Bainbridge said. "Can we start again? The truth this time."

She lowered her head into her hands. She did not speak for several moments. When she did, her voice was cold and hard. "She deserved it," she said through gritted teeth. "Rosie deserved to lose her children. I'm only sorry it wasn't both the girls Claudia took."

Bainbridge leant forward with his hands fanned out on the

table. "Why?" he asked. "Why do you hate Rosie so much?"

Cheryl stood up and unbuttoned the first three buttons of her blouse. "Because of this," she said, opening the gap in the blouse. "Rosie did this to me."

Bainbridge looked at the scarred flesh of her chest. "How…? What happened?"

"Stupid Rosie doused me with sulphuric acid in a science lesson at school," she said. "Two skin grafts I've had, and it still looks horrendous."

"But surely it was an accident? She wouldn't have meant to hurt you."

Cheryl sat back in her chair and fastened her blouse, her eyes narrowing into slits. "It's not fair," she said, tilting back her head. "Rosie has everything I don't. She's beautiful. She has a husband and children, a home." She removed a tissue from her bag and dabbed her eyes. "It's not right. I'm the clever one. It should be me."

"You were jealous of her?"

Cheryl banged her fist on the table. "I hate her," she said. "Rosie had all the good-looking boys after her at school. I never got a look in. I had a fling with Eddie soon after Claudia left him. Did you know that? Eddie loved me. I know he did."

"And then Eddie met Rosie?"

Cheryl nodded. "He didn't know I existed after that. Then she got pregnant, so Eddie and Rosie had their perfect little family." She fidgeted with the chain around her neck. "Claudia asked me to send her photos of Bobby when I was in Redcar. I think she still cared for the little monster."

"So that's when you started drip-feeding her stories of Bobby abusing his sisters?"

She scowled. "Claudia is so naïve. I told her about Daisy coming off her trike and Poppy falling out of her swing. I told her Bobby was responsible."

"And was he?"

She shrugged. "I don't know, I wasn't there. He could have been."

"But he certainly didn't put the girls in the inflatable, did he?"

She lowered her head but remained silent.

"Come on. You've got this far. You might as well tell the truth."

She blinked rapidly, then turned to face Bainbridge. "I… I wouldn't have let them drift too far out. Before I had the chance to rescue them, a man on the beach saw them and swam out and brought them back to shore."

Bainbridge frowned. "Those little girls could have drowned."

"Well, they didn't, did they? If Rosie had been more responsible…"

"So, you rushed to tell Claudia that Bobby had set the girls adrift?"

"That's right. Claudia was horrified. She said she was coming up to Redcar herself. I never dreamt she was planning to kidnap the girls."

"But when you did know what she was planning, you were prepared to help her, weren't you?"

She shrugged but remained silent.

"Weren't you, Cheryl?" Bainbridge repeated.

"Rosie took Daisy with her to get ice cream. So, Claudia could only take Poppy away."

"While you sat back and watched that girl's parents go through hell at losing their child?"

"What of it? Rosie deserved to suffer. They both did."

Bainbridge got up from the table. "Take Ms Lewis back to her cell, sergeant. I'll draw up the charge sheet."

Superintendent Barraclough was waiting in Bainbridge's office when he returned. "How did you get on with Ms Lewis?" he asked.

Bainbridge sighed. "The woman has one hell of a twisted mind," he said. "Wicked doesn't come into it." He proceeded to fill the superintendent in on the interview. "How did you get on with Nigel Johnstone?"

The superintendent curled his lip. "He's putting his hands up to being a perv," he said. "We can nick him for running a brothel, but not much more, I'm afraid."

The telephone rang. Bainbridge listened intently to the caller. "Oh, that's great news. Take a statement right away." He put down the phone and smiled. "That was PC Porter ringing from the hospital. Sally Lomax is starting to remember details of what happened to her, including the conversation between Johnstone and Duffy."

Barraclough clasped his hands, a broad grin across his face. "Good. We've got the bastard," he said. "Conspiracy to murder. Let's see the slimy sod wriggle out of this one."

77

It had been three months since Steven Duffy and Nigel Johnstone had been arrested. Bainbridge, sat at his desk, looked up as Sergeant Brown knocked lightly on his door and entered.

"Sir," he said, a broad grin on his face. "There are two young ladies here to see you."

"Two young ladies? You'd better show them in, sergeant."

Poppy and Daisy Lee bounded into the room, arm-in-arm. Bainbridge got up from his desk and, moving forward, kissed each of them on the cheek.

"What brings you here? Not that you aren't welcome, of course."

"We were passing," Daisy said, flouncing into one of the armchairs, "and we thought we'd call in and invite you to lunch."

He tilted his head. "Daisy," he said, "it's only eleven o'clock."

"Well, join us for a drink then," Poppy said. "We've got so much to tell you."

Bainbridge sat back in his chair. "How is everybody? I've been meaning to call in to say hello, but…"

"We know you've been busy," Poppy said. "We're just glad you've decided not to retire yet and stay on for another five years."

He shrugged. "Well, I thought it's best to keep busy. Now, tell me everything you've been up to."

"Bobby is back with Karen," Daisy said. "Did you know Karen's expecting?"

He nodded.

Poppy grinned. "They're both in France at the moment. Bobby is learning the wine business."

"I take it he's made up with Claudia?"

Poppy hunched her shoulders. "Things are still a bit strained, I think, but they're getting there. I'm grateful you spoke up for Claudia in court," she said. "She got away pretty lightly, really, with two years' probation."

"Well, there were extenuating circumstances."

"I'm glad Cheryl got sent to jail," Daisy said. "Lying about Bobby like that was a wicked thing to do."

"Talking of wicked," Poppy said, "is it true Steven Duffy hanged himself in his cell last night?"

Bainbridge nodded. "Yes. The thought of spending the rest of his life in prison was just too much, I suppose."

Daisy sighed. "They've started demolishing The Coppers Inn. I still have nightmares thinking about what Duffy had done to those poor women."

"Let's not talk about the past," Bainbridge said. "I hear Rosie and Eddie have got a shop on the high street now."

Poppy began to giggle. "Yes, it's next door to Boots. We persuaded Dad to give up the markets. We've told him we'll need an outlet for our clothing brand when we finish our course."

"Oh, you're going to college?"

"We're going to Milan," Daisy said. "There's a twelve-month course on fashion design. Then, after that, we'll start our own company."

"Have you thought of a name for the company?"

"Petals," they both chorused.

Daisy walked towards the door. "You will join us for lunch, won't you? We thought we'd go to The Park Hotel."

"I'd love to," he said. "I have a couple of phone calls to make first, so I'll meet you there."

Poppy joined Daisy by the door. "Don't be long," she said.

Half an hour later as Bainbridge put on his jacket the telephone on his desk rang.

"Bainbridge," he said.

Silence.

"Detective Chief Superintendent Bainbridge," he repeated.

Again silence.

"Who is this?"

It was a gruff, male voice that answered. "Are you that copper that caught Steve Duffy?"

"Who is this?" Bainbridge repeated.

"There's someone a lot more evil than Duffy roaming around Redcar," the voice said.

"Do you want to report a crime?"

Silence.

"Hello?"

"He's already killed twice," the voice said. "He's about to kill again."

"Who are you talking about? Who's killed someone?"

"Me. And I'm going to do it again and again, and you can't stop me. Nobody can."

About the Author

Eva Carmichael followed her dream to live by the sea when, along with her husband and miniature schnauzer, she moved to Redcar in 2016.

Eva comes from a legal background, working first as a shorthand/typist for the West Yorkshire Police and then as a Special Constable. More recently, Eva worked as a legal PA in Leeds.

Although she has always enjoyed writing fiction, it wasn't until she came to live in Redcar that Eva took her writing seriously. She became a member of the U3A in Saltburn and joined the novel-writing group, then joined the Scriveners Writing Group in Guisborough, where she was encouraged to pursue her dream of writing a book.

Eva's first novel, *'Bad Blood Rising'* was published towards the end of 2019. Her current book, *'More Bad Blood'* follows the same gritty path, delving into the seedy underbelly of the sex industry in the north of England.

Other Books by This Author

Bad Blood Rising – A Northern City… Money… Girls… Crime… Murder… And Bad Men

When a young prostitute is murdered by her pimp, Karl Maddox, he thinks the terrible secret she had threatened to expose is buried with her.

But when the murdered prostitute's daughter arrives in Leeds eighteen years later, she is seeking answers.

Slowly but surely, Karl's life as the wealthy, powerful kingpin of his clubland empire begins to unravel as loyalty is replaced by treachery, and friendship is replaced with hatred.

Is Karl about to find out that no secret can remain buried forever?

An exciting romp through the criminal underworld.

More Bad Blood – When a young prostitute is murdered by her pimp, Karl Maddox, he thinks the terrible secret she had threatened to expose is buried with her.

But when the murdered prostitute's daughter arrives in Leeds eighteen years later, she is seeking answers.

Slowly but surely, Karl's life as the wealthy, powerful kingpin of his clubland empire begins to unravel as loyalty is replaced by treachery, and friendship is replaced by hatred.

Is Karl about to find out that no secret can remain buried forever?

Printed in Great Britain
by Amazon

71442836R00166